Cole sa... ...ber, saw it was a honky-to..., a roadhouse. He decided that he could use a beer.

He pulled into the gravel drive and looked around in surprise. ''Well, this is sure weird,'' he said aloud. There wasn't a vehicle there less than thirty-five years old; IH and Studebaker pickup trucks, turtleback Mercurys from the late forties and early fifties. There were even a couple of Hudsons. They were all in good to excellent condition.

Then the band inside started up, and the music was pure rockabilly—drums, bass, lead guitar, and rhythm guitar. The song was something Cole had never heard . . . something about a rock house. Cole chuckled—had to be a meeting of some classic car club. Had to be.

Cole opened the door and stepped inside. Every eye in the place was on him as he walked up to the bar. Suddenly, every cop antenna he had developed over the years was up and receiving signals—this was the roughest-looking bunch of ol' boys and girls he'd ever seen all gathered up in one place.

Strange, he thought. Then swiveled to face the bar.

That's when he saw the calendar. A light sweat broke out on his forehead.

The calendar read, October, 1957 . . .

. . . AND SO WOULD ROY ORBISON

WILLIAM W. JOHNSTONE

ROCKABILLY HELL

ZEBRA BOOKS
KENSINGTON PUBLISHING CORP.

ZEBRA BOOKS are published by

Kensington Publishing Corp.
850 Third Avenue
New York, NY 10022

First Printing: November, 1995

Printed in the United States of America

Dedicated to Mike and Connie Aubuchon
(Brandy, Digger, Joplin, and Blue insisted I do this).

Book One

Nothing changes more constantly than the past; for the past that influences our lives does not consist of what actually happened, but of what men believe happened.

—Gerald White Johnson

One

"Who is this guy?" Deputy Younger asked, holding up the extradition papers.

"A nobody, really, Captain. He's never committed a violent act that we know of. But he's hung enough paper around to fill the local stadium. Are you sure you want to drive all the way up into Illinois for this loser?"

That brought a smile to the man's lips. "I've got five more months to go until I pull the pin. I'm tired of sitting at that desk the sheriff put me behind last month. This will at least get me out of the office for a few days."

The deputy leaned back in his chair and grinned. "What are you going to do when you retire, Cole?"

Jesse Cole Younger shook his head. He was named after his grandfather on his dad's side and his great uncle on his mother's side, but everybody always assumed he was named after the famous outlaws—and he suspected he was, too, for his dad had always possessed a weird sense of humor. "I really haven't given it much thought, Dale."

"Forty-five is too damn young to retire, Cole."

"I've spent nearly twenty-five years wrestling drunks, getting puked on, chasing punks, sweeping up teeth, hair, and eyeballs after wrecks, and getting shot twice. It's time to pull the pin. Besides, I don't really need the money.''

The deputy glanced at his watch. ''It's sorta late. You going to leave now?''

''Might as well. I'll get a room somewhere up in northern Arkansas or southern Missouri.''

Cole headed east out of Louisiana, heading for the Mississippi River bridge crossing, and then cut north on Interstate 55.

Dale was right, of course. Forty-five was far too young to retire altogether. He'd have to think of something to do. Not that he had to. Cole was comfortable, as far as finances went. His parents had been killed in a fiery automobile accident a few years back and had left everything to Cole, their only child. The estate had been substantial.

Dale had joined the Army at seventeen, spent two tours in Vietnam, gotten wounded, and then discharged. He'd gone to college for a year, didn't like it, dropped out, and joined the Sheriff's Department. He'd been there ever since. Married, divorced after five bitter, stormy, argument-filled years. No children. He didn't know where Janet was now. Last he'd heard she was out in California. Good place for her, Cole had concluded.

Cole usually picked a marked and fully equipped unit for any out-of-state run: that way he could stay just above the posted limit and be left alone by other cops, receiving only a wave or a quick flash of lights in greeting. Cops look out for other cops. But this time he was driving an unmarked unit.

Night had covered the land for several hours when he crossed the river again at Memphis and rolled into Arkansas. He had gassed up in north Mississippi and grabbed a cheeseburger, so he wasn't hungry (but his stomach did feel queasy); he decided he'd pull in somewhere and get himself a Coke. And get off this damned interstate for a few miles; it was getting boring.

He took the next off ramp and pulled onto Highway 61. His appeared to be the only car on the old highway—once a main north-south link—and that suited him just fine.

Cole turned off the radio and drove in silence for a time, his driver's side window down and his elbow sticking out. The early fall air rushed in and blew cool on his face.

When his radio clicked on and the 1950's rockabilly music slammed into his ear, he nearly lost control of the unit. Shaken, Cole pulled off on the shoulder and sat for a time, eyes fixed on the lighted electronic dial of the radio. He almost never listened to AM, except for a news and talk station out of Shreveport, but there it was, the numbers clearly indicating an AM station. But it sure wasn't KEEL from Shreveport. And the song was not at all familiar to him.

"What the hell?" he muttered.

The announcer came on. The guy was using terms like daddy-o, and toe-tappin, and rooty-tooty.

"Rooty-tooty!" Cole said.

Then he smiled. Had to be a tape from years back, some golden oldie program.

Then he frowned.

But how the hell did the radio just come on all by itself?

He reached over and punched the on-off button. Nothing happened. The music continued to play. Thumping, hard-driving, early rock and roll—rockabilly. That unique brand of music that was pure Southern. He punched a preset selector button. The station didn't change. Another one. Same results. He punched all the selector buttons. The station would not change.

Cole turned off the engine. The radio did not go off with it.

Cole felt himself getting a bit spooked by these strange happenings. He shook his head, got out of the car, and walked around it several times. The music continued to play as he walked.

Then it stopped.

The night was very silent.

Out of habit, Cole slipped his right hand under his jacket and touched the butt of his Sig Sauer 9 mm. It was there, nestled snugly in a shoulder holster. It was comforting.

He got back into his unit and cranked up. The radio stayed off. He reached over and punched it on. A Memphis station, playing music from the sixties, seventies, and eighties. No fifties rockabilly.

Cole shook his head, expelled air, sighed, and slipped the unit into gear, pulling back out on the highway. He occasionally would fix the radio with a very jaundiced glance.

Cole had been born in 1950, and he only vaguely remembered the early days of rock and roll. His music was the Beatles, the Stones, the Righteous Brothers, Neil Diamond, the Beach Boys, Fleetwood Mac.

He didn't know shit about early rockabilly.

He saw lights up ahead and, as he drew closer, saw it was a honky-tonk, a roadhouse. He wasn't in uniform and decided he'd pull in and get a beer. He needed one after that odd business with the radio. And his stomach still felt queasy. Bad cheeseburger.

He pulled into the gravel drive and sighed. "Well, this is damn sure a night for weird," he said aloud, his eyes taking in all the cars and trucks parked around the honky-tonk.

There wasn't a vehicle there less than thirty-five years old. IH and Studebaker pickup trucks. Turtleback Mercurys from the late forties and early fifties. A couple of Hudsons. One Henry-J.

Cole had never seen one of those except in picture books of classic and antique cars.

And all of the old cars and trucks ranged in condition from good to excellent.

Then the band inside started up, and the music was pure rockabilly. Drums, bass, lead guitar, and rhythm guitar. The song was something about a Rock House. Cole had never heard it.

Cole chuckled as what was happening came to him. Had to be. The cars and trucks belonged to members of a classic car club, and this was their monthly meeting. The band was playing songs from the era of the old cars and trucks.

Sure.

"Well, it's easy when you figure it out," Cole muttered, getting out of his unit and making sure the doors were locked.

He opened the front door and stepped inside. He immediately

got the feeling he was entering a time warp of some sort. Rod Serling would have felt right at home. Cole felt every eye in the place on him as he walked to the bar.

"Bud Light," he told the bartender.

"What?" the man said.

Cole looked up and down the bar. The beer was all in bottles, long-necks. He didn't recognize a single brand. He cut his eyes to the bartender. "Just give me a beer."

"Stag be all right?"

Stag? Had to be a local brand. "That's fine." Cole put a dollar on the scarred bar, and the barkeep gave him change.

Change? Must be some sort of special night. He slipped the change in his jacket side pocket without looking at it. Beer in hand, Cole swiveled on the bar stool and gave the place a look-over. Suddenly every cop antenna he had developed over the years was up and receiving signals. This was the roughest-looking bunch of ol' boys he had ever seen all gathered up in one place. And the women, most of them attractive in a hard-looking and well-used sort of way, had the same mean look in their eyes. Even those doing some sort of dance on the dance floor. Then Cole recognized the step; or thought he did. It was the bop. He'd seen his parents doing it.

Strange, he thought, again swiveling to face the bar.

Then his eyes centered on the calendar on the wall behind the bar, and he felt a light sweat break out on his forehead. October 1957.

Cole blinked a couple of times. The month and year remained the same.

"I reckon we'll have a war with them damn Rooshins 'fore it's all said and done," he heard a man said. "Ike ain't gonna put up with 'em for long."

"Ike ain't gonna do shit," another said. "We should have whupped them damn Bolsheviks back in '45. Patton wanted to, but Ike didn't have the balls for it then, and he don't now."

Cole put a hand to his forehead. He felt feverish.

Cole stood up, beer in hand. One of the men looked at him. "What do you think about Ike, buddy?"

"I, ah, I'm not political," Cole managed to say.

The man turned his back to him and resumed the conversation with his buddy.

Across the room, two men in jeans and cowboy boots suddenly lunged to their feet and began fighting. Barroom fights usually happen that way, the viciousness coming so fast no one around them has time to get out of the way. For the most part, the combatants were ignored. One of the pool players reversed his cue stick and smashed the heavy end of it against the head of one fighter. The blood sprayed the wall, and the man went down in a boneless heap.

"I never did like that son of a bitch," the cue stick-wielder said, then tossed the broken cue stick to the floor and walked to the rack, picking out another one.

The band never missed a beat.

Cole knew he had to get out of this joint. He was coming down with something. Flu, maybe. "Have a nice evening," he said to the bartender.

"Whenever we're here, they usually are," the man replied strangely, a very mean look in his eyes.

The band was playing and singing some song about a Rock and Roll Ruby.

Cole made it to his unit and unlocked the door, falling into the seat. He slammed the door and locked it. *"Jesus Christ!"* the words exploded from his mouth. What the hell was this, the Twilight Zone? He set the long-neck bottle in the beverage holder and sighed heavily.

Cole sat for a time, listening to the music and calming himself. It was a joke, he finally concluded. The locals were having fun with the stranger. *Had* to be.

Cole stuck his hand in his jacket pocket and took out the change the bartender had given him. Sixty-five cents. Thirty-five-cent beer? He tossed the change into a section of the console between the firewall and the seat, and cranked the engine.

Cole backed out onto the highway and took one more look at the roadhouse.

But it was gone.

There was no music, no old cars and trucks, no building. The gravel parking lot was all grown over with weeds, and only a cracked concrete slab remained of the honky-tonk.

Cole put a shaking hand down to grab his long-neck and take a swig.

But the bottle was not there.

Cole felt his heart rate surge. He took several deep breaths and looked up and down the highway. No lights in sight. He pulled back into the parking lot. The roadhouse reappeared, the lot filled with old cars and trucks, the music loud from inside the joint.

He put his hand down for the bottle of beer and his fingers closed around the condensation-covered bottle. Cole took a deep pull and could not recall any beer ever tasting so good. He watched as the front door opened and a man was hurled outside, landing hard on the gravel. He did not move. The back of the man's head was bloody, where he'd been hit with the cue stick. He looked dead.

"This is a nightmare," Cole muttered. "Just a nightmare. This is not happening. Either that or I've got the flu and am hallucinating very badly."

He sat in the parking lot and drank his beer, while the loud rockabilly music wafted all around him. He waited for a sheriff's department car to show up. After a few minutes, he decided that no one had called the police. Cole drained his bottle of beer and started his car, backing out of the parking lot and pointing in the direction from which he'd come. There was a town just a few miles back. He'd call in the incident from there.

But when he looked to his right, the club was not there. No lights blazed, nobody on the ground, and as before, the parking lot was overgrown in a maze of weeds.

"Goddamnit!" Cole yelled, spinning the steering wheel and once more turning into the old parking lot.

Nothing happened. He drove right up to the edge of the concrete slab and stopped, cutting off his lights and killing the engine. He reached down to touch the empty bottle of beer, but it was gone. He fumbled in the tray for the change he'd received from his dollar bill. The tray was empty.

Cole sighed heavily. "I gotta find a room for the night. I'm sicker than I thought."

He spent the night in a motel in Blytheville. When he awakened the next morning, he felt fine, the strange events of the preceding night only an unpleasant memory, brought on, he was sure, by that bad cheeseburger he'd eaten earlier in the day. He showered, shaved, and felt much better. After breakfast, he paused at the checkout desk.

"Back down the road about ten miles or so, there used to be a honky-tonk there. What happened to it?"

"On the right-hand side heading south?"

"Yes."

"Burned down years ago. Golly, I guess . . . oh, fifteen years ago. Maybe longer than that. Most people around here were glad it did."

"Tough place, huh?"

"I guess. I was too young to go there. But I've heard some really wild tales about it."

Cole pulled out and headed north.

The prisoner Cole picked up was a small, very pleasant-speaking man in his late fifties. "He won't give you any problems, Deputy," Cole was told. "We just received word this morning that he's been given a grant of immunity in exchange for his testimony in another case. As soon as he testifies, he walks out a free man."

"With that kind of deal, it would be kind of stupid for him to get cute on the last leg home now, wouldn't it?" Cole said with a smile.

Like many prisoners Cole had transported over the long years behind a badge, this one was, at least on the surface, a likeable man, and possessing above average intelligence. As they approached Cairo, Illinois, the man really started talking, lost in memories.

"I used to know every joint between here and Jackson, Mississippi, Captain. But most of your real good roadhouses were between here and West Memphis, Arkansas."

"Oh, yeah?"

"Yeah. Really. I know, I made them all. I used to be a hell of a gambler. There were back rooms in most of those clubs, and the games got pretty damned high-stakes, let me tell you."

And tell it he did, entertaining Cole with all sorts of stories. At Sikeston, Missouri, Cole cut off of the interstate and took Highway 61.

"I'm glad you did that, Captain," the prisoner said. "Lots of old roadhouses on this stretch of highway."

"So I've heard. You knew them along this stretch, too, huh?"

"Everyone of them."

"Well, I had another reason for taking 61."

"Oh?"

"Yes."

At New Madrid, Missouri, Cole stuck the man in the county jail and slept for six hours, then was on the road again.

"That was mighty cold of you, Captain," the man bitched, once they were back on the road.

"What'd you expect, Holiday Inn?"

The prisoner thought about that for a moment, then chuckled. "You're right. You want to hear more about the clubs?"

"Sure."

The man talked about the clubs in New Madrid County, then about the club where Elvis played when he was just getting started, here in the bootheel of Missouri. "Used to call that one the Bloody Bucket. I remember it well."

They crossed over into Arkansas, and the man fell silent.

"What's the matter?" Cole asked.

"Club used to be right down here a few miles. Brings back bad memories for me."

Cole felt a cold tingle in the pit of his stomach. "Oh?"

"Yeah. Over the years it had a lot of names. Stateline, the Spur, the Cowboy Club. I remember it as the G & K Club. Locals called it the Gun and Knife Club, all the shootings and killings that went on there. Mean bunch of bastards hung out there. And their women weren't any better."

Cole felt slightly sick at his stomach as he recalled the sign over the club entrance in his feverish hallucinating. G & K Club.

"You sound like it's personal to you."

"It is. My first cousin was killed there. Man hit him on the back of the head with a cue stick. Fractured his skull; drove bits of bone into his brain. He died right there in the parking lot. Those sorry bastards and bitches just tossed him out the front door and left him. Oh, my cousin was no saint; he was mean as a snake himself. It's just . . . well, *kin*, you know?"

Cole didn't trust his voice to speak. He nodded his head. Clearing his throat, he asked, "You remember the date that happened?"

"Sure. October 1957."

Two

Cole never mentioned his strange experiences at the roadhouse to anyone for at least two reasons: He was not at all certain the events had actually happened, and he didn't want his friends on the sheriff's department to think he was a nut. But Cole never forgot that night at the G & K Club, either. He just tucked it carefully away in the back of his mind.

Fall drifted into winter and the new year came and went. A month before Cole was due to retire, the sheriff walked by his desk and dropped an envelope in front of him. Pausing, he said, "Law enforcement convention in Memphis next week. You go. Hobnob with real people for the last time before retirement."

Before Cole could state his objections, and that he really didn't want to go, the sheriff had walked on. Cole studied the brochure and decided the convention might be fun after all. And for a fact, it would be the last time he could get together with like-minded people and talk shop. He would miss that.

Whether the department is large or small, cops belong to a closed club. You don't wear a badge, you don't get in. Period. If it's a town of any size, cops have their own watering holes, and much of the time, cops associate with other cops. Us against

Them mentality—it comes with the territory and goes with the job.

Suddenly, Cole began to look forward to the convention. But getting away from the office and having fun was not among the reasons.

Cole wandered around the hotel until he located some law enforcement people from north Arkansas and southern Missouri. They greeted him warmly and immediately made room for him in their little klatch. After listened to this and that for a few minutes, Cole said, "I was through your part of the country a few months back, hauling a prisoner from Illinois. That ol' boy told me some pretty wild tales about the old roadhouses in this part of the country."

The cops all smiled and nodded their heads, one sheriff from north Arkansas saying, "He was right about that, friend. Back in the fifties and early sixties, there were some wooly buggers along highway 61."

"Any unsolved cases that might involve those roadhouses?" Cole asked innocently.

There was a moment of reflection, then the cops all started nodding their heads affirmatively. "Both directly and indirectly," a deputy from the bootheel of Missouri said.

"Disappearances, mostly," a deputy from Arkansas said. "Why?"

"I'm going to retire soon. I've been thinking about writing a book about these old roadhouses." Cole lied easily; many cops are good at that, too. "And maybe some bizarre crimes that might be linked to them. You guys mind if I come visit and look through the old files?"

They all assured him he'd be welcome any time. Then they joked about Cole retiring so young, exchanged business cards, and soon the group broke up, the men—and it was mostly men there—wandered off to seek out old friends and make new ones.

"Bullshit!" the female voice spoke from just behind him and to his right.

Cole turned to face the voice. "I beg your pardon?"

The face behind the voice was interesting. She was not beautiful in the classic sense, but she was very attractive. Light brown hair, hazel eyes. Very nice figure. About five-five, Cole guessed. Her nametag read KATTI BAYLOR. She met his gaze and wasn't about to blink first.

"That was a very interesting opening line, Miss Baylor. I don't believe I've ever been approached with that particular phrase."

"It's *Ms.*, thank you. And I don't believe that book business."

"Wonderful," Cole said drily. "Did you bring Gloria with you?"

"What?"

"Never mind. Were you slinging that bullshit at me, *Ms.* Baylor?"

"Who is Gloria?"

"Steinem."

"You're pretty sharp for a flatfoot."

Cole laughed at that. "Ms. Baylor, the term flatfoot went out years ago. I believe it was replaced by pig." He studied her name tag and let his eyes drift to what lay just below the name tag. That was even more interesting. "You're a reporter?"

"Freelance writer. Are you all through eyeballing my tits?"

Cole met her eyes. "I'm sort of old-fashioned, Ms. Baylor. I never thought profanity was very becoming for a lady."

"Who the hell said I was a lady?" She studied Cole. Just a shade under six feet tall. Solid. Brown hair specked with gray. His eyes were so blue they were almost black. Big hands and thick wrists. Trim waist. No pretty boy, but handsome in a very rugged sort of way. A lot of character in the face.

Cole smiled. "We're really getting off to a lousy start, Ms. Baylor. Can I buy you a cup of coffee?"

She stared at him for a moment. "No. But I can buy you one. And the name is Katti."

* * *

She was lost. And these damned Arkansas back roads were the pits. If they were marked, she couldn't find the signs. She should have stayed on the interstate, but she wanted to see that historical marker and was pressed for time. She hadn't found the marker and now it was dark and she was all turned around. Then she saw the lights just up ahead and her spirits lifted. Civilization at last.

Pulling into the poorly lighted gravel parking lot, she didn't notice that all the cars and trucks were very old. But she did notice the music thumping through the walls of the joint. Hillbilly crap. God, she hated that country corn. She got out, locked her car, and walked up to the front door of the roadhouse. Just for a second, she hesitated, then opened the door.

She stepped into Hell.

Cole found the article in the state and local section of the paper. It had come in just in time for the morning edition. The nude body of a young woman, between twenty and twenty-five, had been found by the side of the road about forty miles north and slightly west of Memphis. She had been brutally raped and then beaten to death. She was in a ditch just across the road from her car. Her clothing and purse had not been found. The police were withholding her name, until next of kin could be notified.

"Find something interesting in there?" the voice jarred Cole out of his musings.

He looked up and smiled at Katti. "Decided to take me up on breakfast, hey?"

"Why not?" She sat down and poured coffee from the service on the table. She sugared and creamed and lifted the cup, her eyes amused and mocking him over the rim. "You didn't hit on me last night, Deputy. Why?"

"I told you, I'm old-fashioned."

"That is . . . very refreshing in this era of jumping in and out of bed before you know someone's last name."

"That's what you do, hey?"

Her eyes flashed and then softened, as she saw the smile on Cole's lips. She laughed. "Okay. Touché. Truce?"

"Sure. Order breakfast and then we'll take a ride. That is, if you meant what you said last evening."

"About working with you on my book? And it is *my* book."

"I don't know the first thing about writing books, Katti. But I'll be a cop until the day I die. It's your book."

"Fine. Where are we going?"

"Eat. Then we'll go."

Katti's older brother had disappeared ten years back, when she was twenty-eight years old and working as a reporter for a Memphis newspaper. He was ten years her senior. His body had never been found. But his car had been found in the parking lot of what used to be a roadhouse a few miles off Highway 61. Katti had left the paper a few years later, after finding out she could make a living writing romance novels. But she still did short pieces for the paper and for various magazines. Because of the disappearance of her brother, she had compiled quite a list of people who had disappeared over the years, all of them either on or close to the old highway. But until now, she could not find a cop, active or retired, to help her dig into the mysteries.

"Cops are swamped with work, Katti," Cole had told her. "Everywhere. Big towns, small towns. Makes no difference. They've got to work on current cases. Something that happened twenty years ago might interest them, but they just don't have the time to look very hard at it . . . or look at it at all."

"You never remarried, Cole?"

"No. You?"

She had confided in him about her own miserable failed marriage. She shook her head. "No. When I do find someone who interests me, he turns out to be gay, someone who misses his mother, wants to lay up in front of the TV all weekend watching sports and drinking beer and belching, or is unhappy about his fading youth or some such crap as that."

Cole had never really figured out exactly what women wanted in a man, so he had no comment to make. But he had reached the conclusion a few years back that most *women* didn't even know what they wanted in a man. So how the hell was a man supposed to know?

While finishing their coffee after breakfast, Katti read the article. "You think this has something to do with the disappearances?"

"I don't know." He had not told her (or anybody) about his own strange experiences at the ghost club, as he had started calling it, some months back. "But we have to start somewhere."

"What about the meetings here at the conference?"

"I'm retiring in a couple of weeks, Katti. I don't care doodly-squat about these meetings. I don't need some chair-bound cop to tell me we're losing the war on crime. I know it firsthand. If I have to listen to some damn psychiatrist tell me one more time about the need for sensitivity training in dealing with minorities, I'll puke. All people of any color have to do is obey the law . . . don't get me started. Let's get out of here."

Cole had driven his own vehicle to the convention, a new Ford Bronco. On the floor, between the firewall and the console, there was a bank of electronics: a scanner, a CB, a police radio, and a mobile phone.

"You do come prepared, don't you?" Katti said, eyeballing all the gear.

"Just like a Boy Scout."

She arched one eyebrow and smiled. "My, my! All the time?"

Cole sighed and pulled out into the street, heading for the interstate and, eventually, Highway 61.

An area on both sides of the poorly maintained farm to market road were still sealed off—loosely speaking—with yellow and black CRIME SCENE DO NOT CROSS tape. The victim's car had been towed off, and no deputies were in sight. The first thing Cole noticed was the long rectangular outline of concrete blocks just past the weed-grown parking lot.

"Ten dollars says that used to be a honky-tonk," Cole said.

Katti stared at him for a moment. "Is that important?"

"Yeah. It sure is." He kept on driving until he reached the next town, population about fifteen hundred. He pulled into a self-service station and decided to gas up and get a little information. "Big doin's down the road, hey?" he asked the old man who came out to watch him pump the gas.

"Yep."

"I was through this part of the country some years ago. I could swear I stopped and got a beer at a nightclub back down the road."

"Prob'ly did."

"I think it was right about where all that yellow tape is."

"Yep."

"Can't recall the name of it."

"Don't matter now. It's gone."

"Burned down, huh?"

"Nope."

"Fell down?"

"Nope."

"Moved?"

"Nope."

"Well, what the hell happened to it!"

"Bulldozed."

Cole blinked at that.

"Man got cheated at cards there one night. Came back when the place was closed and splintered the damn place. Wasn't enough of it left to use for kindlin' wood. That'll be eleven dollars please."

Cole paid him. "Thank you."

"You're welcome."

"That would make for a very interesting chapter in my book," Katti said, once they were back on the road.

"Old fart!" Cole muttered.

And Katti laughed at the expression on his face.

* * *

Cole and Katti talked nearly every night for two weeks after the convention. But he still had not told her about his strange experience at the G & K Club. And while he had never so much as kissed the woman, something was building between them, and although neither would admit it, it scared them both.

The sheriff's department gave Cole a retirement party. He turned in any equipment he had that belonged to the department or the parish, and a day later had closed up his house and was on the road to Memphis.

Three

Katti's home was unpretentious, but very nice and comfortably furnished, located about five miles outside the Memphis city limits, on the east side of the city, off I–40.

"I'll get a room at that motel just down the road," Cole told her.

She was making coffee and paused, looking at him. "You don't need to do that, Cole," she said softly. "Go bring your luggage in."

He stared at her for a moment. "Which bedroom is mine?"

She turned back to her coffee-making. "That's up to you."

That was the easiest decision he ever had to make.

Cole spent the next several days going over Katti's notes—they were extensive and detailed. When he finished, he leaned back in his chair and shook his head in disbelief. "Almost five hundred people have disappeared over the past twenty-five years. Five *hundred* men and women?"

"It's probably twice that, Cole. As you can see, I've only been able to verify two hundred and thirty-five. I'm positive of the others, but can't prove it. But just think about the number of hitchhikers and hobos and so forth that have traveled this stretch of highway over forty years. No one to report them missing, or even if they had kin, odds were good the family had no idea where they were. Now figure in the number of unsolved rapes and assaults and murders over a twenty-five-year period, along a stretch of highway a hundred and fifty miles long, working say, twenty miles east and west from the highway, and you'll see what I mean about the number being higher. We're talking hundreds of square miles, several dozen counties, and two or three states, at least.''

''This is incredible, Katti.''

She sat down at the table and fixed her eyes on him. ''Now you level with me, Cole. What about this fascination of yours with old honky-tonks?''

He nodded his head and, as unemotionally as possible, told her about his strange experience at the G & K Club, and related to her what the prisoner had told him.

She got up and walked around the table a couple of times. She stopped her pacing and said, ''I . . . have another set of notes, Cole. Just as extensive as those in front of you. They are reports of strange sightings, the paranormal, things of that nature.''

''What the hell are we dealing with here, Katti?''

She screwed her face all up, making a horrible expression.

''I wish you wouldn't do that,'' Cole said.

She smiled and said, ''I guess we're dealing with ghosts, Cole.''

He stared at her for a moment. Sighed. Finally said, ''Is it too early in the day for a drink?''

''Fifty or so years ago,'' the cop said, ''this area used to be called Frog City. I don't know why, it just was.''

Cole and Katti had decided to work south from Cairo, Illinois.

The friendly Illinois cop that Cole had met at the convention waved his hand. ''There used to be nightclubs all around this two/three block area. A lot of them are gone now. Honky-tonks, strip joints; you name it, we had it. You and me, Cole, we were just grade-schoolers when this area was jumping." He looked at Katti and smiled. "And you, Katti, weren't even born! Well, I've got to get back to work. You two nose around all you like. I've told the guys and gals patrolling this area that you're here. You won't be bothered. Have fun."

They sat in the Bronco in front of what used to be a notorious nightclub. Now there was nothing left except for a building that looked to be ready for demolition.

Katti said, "Along the way, we've pulled over and paused at the ruins of—or just the land that used to be the home of— the Do-Drop-Inn, the Stateline, the G & K, the Courts, the Bloody Bucket, and a dozen others. The feeling is the same at each one. Do you agree?"

"Very reluctantly."

"But you do agree?"

"Yes."

"So what is it we feel?"

"I don't know."

"The files we looked at this morning tell us that since this club finally closed its doors, fifteen years ago, there have been two disappearances and three unsolved murders here, right?"

"Yes. Right where we're sitting."

"And right across the street, in that vacant lot, there used to be a club called the Glass Slipper, right?"

"Right."

"Two teenagers—a boy and girl—vanished there one night, right?"

"That's right. Their bodies were never found. Before the building was torn down, it used to be a favorite place for kids to park and smooch."

She giggled. "Smooch, Cole? *Smooch?*"

"That's what I said."

"You're a little behind the times, dear."

"Well . . . suck-face, then. Is that better?"

"No. Are you ready to head back to the motel?"

"What do you have in mind?"

"I'll think of something."

"I just bet you will."

They had stated their intentions to both the city police and the sheriff's department, and there were no objections from either department. Just to be on the safe side, the sheriff informed the Illinois State Police about what was going on, further insuring that Cole and Katti would not be bothered that night.

There were a few houses along the two-block area, but they were all unoccupied. A realtor had very reluctantly told them that people did try to live in the homes from time to time, but always moved out after a few months.

"Why?" Katti asked.

The realtor had looked pained, like he needed desperately to fart. "Things that go bump in the night," he finally said. "It's all nonsense, of course. There are no such things as ghosts. We're going to have to eventually tear those houses down. The insurance premiums for unoccupied dwellings are killing us."

Cole and Katti had picked up a dozen cassette tapes before leaving Memphis—the remastered originals of early rock and roll. Elvis, Orbison, Jerry Lee, Rich, Cash, Perkins, Smith, Feathers, Riley.

They were now parked in the grassy lot where the Glass Slipper used to stand. Cole checked his 9 mm.

"What are you going to do with that?" Katti asked. "Shoot a ghost?"

"I feel better with it."

"I'd feel better with an exorcist."

"Tell you the truth, I feel like an idiot."

"That makes two of us."

There was very little traffic, and the skies were overcast. A couple of the street lamps along this particular section of town were not working, and it was very dark. The only light came from the interstate that ran close by.

"You ready for the tape?"

Katti sighed. "Why not?"

Cole hit the play button, and the Bronco and the night all around it for twenty or so yards was filled with the sounds of early rock and roll—rompin', stompin', pure rock and roll. Drums, bass, lead, and rhythm, without any of the electronic gimmicks that eventually bastardized the music and changed it into so much clashing, banging, fuzzy-noted crap.

"Jesus, Cole!" Katti said, clutching at his arm. "Look over there!"

A shadowy form had materialized out of the brush and weeds. Whatever it was, it was indistinct in the gloom of night. From their distance, it was impossible to tell exactly what it was.

"Katti," Cole said. "You are paralyzing my right arm."

"Oh!" She relaxed her death grip on his forearm. "What is that thing?"

"I don't know. But it sure appeared out of nowhere."

Cole felt the comforting weight of the 9 mm tucked behind his belt, and then realized that maybe it wasn't so comforting. What good *was* a bullet against a ghost?

"It's coming this way!" Katti said, real fear behind the words.

Cole watched the . . . thing, not really feeling all that brave himself. The dark shadow drew closer, moving very slowly through the weeds. They both watched as the shadow reached down and picked something up off the ground.

"Whatever it is just picked up a club," Cole said.

"Why would a ghost want a club?" Katti asked, reaching over to turn down the volume of the music.

"That's better," came the voice from the strange form. "It's bad enough I have to sleep on the ground like an animal, but puttin' up with that damn racket is just too much. Why don't you kids go somewheres else to make out?"

"Homeless," Cole said, after expelling some pent-up air. He opened the driver's side door and stepped out. "Come over here," he called. "I want to talk to you."

"You the cops? I ain't done nothin', man."

"I'm not the cops. I just want to talk to you. I'll give you a couple of bucks for a few minutes' time."

The man drew closer and Cole could smell a strange odor. He knew that in many cases, that was not the individual's fault—not entirely. Where can the homeless go for a hot bath? Over the years, Cole had personally seen dozens of homeless men and women who were made that way through no fault of their own. Hundreds of thousands of Americans live just one paycheck away from disaster.

Cole dismissed the smell as he laid a five dollar bill on the hood of the Bronco. "There's five bucks. Can we talk?"

The man stepped closer and snatched away the bill. "All right. What'd you have on your mind?"

"How long have you been . . . living out here?"

"Couple of months or so. I got me a cardboard house over there," he pointed. "I take it down durin' the day, so's the cops won't see and roust me away. 'Course I have to replace it ever' time it rains."

"You ever seen anything, well, odd, around here at night?"

The homeless man thought about that for a moment. "Seen, no. Heard, yeah. Twice in last two and a half months."

Seated in the Bronco, Katti had punched on a cassette recorder and was taping every word.

Cole stared at the man through the darkness. He figured the guy to be in his mid- to late-thirties. "What have you heard?"

The man hesitated, then said, "The same goddamn music that you was playin', that's what. Not necessarily the same songs, but the same beat—the sound, you know what I mean? Kinda hillbilly, but more rock and roll. Then I hear laughin', jokin', talkin'. Then the sounds of what seems like fightin'. A scream. Then . . . nothin'. I hear all this, but I can't figure out where it's comin' from. There ain't no place around here where it *could* be comin' from. There ain't nothin' out here."

"Does this happen at about the same time each month?"

The man laughed, but it was a bitter sound, void of any trace of humor. "Man, how the hell should I know? I ain't got no calendar. I swapped my watch for a pair of shoes last year. All I know is I've heard the same sounds twice. It's spooky, that's what it is."

"How long have you been down on your luck?" Cole asked.

The homeless man grunted. "Three years, I think. I had me a good job up in Chicago. Home, wife, kid, all that good stuff. Lost my job, went through the savings in two months. Couldn't pay the mortgage. Couldn't find a job. Unemployment ran out. First the car went, then my old pickup. When the mortgage company took the house, the wife took the kid and left. It's still all . . . unreal, you know? It all happened so fast. One day I'm a regular workin' guy, with a home and everything. Just like regular people. The wife and I could afford to go out maybe once a month or so, for supper and a movie. Maybe down to the tavern for a few beers and some laughs with the neighborhood crowd. Then I look up, and I don't have anything. I'm wiped out. When the shop started hirin' again, you know who got my old job? A fuckin' foreigner, that's who! Comes into this country without a pot to piss in, stays on welfare for a year, then the son of a bitch gets *my* job. I been a welder all my life. Ever since I was fifteen years old. I don't know nothin' else. When everything else run out, I borrowed money from a finance company against my equipment. I couldn't pay the notes, so they come got that. I been payin' taxes and obeyin' the law all my life. And this is what my country does to me. I'm ruined, and my job goes to some fuckin' foreigner. Something is awful wrong with the way this country is run, man. Really bad wrong." He turned to go, then paused, and turned around. "Thanks for the money, man. That'll buy some pork and beans for me and some food for my little dog . . ." The man's voice caught in his throat. "Well, I forgot. I don't have my little dog no more. He got run over, and the son of a bitch who hit him didn't even stop to see about him. I buried him right next to my cardboard house. I got to find me another dog. They love you no matter what you have or don't have. Animals are better than people, man. You know that? It's true. I never realized that until I got put out on the street." The man walked away, back to his cardboard house, by the grave site of his little dog.

Cole stepped back into the Bronco in time to see Katti put away the tissue she had used to wipe her eyes.

"Yeah, I know, Katti. It gets to me, too. And I've seen a lot more of it up close, than you have."

"Why doesn't the government do something to help people like that?"

Cole cut his eyes to her, glad that she couldn't see his expression in the darkness. After a few seconds, he said, "I warn you now, dear: don't get me started on this wonderful government of ours."

Katti cut off the music, and they sat in silence for a time. After a moment, she said, "If what that homeless man said is true, we're on the right track."

"It looks that way. But if so, what triggers the appearance of the clubs? Why could he hear the music, but not see the building and the people, like I did down in Arkansas. I'm way out of my league here, Katti. This is paranormal stuff. I was just a plain ol' cop. A pretty good investigator. I don't know anything about ghosts."

"Neither does anybody else, Cole. Not really. There are a lot of theories, but no facts. I've done a lot of research on the subject over the past few years. Even the so-called experts can't really agree on much."

"If those . . . clubs do exist—and I'm convinced that they do—why have the . . . hell, *spirits,* left that homeless man alone?"

"Maybe they haven't," Katti said, after a few seconds' pause.

"What do you mean?"

"You got a flashlight?"

"Sure. Two of them. One in the glove box and another in the console."

"I forgot. Always prepared, that's you."

"Just like a Boy Scout."

"I'll remind you of that in a few hours."

"What if I have a headache?"

"I'll give you two aspirin—among other things." Katti got the flashlights and handed one to Cole.

"What are we doing?" Cole asked.

"Come on. I've got an idea."

They walked all over the weed-grown area, covering every foot of it, then went over it again. There was no cardboard house, no grave site of the little dog, no ashes from old fires, nothing to indicate that the homeless man lived anywhere near here.

"You people are getting just too damn smart," the disembodied voice sprang out of the darkness.

Katti and Cole spun around, spearing the darkness with narrow beams of light. There was nothing out there. But there was *something* out there.

Cole instinctively reached for his pistol. Grimacing, he pulled his hand back. No point in that. The wild thought came to him that perhaps he should to try to get some silver bullets. But then he recalled that only worked on werewolves.

"Cole?" Katti's voice was decidedly shaky.

It was only with a great effort that Cole kept his own voice strong. "I'm right here. Take it easy. Start working your way back to the truck. Go on, I'm with you."

They made it to the Bronco without incident, with no more ghostly voices springing from the night.

Cole started the engine and cut on the lights. The homeless man was nowhere to be seen. Cole hit the button on his side panel that locked both doors. He turned to face Katti. "That was probably that homeless guy, having a little fun with us."

She did not respond vocally to that. But she did shake her head in the negative.

"All right. Let's say it was . . . someone from the other side, for want of a better description. Katti . . . this is only the beginning of the investigation. Judging from what I saw in that joint down in Arkansas, I can assure you, it's going to get a lot worse as we progress. Are you sure you want to go on?"

She sat quite still for a moment, her hands in her lap. When she spoke, her voice was low, but steady. "Yes. I'm quite sure, Cole."

"All right. Now then, do you have books at your house on ghosts and spirits and so forth?"

"Dozens of them. Why?"

"I want to read them."

"*All* of them?"

"Yes. I'm a fast reader."

"What are you looking for?"

"I don't know. A thread . . . some common link—I'll know it when I see it."

"You're talking about ghosts?"

"Yes."

"There is no common thread. Not one that will do us any good."

"There has to be. And I'll find it," he added stubbornly.

Suddenly, from the darkness on either side of the Bronco, out of the glare of the headlights, music began, a wild guitar piece that hammered and shattered the night.

"I guess that lets out the homeless man playing games with us," Katti said. "If he was a homeless man."

"Which I doubt."

"Yeah. Me, too."

"What is that song, Cole?"

"I can't place it right off. Wait a minute." After a moment, he strung together some pretty impressive cuss words.

"What's the matter? Other than the obvious, that is."

"That song. Somebody has a really sick sense of humor."

"Why? What is it?"

Cole looked at her. "Ghost Riders In The Sky."

Four

Before leaving town the next morning, Cole and Katti drove back to the vacant lot and walked the area, double-checking. Absolutely no trace of any cardboard house, no ashes from old fires, no little dog's grave site they could find, no sign that anything human ever lived in the weeds and the brush.

Neither one of them said anything, just exchanged glances, returned to the Bronco, and pulled out, heading south. They were back in Memphis in time for lunch.

Cole began reading the books on psychic phenomena, haunted houses, ghosts of the south, poltergeists, and various other books about things that go bump in the night.

After two days of reading and making careful notes, Cole left the house one morning and went to a Memphis police supply house. He was still a fully bonded and commissioned deputy, so he had no trouble buying what he wanted. He said nothing to Katti about his purchases, for he was playing a long shot and had no idea if it would work.

Over drinks that evening before dinner, Cole asked, ''Exactly where did your brother disappear, Katti?''

She found a road map and pointed. '' Right there. Used to

be a roadhouse called the County Line. His car was in the parking lot, but no trace of him was ever found.''

He studied her face. ''You've been there?''

''Once. Just before it closed down. It was a really, well, seedy place. Strictly low-class types hung out there.'' She smiled. ''You know what we call them here in the South.''

''White trash.''

''Of the worst kind.''

''Is the building still standing?''

''No. It was torn down about a year after it closed.''

''What in the world was your brother doing in a joint like that?''

''I never could figure that out. Tommy hated places like that. He was a bourbon and water man. He couldn't drink beer; it made him sick. The County Line was a beer joint, not a bottle club. No hard liquor sold or allowed on the premises. Of course, it was consumed there, but on the sly.'' She shook her head. ''I never understood what he was doing there.''

The next day, Cole did some checking on the County Line club.

''Back in the fifties and early sixties,'' he told Katti, ''there was a roadhouse there called the Corral. In 1965 it was torn down and another building put up. The second building was named the County Line. But a lot of the materials from the Corral was used to build the County Line—cypress, mostly.''

''Well, now. How come I couldn't find that out?''

''You did not make a good impression with them after your brother went missing. They remember you well.''

''So I was a pain in the ass. What else did you find out?''

''The joint was a rough place in its day. Started out nice, but the 'necks took it over and soon the original clientele stopped going there. That's when the shootings and knifings and brawls started. Several people were killed there before it was closed down.''

''Disappearances?''

He nodded his head. ''Several. The cops really didn't want to talk about that, but I got the important facts out of them.

The rest I got from the newspaper morgue." He leaned back and sipped his coffee, smiling.

"Come on, Cole. Give. There have been sightings, right?"

"Plenty of them. But most of the locals don't like to talk about them." He set his cup down. "The one sighting that appears most often is of a man, between thirty-five and forty, nicely dressed in a blue blazer, light gray slacks, white shirt, and striped tie."

The blood drained from Katti's face. For a moment, Cole thought she was going to faint. She steadied herself and sat down in a chair. Collapsed, was more like it. Seconds ticked past until Katti found her voice.

"That's . . . that's what Tommy was wearing the night he disappeared."

"I figured as much."

"What is . . . what does this . . . sighting do? I mean . . ."

"I know what you mean. He's running down this county road. His face is bloody. He's waving his arms, as if trying to get someone to stop and help him. Then he vanishes."

"Does the sighting occur at regular intervals? I mean . . ."

He held up his hand. "No. People have reported it throughout the year."

Katti stood up and walked into the kitchen, pouring herself a cup of coffee and bringing the pot to refill Cole's cup. She sat down, a strange look in her eyes. "His still . . . well, *being here,* so to speak, could mean a number of things. Many of the so-called experts can't agree on that."

"There is one more thing, Katti."

She looked at him.

"The sightings always occur at approximately the same time. Between nine-thirty and ten at night."

"I want to see him, Cole."

"We can try. If you're really sure you want to do this."

"I'm sure."

"We'll drive up there tomorrow. Get a room at a local motel. Drive out to the place and get the feel of it. Then go back that evening. I've already spoken with the sheriff and the deputies;

told them we were doing a book and might show up in odd places in the middle of the night. We won't be bothered."

"I want to find the people who killed my brother, Cole. I want them punished!" She paused, realizing what she was saying.

"Katti, the people who killed Tommy are being punished, in a manner of speaking."

"I'll accept the first part. What do you mean by the last?"

"I think they knew when they killed him that they had given their souls to the devil. Maybe not Tommy, but a lot of the others who have vanished without a trace over the years, wandered into the same situation I did. But I got out in time."

"Trapped between worlds?"

"That's one way of putting it."

"Well, why doesn't God do something about it, then?"

"Maybe God doesn't have anything to do with it, Katti."

This time it was her turn to hold up a hand. "Wait just a minute, Cole. Hold on. You're saying, you're saying . . . what?"

"I'm not a religious man, Katti. I haven't been to church, any church, in years. I'm sort of like that old Tom T. Hall song: Me and Jesus got our own thing going. But I do believe strongly in God. I believe in Satan. I believe in the hereafter. I believe God punishes sinners. But I also believe there are levels of Heaven and Hell. And I believe that some people knowingly and willingly sell their souls to the Devil. Now, I don't believe in vampires or werewolves or things of that nature. But I do believe with all my heart and mind that evil walks this earth. Am I making any sense to you?"

She nodded her head. "Yes. Yes, you are. I think. You're saying these people, these *things* that live on in these ghost roadhouses, are the Devil's work."

"Yeah. I guess that's what I'm trying to say. But more than that. This is their punishment. They sold their souls to the Devil. Maybe they were so evil even the Devil didn't want them in Hell. So he left them here, but did so for a purpose——"

"Flaunting his power in the face of God?"

"Right. I think this is an ageless game between God and

Satan. They've been playing this since the beginnings of time. Maybe that's how they amuse themselves."

"Cole, that's . . . sacrilege. That's like saying we're just . . . pawns in some cosmic game."

"Some of us, yes. As a cop, Katti, I firmly believe in the Bad Seed theory. I've seen evil in kids six and seven years old. Down in Louisiana we recently put to death a man whose arrest record goes back to when he was six years old, stealing bicycles. He came from an upper-middle-class home. Good people. Plenty of love in the family. That kid was just no . . . fucking . . . good. Right from the git-go. And I've seen plenty of others just like him. I firmly believe something supernatural planted that evil seed in them." He sighed heavily and rubbed his face with big hands. "Like most people, I've denied the existence of ghosts ever since I was old enough to reason. But I guess I was just kidding myself all along. Hell, I know I was."

"You said that God didn't have anything to do with these . . . things."

"It's out of His hands. They sold their souls. They now belong to Satan. I don't believe that a person can live a life of depravity and degeneracy and then on their death beds mumble a few words and be absolved of all sins. I think that's crap. I think to attain Heaven, a person has to work at it all their lives. Not to be perfect, for that's an impossible goal for a human. But try to do the best they can. My dad used to say that Heaven was going to be a very sparsely populated place. And come Judgement Day, there were going to be a lot of very disappointed and unhappy people. I think he was right."

"This is a side of you I didn't know existed."

"I've watched too many people die pinned in wreckage; seen the light of life fade from their eyes. Innocent eyes. Then look up to watch some stinking drunk or some worthless damn punk walk away unharmed from the wreck he or she caused. I've seen victims of incest, rape, torture, drive-by shootings, robberies. You can't but think about the hereafter. Maybe cops won't admit they do; maybe they aren't even aware of it at the time. I always was."

"Have you killed people, Cole?" she asked softly.

"Yes. In 'Nam and on the job as a cop. On the job I've killed two and wounded two." He smiled, but it was a hard smile. "And beat the shit out of several."

"One of those kind of cops, huh?" But it was said with a twinkle in her eyes.

Cole smiled. He was happy to shift the conversation away from Katti's brother. If for no more than a moment or two. "You have to get some folks' attention. No, truthfully, in over twenty years behind a badge, I had very few complaints from the public. I don't believe in hassling people, and don't have any use for cops who do."

The twinkle in her eyes faded, and she lost her smile. "Cole, are you certain in your mind that you want to pursue this investigation?"

He nodded his head. "Yes. Very certain. Pack enough for a week's stay. Let's get to the bottom of this mystery."

They checked into a small but clean and well-kept motel in a town close to the site of the old roadhouse. They ate lunch and drove out to where the roadhouse used to stand. The concrete slab was plainly visible, although the parking lot was grown over with weeds. Together, they walked around the several acres. It was then that Katti noticed Cole was not wearing his pistol. But he was wearing what looked like some sort of walkie-talkie in a leather holder.

"What is that thing?"

"Stun gun. The best and most powerful one made. Delivers several hundred thousand volts."

Katti thought about that for a moment. "You're going to stun a ghost?"

"I don't know exactly what it's going to do. But if it works, I've got several more in the truck. I'll show you how it works, and tonight I want you to carry one."

"Stun a ghost," she muttered. "Right."

Cole smiled and said no more about it.

After walking around the area, they both sat down under a huge old oak tree. After a moment, Katti broke the silence. "Cole? Are we a couple of idiots, or what? The more I think about what we're doing, the less certain I am."

"I know the feeling. I also know what I saw that night. Not that many miles from where we're sitting, I might add."

"Cole?"

"Ummm?"

"What if we do . . . find Tommy? What can we do?"

"I don't know. I didn't find many answers in those books of yours. But it's obvious that he's trapped—for some reason— between worlds. What kind of a person was your brother?"

"Basically a good person. He enjoyed being around people, liked most people. He seldom had a bad thing to say about anybody. He was a teacher. But a very special kind of teacher. He worked with retarded kids. Tommy was a very patient sort of man. The kids loved him."

"Married?"

"Divorced. They were married while they were both in college. It was a mismatch from the beginning. They called it quits after a few years. No kids. He was seeing a real nice lady before he . . . vanished. She finally moved away. I don't know where she is now."

"What happened to Tommy's car?"

She smiled. "I still have it. In storage. It was a restored 1965 Mustang. Tommy loved that car."

"If things work out this evening, tomorrow we'll go back to Memphis and get that car. Bring it out here with us at night and park it. Is that all right with you?"

"Sure. But why?"

He shook his head. "I don't know. Just a hunch. I want to play every angle I can think of."

"What if . . . what if we don't see anything tonight?"

"We come back every night until we do."

"Maybe we should contact some religious person. What do you think?"

"I thought about that. But I'm not sure that religion has

anything to do with what's happening at these old honky-tonks. I think it's beyond that, past it." He was silent for a time, then said, "The past . . . the past. Who are these people who live on and on in these honky-tonks? Are they local people? How did they die? What kind of lives did they lead? We may be tackling this thing from the wrong angle." He stood up and held out his hand, pulling her to her feet. "Come on. We've got hours of daylight left. Let's go find some local folks who love to talk."

"What if we get tied up and can't get back out here in time? What about Tommy?"

"He's been here for ten years, Katti. He's not going anywhere."

"But—"

"He's dead, Katti. That's not flesh and blood that people see. That's Tommy's soul. Trapped where it doesn't want to be. These other people, the one's who permanently inhabit the old roadhouses, they *sold* their souls. They're where they chose to be. The more information we have about who, what, where, why, and how, the better prepared we'll be to help your brother. If that's possible."

"You mean we might not be able to help him? I don't even want to think about that!"

Cole put both big hands on her shoulders. "Katti, we're dealing with the *dead*—the afterlife. The only thing I know about the supernatural is that I don't know anything at all about it. No one really does. No, there is something I do know about it: frankly, it scares the crap out of me. So far, we've been stumbling around blind. Let's do some talking with the locals and find out all we can. We've got the time, and Tommy sure isn't going anywhere."

She shuddered under his hands. "He might be listening to us right now."

"He might be. I guess that's possible. I don't know what's possible and what's impossible anymore." Cole took his hands from her shoulders.

She walked a few feet from him and looked all around her, sudden tears misting her eyes, making the green farmland wavy and indistinct. She turned back to Cole. "What is it?"

"Pardon?"

"What do you want?"

"What are you talking about?"

"You just tapped me on the shoulder."

"I didn't tap you on the shoulder."

Katti's face drained of color, and for a few seconds, Cole thought she was going to faint. "Oh, god!" she whispered.

Cole felt a hard chill wash over him as a scream of anguish cut the warm air. He'd never heard anything like it in his life. The air suddenly contained a putrid smell that almost caused him to vomit. It was the smell of death. He was very familiar with the smell. It was the same odor he'd smelled up in Cairo, from the man who said he was homeless.

"Katti!" the cry sprang out of the summer air.

Katti turned around and around. "Tommy!" she called. "That's Tommy! Damn it, Cole, do something!"

Cole stood helpless. There was nothing he could do.

The wind picked up, blowing hard all around them. Cole's ball cap flew off his head and sailed away, spinning and spinning until he lost sight of it.

Loud music filled the windswept area. Cole remembered the song. Raunchy. Laughter was behind the music. But it was taunting laughter . . . evil . . . hate-filled.

Katti screamed as her blouse was ripped down the front, the buttons flying. Something hit Cole in the back and knocked him sprawling to the ground. He tried to get up and could not. Something, some . . . force was pinning him down.

He watched helplessly as Katti was lifted off her feet and tossed to the ground on her back. Her bra was ripped from her, and it went sailing off into the hard wind.

"Get your hands off me, goddamn you!" she screamed. "It's cold," she wailed. "It's cold. Stop it."

Cole summoned all his strength and bulled away whatever

it was holding him down. He ran over to Katti and slammed
into some invisible object. He heard a grunt as . . . whatever-
the-hell-it-was was knocked off of Katti. "Get up!" he shouted.

"No. Don't leave me!" the voice of Tommy lashed out at
them.

"Get up!" Cole ordered, reaching down and jerking Katti
to her feet. "Run for the truck. Run, damn it!"

"Sis!"

"Move, damn it!" Cole shouted at her, giving her a shove
toward the Bronco. He grabbed her hand and pulled her along
with him.

At the edge of the parking lot, the wind ceased its hard
blowing, the music faded, the laughter died away. Silence surrounded them.

Holding her ripped blouse together, Katti said, "Cole, that
was Tommy calling for me." Her face was very pale.

"We'll come back tonight. The joint ought to be jumping
about nine o'clock."

"Come back?" the words were almost a shout. "Cole, some
. . . *thing* was fondling me. Those were real hands. As cold as
ice. But hard and callused. You want me to come back *here?"*

"You want to quit?"

She leaned up against the Bronco and tried to compose
herself. She took several deep breaths. "Of course, I want to
come back. Forget what I just said. Jesus Christ, Cole! I've
never been so frightened in all my life."

"I don't think I had time to be scared. But I'm getting
a delayed reaction now." He held out his hands; they were
trembling.

"Well, you didn't have some redneck ghost pawing at your
tits!"

"And I certainly hope I never have that experience," Cole
said drily.

"That was Tommy's voice, Cole. It was really his voice.
He's here."

"We'll come back tonight. Come on. Let's get you back to
the motel for a change of clothing. Then we'll go find some

talkative local. And I want to show you how to use a stun gun. That was a real solid object I hit out there. I think my idea just might work."

"I'll kick him in the nuts, if he tries that again," Katti muttered, anger replacing fright.

Cole started laughing at the ludicrousness of the situation, and Katti looked at him as if he'd lost his mind. Then she started giggling at the idea of kicking a ghost in the balls.

"It's not funny, damn it!" she shouted at him, trying to contain her laughter. "How would you feel if some redneck chick grabbed you by the crotch?"

"Flattered," he said, and dodged the punch she threw at him.

Five

Katti was silent on the way back to the motel. After their laughter died away, she had sobered and not smiled since.

"You're sure that was your brother's voice back there?"

"Positive. It was Tommy."

Cole turned into the motel parking lot and pulled up in front of their room. "You feel like talking to people, Katti?"

"Now, more than ever," she said tight-lipped, one hand holding together her ruined blouse. She opened the door. "I'll be right back."

"Land, yes, I recall that dreadful honky-tonk," the woman said. "Mind you, now, I was never in that sinful place. But I know some of those who did drink and gamble their paychecks away out there."

Her name was Idabelle, and Cole had found her sitting with her sister, Clara Mae, on the front porch of their home on the outskirts of town. It was hard to tell how old the sisters were, but Idabelle looked as though she might vividly recall the Spanish-American War, and her sister looked like she might be able to talk at length about the Indian Wars.

"Terrible goings-on out at that place," Clara Mae said. "When it first opened, oh, forty or so years ago, it was a nice place—so I'm told. Then the trash of the county took it over—Ace Black and Curly Williams and Steve Deal, and those types of people. Drunkards and gamblers and thugs—bad blood in those men . . . and the women they caroused around with."

"Oh my, yes," Idabelle said. "Joyce Rushing and Paula McCord and Gloria Kendrick . . . to name but a few. They all met with tragic ends. Every last one of them."

"Not all of them, dear," her sister gently corrected her. "Billy Jordan is still alive."

"That's right! He sure is. My, but he was a bad one in his day. Now he could tell you some tales about the roadhouses up and down the highway. He sure could."

"Does he still live around here?" Katti asked.

"He certainly does. Right down this road about five miles. Little white frame house on the left side. Name is right on the mailbox. Arthritis slowed him down." She looked hard at Cole. "The Lord will punish sinners, Mr. Younger. Always. You remember that."

"Yes, ma'am. I sure will."

"And, then, there is our cousin," Clara Mae said.

"You hush your mouth!" Idabelle said.

"No, I won't. For just as sure as God made little green apples and little boys to eat them, Cousin Ray was one of the rounders who frequented that horrible place." She looked at Katti. "Ray was a bad one, child. But prison changed him. He found the Lord. He preached right up to when he retired."

"Is he still alive?"

"Oh my, yes. He lives on the other side of town. 'Bout two miles out. Right on Route 120. Name's on the mailbox. Ray Sharp."

"And he was a bad one?" Cole asked. "A patron of the Corral and the County Line?"

"My word, yes," the old woman said softly. "Up until he got out of prison, Cousin Ray was probably the sorriest son of a bitch in the county."

Idabelle picked up the tray and held it out for Cole and Katti. "Have another cookie," she said sweetly.

"You got the mark of the law on you," the old man in the wheelchair said sourly. "I don't cotton much to lawmen. What the hell do you want?"

"Some information," Cole said. "And I'm retired from the law."

"You ain't been retired long, boy. You still stink of the badge."

"If you don't want to talk to us, we'll leave," Cole told the man.

The old man waved a gnarled hand at the porch swing. "Oh, hell, sit down. Talk is cheap. What do you want to talk about?"

"The Corral and the County Line."

Billy's eyes softened in remembrance. "Hell of a place back in its day. Rough place. But a lot of good times was had out there. And some mighty bad ones, too."

"Let's talk about the bad ones."

"What's in it for me, if I do?"

"Nothing."

Billy chuckled. "You're right out front with it, I'll give you that. All right. You got a bad time in particular in mind?"

"Ten years ago," Katti said.

Billy shook his head. "I'd quit my runnin' around some years 'fore then. I been in this damn chair for more'un ten years. But I bet I know the incident you speak of. Young man, 'bout thirty-five years old disappeared after bein' out there, right?"

"That's right."

"Way I heard it, Steve Deal killed him. A local road whore name of Joyce Rushing come on to that young man. But Steve, he fancied Joyce was all his. He was wrong 'bout that. Joyce wasn't never gonna be tied down to no one man. Hell, boy, the cops know all this. They should have told you." He smiled at the expression on Cole's face. "But they didn't, did they?

Dirty little secrets—every town and county has 'em. Well, what the hell? I'm an old man fixin' to meet his Maker. Eat up with cancer. On top of everythin' else, cancer is gonna kill me. I ain't got long. Six months at the most, the doctors tell me. I figure less than that. It's a feelin' I got. And I think I'll feel better gettin' this story out of my craw. So you turn that machine on, Missy. I'm fixin' to tell you some stories about roadhouses from West Memphis to Cairo, Illinois. Now, you ain't gonna believe me, but it's the truth. Ever' goddamn word of it."

Katti turned up the volume and leaned back in the swing.

Several hours later, just as the sun was going down, Cole and Katti sat in their motel room, listening to the tapes as Cole was making dubs of them on another recorder. Billy had been careful not to mention his name anywhere in the more than two hour relating of past events in roadhouses all up and down the line. But he had named several dozen other names, including some rather prominent people and more than one law officer.

"Monstrous," Katti said. "Rape and murder and beatings and torture, spanning twenty-five years."

"And we've got men and women involved in this who are now judges, lawyers, millionaires, half a dozen state senators, and several past and current sheriffs," Cole said. "Jesus!"

"Five states, Cole. Stretching from Cairo, Illinois, down to Jackson, Mississippi."

"And Billy certainly couldn't have known everybody involved. There are probably a hundred more people mixed up in this that he didn't name."

"That woman, Joyce Rushing, she came on to Tommy, and Steve Deal beat him to death because of a little flirtation."

"But Steve wasn't alone in this. The Sheriff's son was right in there with Steve, punching and kicking your brother . . . along with several others." The taping was finishing and Cole took the second cassette and leaned back with a sigh. "Not one word of this would ever make it to a court of law. It's hearsay. Katti, the sheriff *then* is still the sheriff *now*. And the chief deputy *then* is still the chief deputy *now*."

"What are you saying, Cole?"

He leaned forward and whispered, "This tape, even though it's not admissible as evidence, is damning. It could ruin careers. We were followed today, by at least two people who were pretty damn good at it. But not good enough. It was a two-vehicle soft tail. We leave everything except these tapes right here in the room. We walk out of here like we're going to supper, and we keep right on going and don't stop until we get to Memphis."

She put her lips against his ear and softly asked, "Why are you whispering?"

"The room might be bugged."

Her lips formed a silent O.

"Well, I'm hungry," Cole said in a normal tone of voice. He stood up and motioned for Katti to do the same. "Let's go get something to eat. Then we'll head out to the old roadhouse site, and see what happens."

Cole slipped one set of tapes into his jacket pocket, and gave the other set to Katti to put in her purse. They left the room and stepped outside.

Cole put a hand to his mouth in case a lip-reader watching them and said, "When you get in, buckle up. This might be a wild ride."

"I feel awful, deserting Tommy."

"We'll be back. I promise you that."

Dusk was settling over the land as they drove away from the motel.

Billy Jordan felt the sudden drop in temperature and saw the sparkling dots light up the room. He looked up from the TV. A smile creased his lined face. "Once you get away from that goddamned old honky-tonk, you're visible, you know that?"

The hundreds of sparkling dots that vaguely formed a once-human shape brightened and dulled in reply.

"You think I fear death?" Billy said, his voice calm and steady. "Hell, Curly or Steve or Ace or whoever the hell you are, I look forward to it. The pain is getting worser ever' day."

The sparkling dots moved closer, and Billy could feel the air grow colder and the smell of rot filled his nostrils.

Billy smiled. "I always said you didn't take baths regular enough, Curly. And it is Curly. I recognize the smell. You stink worse now than you did before."

The dots flashed in anger.

"Fuck you," Billy said. "And them that use you. They're the worst. You're just pawns in their game."

The television set was picked up and hurled across the small room, shattering against a wall.

"I never liked that program no way," Billy said.

The temperature in the room dropped another ten degrees, as a second sparkling form appeared.

"Ace," Billy said. "I got to say this is an improvement. You always were an ugly son of a bitch."

Billy felt himself picked up from the wheelchair and flung across the room. He screamed as a hundred points of pain flashed through him, when he impacted against the wall. He flopped on the floor and managed to pull himself up to a sitting position, his back to the wall.

"Get it over with," Billy gasped. "Hell, it'll be a relief."

His wheelchair was picked up and the metal twisted in grotesque shapes. One wheel was torn loose and the wheel slammed down on Billy's head, the spokes wrapping around his now bloody face and neck.

"Perverted sons of bitches," Billy blubbered the words past bloody lips. "Bullies and cowards, ever' damn one of you."

What was left of the wheelchair was slammed down on Billy's legs, breaking his knees. He screamed in agony and waves of pain-filled shadows tried to engulf him. He fought the darkness and swam back to the sparkling dots that confronted him with evil.

"Bastards!" Billy whispered. "I never sold my soul. I wasn't much good, but I fought the devil and I'll *still* fight him. You're all pieces of shit. Ever' one of you."

Billy's tongue was ripped from his mouth, and the blood gushed out in spurts. He silently screamed his agony.

The sparkling dots seemed to laugh.

Cole shook the tail and when he reached the interstate, he cut north, knowing that was the unexpected thing to do. "We'll cross the river north of here at Caruthersville, then cut south through the western part of Tennessee."

"Are you exaggerating the danger, Cole?"

"No. If anything, I downplayed it. This is big, Katti. Real big. Lots of players in this cover-up. Hell, we might not be safe *anywhere*."

"Why?"

"I've got a nasty feeling this thing is going to mushroom on us, Katti. We're capable of opening up closet doors and uncovering skeletons that have been long hidden. And like Billy told us, it stretches all up and down the line. A lot of people who had back room dealings with those old roadhouses have real money. I'm more than comfortable financially, but some of these people have *millions* of dollars. And big money can buy lots of trouble."

She looked at him. "For us, you mean."

"Yeah. I've got a buddy I was in 'Nam with, who is a top flight private investigator in the Memphis area. I saved his ass twice in 'Nam and helped set him up in business; he got hurt as a Tennessee highway cop and had to retire on disability. Jim would walk through hell for me."

"And we just might have opened that door, Cole."

"That thought has occurred to me."

"I'm suddenly very scared."

"Stay that way. It'll help keep you alive. Only fools or liars say they're never afraid."

"I can't imagine you being afraid, Cole."

He chuckled. "Cops are sort of like crop dusters, Katti."

"Crop dusters?"

"Yeah. Ag pilots. I had one tell me once that there are old crop dusters and there are bold crop dusters, but there are very few old, bold crop dusters."

"We still going to take Tommy's old Mustang out of storage?"

"No point in it now. I was going to use it to lure those . . . *things* out to us."

"I believe we've been successful in doing that," Katti said, then shivered in remembrance of recent events, and in what might lie ahead for them. "Are we being followed, Cole?"

"I don't think so."

"We are going back there, aren't we?"

"You bet."

"But we're sure to be spotted ten minutes after we go back."

"That's right. But we won't have the tapes. They'll be in a very safe place in Memphis. And if, or probably when, we're stopped and questioned, those in power will be told that if anything happens to us, the tapes are to be released to the press and the police."

"Providing, of course, the order hasn't gone out to shoot us on sight."

"That is something to be considered. Do you know anything about guns?"

"No. They scare me."

"Ever fired a gun?"

"Hell, no!"

"Well, if the need ever arises that you have to, just point the little end at the target, hold on, and pull the trigger."

"I know that much, Cole. I watch John Wayne movies."

"I wonder what the Duke would do in this situation," Cole mused.

"Charge," Katti said.

Cole smiled and cut his eyes to her. "You know, that might not be such a bad idea."

"Oh, lord!" Katti said.

"But one thing really puzzles me."

"Just one thing?"

"Why did it start twenty-five years ago? What triggered it?"

"I haven't thought about that."

"We'd better start thinking about it."

She glanced at him.

"Our lives might depend on it."

Six

Jim Deaton listened to the tapes, his eyes widening in shock more than once. He made careful notes as the tape wound on.

Katti had liked the P.I. from the first. Jim did not look at all like the Hollywood version of a private investigator. He was not a big man, standing several inches under Cole's nearly six feet. His hair was sprinkled with gray. But Katti could sense a certain strength about the man. She decided that Jim could be a very rough customer, when pushed past a certain point.

Jim sighed and leaned back in his chair when the conversation with Billy Jordan was over. He fixed Cole with a strange look. "Ghosts, Cole? Really?"

"Really. They exist, and you can tattoo that on your arm."

Jim nodded his head. "I'll have another copy of these made and secure them in a safe place. Ghosts, Cole?"

"Yeah, Jim. Ghosts. Very dangerous ghosts."

"I recognize some of the names on those tapes. Some of them are monied people in high positions. We start shaking their tree, they'll shake back. You realize that, don't you?"

"Oh, yeah."

"I want the sheriff's son and everyone else involved in my

brother's death punished for it," Katti said. "I don't give a damn how many trees we have to shake."

Jim smiled at her. "There is no statute of limitations on murder, Katti. But these tapes are useless in a court of law. We're going to have to have more than that."

"Then we'll get it."

"Are you licensed to work in Arkansas, Jim?" Cole asked.

"Oh, yeah. And Missouri and Mississippi, too. I'm not going to charge you anything for my services, Cole, but we're going to need some help on this."

Cole held up a hand. "Whatever is necessary, Jim. I'm not exactly a poor man."

Jim smiled, punched a button on his intercom, and spoke to his secretary. A moment later, a man and a woman walked into the office, both of them in their early to mid-thirties, and both of them positively shining with health. The man was quite handsome, and the woman very attractive.

"Gary Markham and Beverly English. Bev for short. They're both experienced operatives. Both are experts in the martial arts, and both are expert shots with rifle and pistol. Although none of those qualities are worth a damn against ghosts."

Bev and Gary blinked. "Ghosts?" Bev asked.

"Ghosts," Jim repeated. "Both of you caught up on projects?"

They nodded.

Jim held out the cassette tapes. "Both of you listen to these tapes; then come back in here and we'll talk."

Bev and Gary took the tapes and left the room.

"Beverly looks . . . well, very capable," Katti said, when the door had closed.

"She's more than that. Army brat. Her father is a retired general. Before he got his stars, he was commander of various Airborne, Ranger, Special Forces units—the whole bag. Bev was jumping out of airplanes before she was fifteen. She got really irritated when the army wouldn't let her become a Green Beret. After high school and during college, she took about a dozen of the civilian survival courses around the country. She's climbed mountains, waded through swamps, eaten things that would gag a maggot, and killed two men. One with a knife and the other with her hands. Gary is tough as a boot. Ex-Marine Force Recon. Was on some clandestine ops down in Central America . . . and other places. The CIA wanted him real bad. Gary said there were too many limitations in working for them. He's worked for the Pinks, Wackenhut, and others. One will go into Arkansas, the other into Missouri, and nose around."

"Jim, you make damn sure they realize this is not a game," Cole cautioned.

"We don't play games, Outlaw," the P.I. said with a smile, using Cole's nickname. "Now, let's hash this thing out . . ."

Millions of dollars were represented in the large conference room. Several sheriffs, several chiefs of police, two state troopers, a sprinkling of deputies, three judges, several state senators and representatives, and one US Senator and one US Representative. There were captains of industry, and men and women who owned huge tracts of land. Their ages ranged from the mid-forties to the mid-seventies.

"I thought we agreed we would never meet again," one older man said, a frown on his face.

"Something's come up," the sheriff of an Arkansas county said.

"Then get it said," a federal judge spoke. "I have a golf game in a few hours."

"You just might want to postpone that, Jeff," the sheriff said. Then he started talking. The gathering fell silent, as hushed as a graveyard at midnight.

When the sheriff finished, the US Senator said, "I haven't been in a goddamn honky-tonk in forty years! This has nothing to do with me."

"The hell it doesn't," a chief of police said. "We know about those old roadhouses. We knew of the danger they posed. And we did nothing about it."

"What the hell could *we* have done about it?" a millionaire industrialist asked. "Go public and tell people we knew where there were ghosts? We'd have been laughed out of the country. None of us would have attained our current positions had we done that."

"Let's cut the bullshit!" a woman said, her voice hard. "We all know that some of us have used those roadhouse to, ah, shall we say, rid ourselves of people who might present a problem to our futures."

"I never have!" the federal judge said hotly.

"You're a damn liar, Warren," the woman said. "How about that bimbo you were humping? What happened to her?"

"How did you know . . .?" the judge bit back his words.

"You told her to meet you where the old Highway One roadhouse used to stand," the woman said. "She told her father where she was going. Then she dropped off the face of the earth. And we all know what happened to her. So don't get high and mighty with us."

"Look," a very senior state trooper said. "So these people have a tape recording from a man who is now dead. That tape is worthless. We didn't kill Billy Jordan, and we didn't order him killed. We had nothing to do with it. Those . . . *things* killed him. But I agree this Cole Younger person and Katti Baylor just might give us some problems. Unless we can stop them." He looked at the sheriff of the county where the County Line club used to be. "Your boys blew it last night."

"We didn't have enough time to set it up, Curtis. And my deputy never dreamed Younger would turn north on the interstate. It wasn't a logical move."

"They never are," the veteran highway cop said.

"Let's don't start bickering among ourselves," a district judge said. "That will accomplish nothing. What we have to decide now, right now, is what to do about these meddlers."

"There is only one thing to do," a state senator said. "And we all know what that is."

"I agree," a man said. "I am not going to sit idly by and have my reputation ruined by these people."

"Wait a minute," another man spoke up. "Listen to me. Most of us have had no dealings with the honky-tonks in whatever area we're from in years. Any honky-tonk. The only thing we have in common, most of us, is our knowledge of the . . . well, *beings* that linger around those old places. I mean, okay, so a lot of us were rowdy in our youth. We joint-jumped. Big deal, so did a lot of other people. And like us, they've settled down. We're not in cahoots with these . . . creatures. It isn't as if we have any control over what they do, for we don't. I say it's time to go public with what we know, and take the consequences."

"Do you realize what you're saying, Gerald?" a state representative asked. "Or better yet, what you're asking us to do? I couldn't get elected outhouse inspector, if this were made public. We'd all be objects of ridicule and quite possibly any number of lawsuits. And maybe prison. So what if we can't be linked directly with any of the many disappearances over the years. The dumbest cop in the world would smell a rat five minutes after you opened your mouth. He'd start adding it all up, and the next thing we knew, we're all up to our necks in shit. No. I'm sorry, but no. It's unfortunate about these two people—and I'm really sick about it—but I've got kids to put through college, a mortgage to pay off, and a future. No. I say we silence them. Any way we can."

"My pension would go right out the window," the senior highway cop said. "I agree with you, Maxwell."

Only a few sided with Gerald, including Sheriff Pickens, although silently and half-heartedly. The US Senator said, "I'm out of this. As of right now, I don't know any of you people."

"Don't be a fool!" one of the women said. "Most of us are campaign contributors of yours. That alone means we're in this together. I agree with Maxwell. It's unfortunate. I'm sorry about it. I truly am. But we've got to look out for number one." She shook her head. "I have never understood what an educated, well-respected teacher from Memphis was doing in that white-trash joint to begin with."

"Asking for directions," a chief deputy said. "He got lost.

Some road whore started coming on to him, and Steve Deal invited the man outside to fight. When the guy wouldn't fight, Steve sucker-punched him, and that's when Sheriff Pickens's kid jumped in the middle of it and started kicking the guy. The teacher managed to get outside and was running up the road, when the Pickens kid ran over him with his truck. They dragged the body around back and dropped it into an old privy pit.''

"How convenient for your son that you personally led the investigation, Sheriff Pickens," another of the women said acidly.

The sheriff flushed red, but said nothing.

"Is the body still there?"

"The bones are, I'm sure."

"And now we all know about it," a judge said sarcastically.

"Yes," a state representative said. "Speaking for myself, I certainly could have done without that information. We're just getting in deeper and deeper."

"And if one falls, we all fall," the US Senator reminded the group.

"You're an asshole, Bergman," Sheriff Pickens said to the man.

The Senator smiled. "I assure you, Pickens, I've been called much worse."

Cole picked up the ringing phone. "Jim here, Cole. I just spoke with a friend on the Memphis PD. Your Billy Jordan was murdered in his home last night. It was really macabre. He was torn all to pieces."

"They got him for talking to me."

"They?"

"The . . . well, *things* . . . goddammit, Jim. You know who I'm talking about."

"Cole, if they're dead, what harm could come to them by a old man talking to you?"

Cole sighed. "I know it doesn't make any sense. I haven't

worked out that part of it yet. But I will. Anything else happening on your end?"

"Bev and Gary headed for their assignments. You and Katti just relax for a couple of days. I'll be in touch."

Katti worked on her story and Cole read everything he could find on ghosts, the supernatural, unexplained sightings, the Devil, and related material. Katti had a computer with a modem, so Cole had Jim E-mail him any new information he could find on the murder of Billy Jordan. Several people who lived along that lonely road said they saw strange lights the evening Billy was murdered. Sparkling lights, dots, sort of like a kid's lighted sparkler, and sort of all connected.

Connected like what?

They looked sort of like a human shape.

The reports were dismissed as nothing more than overactive imaginations.

But Cole smiled. "Got you!" he whispered. "I believe I can beat you."

Katti looked up from her work. "Did you say something to me, Cole?"

"Just talking to myself."

"I do it all the time. Comes from living alone."

Jim reported that the murder of Billy Jordan was now considered to be the work of drug-crazed hippies, who were passing through, and robbed and murdered the old man in some sort of perverted sexual rite. Hippies being what they are.

"Bullshit!" Katti said. "The sheriff of that county is in this up to his nose."

"Sure he is. Now all we have to do is prove it."

On the fourth day out, Bev returned from Arkansas, where she had been posing as a artist who was looking for a piece of property to buy. Gary was still up in Missouri.

Bev and Jim came out to Katti's house. "A big meeting was held at the estate of one Victoria Staples the day after you two made a run for it out of the county. Practically every name that Billy mentioned on that tape was in attendance. And the list is very impressive.''

''But what do they have to do with these ... well, hell, ghosts?'' Cole questioned.

Bev smiled and sipped her coffee. ''Most of them didn't even know each other until about ten years ago. Right after Tommy was reported missing, and Steve Deal and Joyce Rushing killed each other in a wild gunfight.''

''Billy didn't tell us that,'' Katti said.

''No. People don't talk about that incident. Steve and Joyce were living together, as they had done off and on for years. He was a thug and she was a whore. One night they got into a shouting argument and Steve hit her—this is conjecture— she came up off the floor with a gun and shot him. He staggered over to a dresser or table and grabbed his pistol. Then they stood face-to-face in the living room and shot it out. Emptied their pistols. Each one was shot six times.''

''Nice people,'' Katti muttered.

Bev said, ''Ace Black and Curly Williams were both killed by the father of a fourteen-year-old girl they'd found walking alongside a road. They raped her repeatedly ... among other sexual perversions. The father is still in prison.''

''Whatever happened to justice in this country?'' Katti said, some heat behind her words.

''Paula McCord and Gloria Kendrick were killed during a high speed chase on Interstate 55 ... after they ran over and killed a six-year-old boy. They were both drunk. It would have been Paula's fifth DWI in ten years,'' she added drily. ''But she still had a driver's license.''

''I know that story all too well,'' Cole said. ''A friendly judge.''

''She was fucking him, among other things,'' Bev said. ''Judge Roscoe Evans is rather kinky in his sexual appetites.''

''Is he still on the bench?'' Cole asked.

''Oh, yes. District judge.''

"What finally brought all these people together?" Katti asked.

"A series of coincidences and happenstance. They all were pretty rowdy in their younger days, and that stretches from about 1950 to 1975. Their ages range from mid-forties to mid-seventies. Geographically, my group runs from West Memphis to the Missouri/Arkansas line. Gary is working the bootheel of Missouri on up to Cairo, Illinois. He's pretty much finding the same thing. These people all discovered the . . . well, might as well get used to saying it . . . *ghosts* that inhabit these old clubs or club sites. And it was accidental. By this time, the older ones had given up their honky-tonking and were making careers for themselves. They didn't know what to do with this knowledge of the supernatural. They certainly couldn't go public with it; they'd become the objects of ridicule and their careers would fade like the wind. So they remained silent. But, on occasion, they'd go back to these sites just to see if what they suspected was true. It was, of course, and they began running into each other. That's conjecture on my part, and so is this: They formed a club, and at the beginning, it was all innocent enough. None of them had broken any major laws in their rowdy days. It was just a bunch of mostly highly successful men and women getting together once a month to laugh about their secret. But then the truth began to sink in, as one by one, they realized all the unsolved murders, disappearances, rapes, and assaults over the decades were being committed by these honky-tonk ghosts——"

"But what to do about it?" Cole picked it up. "They couldn't go public now, because they faced the possibility of being charged with accessories to all these charges."

"Exactly," Bev said. "They were all in a trap. Trapped just as surely as these ghosts were trapped."

"I can't believe the charge of accessory would stick," Katti said.

"Oh, I don't either. How the hell could anyone try a ghost in a court of law?" She looked at Cole and smiled.

He nodded his head. "Sure. Some of them made a pact with

these ghosts. How many of their enemies or political opponents or competitors in business have vanished over the years?''

''There you have it,'' Bev said.

''Son of a bitch!'' Jim said.

''Somehow, they lured people to these old places, and let the ghosts do their dirty work?'' Katti asked, very dubiously.

''Has to be,'' Cole said. ''But it must have really gotten scary for them when the sheriff's son got involved in Tommy Baylor's disappearance.''

''I'm sure it did,'' Bev said. ''I spoke to one very disgruntled ex-employee of Victoria Staples. He said that about three years ago, the monthly meetings stopped abruptly. This meeting a few days ago was the first one since that time.''

''So we spooked the group bad enough for them to call an emergency meeting,'' Cole said with a smile.

''Let me say something else,'' Bev said. ''I don't know much about the supernatural; as a matter of fact, I don't know anything at all about it. I don't think my mind has fully accepted what we're dealing with here. I believe everything that Cole and Katti told us, but yet——''

''I know,'' Cole interrupted her. ''Believe me, I felt the same way. Until a few days ago, when those things attacked us at the old club site. Now Billy's been ripped apart like he was fed through a meat grinder. But nothing human did it, right, Jim?''

The P.I. shook his head. ''Not according to what I heard. He was mangled.''

''And the burial was real hurry-up,'' Bev said. ''Closed casket, of course.'' She looked first at Katti, then cut her eyes back to Cole. ''What about these sparkling dots people claim to have seen that night?''

''The souls of the dead,'' Cole spoke the words softly.

Bev suddenly felt cold. She hugged herself and could not contain a shiver of dread at the thought.

''But that also brings up some interesting points,'' Cole said. ''The dead who linger at these old honky-tonks, as long as they stay within a certain boundary, can materialize in whole, or be invisible. But when they wander outside those boundaries, their souls become what they really are: electricity.''

"What?" Jim blurted, clearly startled by the words.

"Many writers about the supernatural agree that the soul is pure electricity. That would account for the sparkling dots that were seen." He leaned back, a smile on his lips. "And I think I know now why they're here, and also how to fight them."

"There are times, Cole," Jim said, "when I wish I had taken my mother's advice and gone into business with my dad. This is one of those times."

"What did your dad do?" Katti asked.

Jim smiled. "He was a mortician."

The tension in the room disappeared as the four of them sat and laughed until tears were running down their cheeks.

Seven

The incessant ringing of the phone woke Cole. He glanced at the clock on the nightstand. Four o'clock. Katti turned and muttered something about the damned phone. Cole fumbled around and stilled the ringing.

"Cole? Jim. I'm at the office. It's been tossed but good. Place looks like a tornado went through it. Here's the strange part: no alarms were tripped. Gary got back into town late and wanted to put his notes away in the safe. He discovered the mess."

"Ghosts don't trip alarms, Jim." Cole was reaching for his pants as he spoke.

Katti sat up in bed at those words.

"Yeah. You're right about that. A taxi driver has come forward and told the cops he saw some strange sparkling objects hovering around the building about midnight. He thought his eyes were playing tricks on him. Cole? Did those damn creatures, whatever the hell they are, follow you from Arkansas?"

"No. Why should they? Think about it. How many honky-tonks were in the Memphis area back in the fifties and sixties?"

Silence on the other end for a few heartbeats. "Yeah. Jesus. Cole! If that's the case, this could be nationwide!"

"Probably is. Hell, I'm sure of that. It would certainly account for the hundreds of unsolved crimes and disappearances each year, wouldn't it?" His eyes caught a flash of sparkling light outside the house. "Jim? They're here." He hung up the phone and glanced at Katti; she was dressing faster than she'd ever had before.

Cole slipped his feet into loafers and pulled on his shirt, then picked up the stun gun on the nightstand. "Now we see if my hunch was right," he muttered. "Stay right with me, Katti," he said.

"Don't you worry about that, buddy. I'm glued to you."

"Let's get out of the house. I don't want these things flopping around in here forever."

"What are you talking about? What's going to be flopping around?"

"You'll see. If this works."

"And if it doesn't work?"

"We're dead."

Katti grabbed his arm. "Listen. Is that humming?"

Cole listened. "Yeah. *Rock Around the Clock.*"

"Very amusing."

"Yeah. Hysterical."

Katti watched another sparkling shape materialize outside the bedroom window. "Which is what I'm very likely to become at any moment."

He handed her the keys to the Bronco. "You get to the truck and crank it up. I'll hold these damn things off. I hope."

The humming of the old rock and roll song abruptly ceased. The early morning was very quiet. Katti's car was in the garage, the Bronco parked behind it, outside. Cole put his left hand on the front doorknob, the stun gun held in his right hand. He had rigged a leather strap with a snap-buckle, so the stun gun could not be jerked away from him. But he could release it if he felt his arm was about to be broken or torn off.

"Ready?" he whispered to Katti.

The sounds of "Ready Teddy" suddenly blasted the night.

"They know what we're thinking and what we're doing," Katti whispered.

"What we're doing. I don't believe they know what we're thinking."

"You hope."

Cole jerked open the front door and was confronted by a huge blob of sparkling dots, more or less in human form. Cole jammed the points of the stun gun into the neck area and hit the button.

There was a very violent flash of light, and the smell of rotting, putrid, and seared flesh became very nearly overpowering. The round mass of sparkling dots that Cole guessed was the head of the thing, was torn loose from the trunk and went bouncing and rolling across the lawn. The arms of the creature flailed the air, grabbing blindly and wildly at the spot where Cole and Katti had been.

But they had ducked around the glob of dots and were running for the Bronco.

The sparkling head began bouncing up and down like a fluorescent basketball, higher and higher. A thin scream of what appeared to be pain filled the air. The two other lighted shapes paused where they were, watching the head bounce high into the air. The headless shape was blundering around, running into trees and frantically ripping up bushes and shrubs and slinging them all about in its blind fury.

Katti jumped into the Bronco as Cole ran up to another of the sparkling shapes and hit it with the stun gun, right in the center of what he hoped was its back.

The thing separated into two parts. From the waist down, the legs went running all about the yard, falling over lawn chairs and slamming into trees. From the waist up, the other part was trying to maneuver along using its arms. It wasn't doing a very good job of that.

The third sparkling shape was running away, becoming dimmer and dimmer in the night.

Cole stepped up to the torso and hit it in the head with the stun gun. The head blew up, sending sparkling dots flying in all directions. The legs were running down the center of the blacktop road, chasing after the third shape, which by now was no longer in sight.

The bouncing head soared higher and higher, until it hit a power company transformer. A brilliant flash of light lit up the early morning hours as the head and the transformer exploded, then the area went dark.

"Will you please stop playing Wyatt Earp and get in the damned truck!" Katti screamed at Cole.

But Cole was fascinated by the scene taking place before his eyes. When the head exploded against the transformer, the rest of the sparkling dots began fading away, and a human form began appearing on the front lawn. The skeletal form was dressed in a ragged and rotted suit, the fingernails had grown several inches in death. But there was no head.

There was, however, the terrible smell of death. Rotting flesh and internal organs.

The other headless torso of dots was flopping around on the ground, flailing its arms helplessly. Cole walked up to it just as headlights cut into the drive. Jim Deaton sat in his car, mesmerized by the scene taking place in front of him. He watched the torso began to fade, and yet another piece of rotting corpse appeared on the lawn.

"Jesus H. Christ!" Katti came storming up to Cole. "What's the matter with you? You're out here playing hero, and I'm sitting in the truck sweating blood and worrying about you, you—Oh!" She threw up her hands in exasperation.

"Well," Cole said, looking at the stun gun. "At least we know it works."

"How are we going to explain these rotting bodies?" Jim said, walking up.

"We're not." He turned to Katti. "You have any tarps?"

"In the shed out back."

"I'll get them," Jim said. He paused. "Then you can tell me what you plan to do with them . . . or maybe I shouldn't ask. Yes, I should ask. 'Cause if we get stopped by the cops and they see a couple of headless, rotting corpses, it's going to get real interesting, buddy."

"Not to mention smelly," Katti added, waving a hand in front of her nose. "Phew!"

"We can always tell them we work for the CIA," Cole said with a grin."

Jim rolled his eyes and walked off muttering.

The shock of the early morning visit hit them all about an hour later, as they were having coffee and breakfast in an all-night place on the outskirts of Memphis. Katti's hands started shaking so bad she had to sit on them.

"Delayed stress syndrome," Jim said. "Cole and me know it well. We were both just kids when we went to 'Nam. I hate to tell you what we both did in our pants the first time we came under a sustained mortar attack."

Cole grinned to hide his own suddenly shaky nerves.

"Well, that makes me feel some better," Katti said, her voice low.

They all looked up as a dozen police and sheriff's department cars went screaming by, lights flashing and sirens blaring.

Jim watched the cars whiz by. "I think it's going to be real interesting around Memphis for a few hours."

"Not if we're really dealing with Satan," Cole said.

Two heads turned slowly toward him and waited for some sort of explanation.

"This is not exactly the kind of publicity Ol' Fire and Brimstone desires," Cole explained.

"Are you serious?" Jim asked.

"Oh, yeah. Dead serious—no pun intended. Lucifer is sort of a low-key guy, I'm thinking."

"Jim, get real, will you?" Katti said.

"You'll see in a few minutes. I'll bet you both a hundred dollars."

"Hey!" the cook shouted out to the dining area. "There's all sorts of weird crap goin' on just east of town. People are reporting seeing strange creatures in the night! Can you believe it? Some are even saying they're ghosts!"

Cole, Jim, and Katti exchanged glances, but said nothing.

A few minutes later several power company trucks rolled past the all-night cafe, heading east.

Music suddenly filled the cafe. Music from out of the fifties. A truck driver, a man in his mid-fifties, looked up and smiled. "It's been years since I heard that one. Now that brings back a lot of memories for me."

Kay Starr was singing "Wheel Of Fortune."

"Yeah," another man said. "Tell the cook to turn up his radio. I like that song."

Cole, Jim, and Katti looked at one another.

The cook came out of the kitchen, wiping his hands on his apron. "The cook ain't got nothin' to do with that. That song ain't comin' from my radio."

One of the waitresses walked over to the jukebox and stared. "It's not coming from here, either."

The music grew louder, the invisible wheel spinning, spinning, spinning.

Jim's hand was slightly trembling as he lifted his coffee cup to his lips.

The waitress pulled the plug on the jukebox. The music did not stop. The cook turned off his radio. The music continued.

"Bernie!" the waitress by the jukebox called. "This is not funny. What's going on?"

The cook stepped out of the kitchen. "I don't know, Rose. Weird, ain't it?"

The song faded away.

"What the hell?" Bernie said.

The voice of Hank Williams filled the cafe, and the plaintive words of "Ramblin' Man" touched them all.

"I think some of them ghosts is *here!*" the truck driver said.

The waitress by the jukebox whirled to face him. "That's not funny."

"It wasn't meant to be," the truck driver replied.

Hank was singing about what to do with him when he died.

A couple seated across the room stood up. "We're out of here," the man said, tossing money on the table. "This is just too weird for us." The man and woman walked to the door. It would not open. The man shoved at the door. It would not open. He turned around. "Hey! This damn door's stuck."

Cole noticed that the glass of the door was green-tinted. "I bet I know what's coming next," he whispered.

The cook and the waitress pounded and shoved at the door to the cafe. It would not open.

The voice of Hank faded away, to be replaced by an old song titled "What's Behind the Green Door." The words and music blasted the air of the cafe.

"I guessed right," Cole whispered.

"Call the cops!" a woman yelled over the loud music. There was real fear behind her words.

Jim walked to the door and shoved at it. It would not budge.

"The damn phone's out of order!" Bernie yelled.

A waitress jerked up a pay phone and held it to her ear. "So is this one. What's going on around here?"

The truck driver picked up a chair and hurled it through a large window, then used another chair to knock out what glass remained on the bottom sill.

"By god, you'll pay for that!" Bernie yelled.

"Screw you," the truck driver said. He climbed up on a booth and stepped out through the window.

He came back in a lot faster than he exited. Some invisible force picked him up and hurled him back inside the cafe. He bounced off a table and slid across the floor, coming to rest against the counter. Cole got up and walked to him, squatting down. The driver was unconscious, but his pulse was strong. "He's alive. The impact knocked him out."

"What threw him back in here?" a waitress asked, her voice shrill with fear.

The music had stopped. The silence was loud.

The cook had stepped back into the safety of his kitchen.

Suddenly he started screaming. He ran out into the dining area, his face ghostly pale. "There's a stinkin,' rottin' body in there!" he yelled. "It don't have a head."

Then he bent over and puked on the floor.

The two corpses from Katti's front lawn had been wrapped in tarps and dumped over the side of a bridge and into a creek.

The three of them wondered where the other corpse might be. They didn't have to wonder long.

It appeared on a stool at the counter, the bony elbow in a ragged and rotted suit coat propped on the counter. "Gimmie a cup of joe and a short stack," a disembodied voice rang out. "Heavy on the syrup."

One of the waitresses fainted at the sight and sound, and the woman customer by the door started screaming hysterically.

A female voice backed by a big band began singing: "I Don't Stand A Ghost Of A Chance With You."

The hysterical woman by the door had her dress suddenly pulled up over her head and her panty hose jerked down. She frantically tried to cover herself. The man with her had his trousers and underwear torn from him. He stood naked from the waist down, a bewildered look on his face.

An unseen Dixieland band began hammering out: "They'll Be A Hot Time In The Old Town Tonight."

The jukebox was ripped apart and records started flying all over the place, smashing against the walls and the ceiling. Jim and Cole hit the floor, Cole jerking Katti down with him.

The cook jumped behind the counter and bellied down on the floor. The woman with her dress over her head found herself completely naked as her clothing was pulled from her.

A cop pulled into the drive just as dawn was breaking. He stepped out of his unit and stood quite still for a moment, staring at the diner, an unbelieving look on his face. He saw the big commercial refrigerator come sailing out of the smashed windows and jumped out of the way just in time to avoid being crushed. The heavy fridge landed on his unit, wiping out both hood and windshield. The horn and siren suddenly started honking and wailing, adding to the confusion. The emergency lights started flashing. The cop drew his pistol, but there was nothing to shoot at. He crawled to his unit and grabbed the mike. ''Officer needs assistance!'' he shouted to dispatch, then gave his location.

Pots and pans and dishes and cups and saucers and flatware were whizzing around in the diner. Music was playing, but it was out of time, out of tempo, and out of tune. The melody was unrecognizable.

The music stopped.

The pots and pans and dishes and flatware stopped sailing about the diner.

The records from the smashed jukebox fell to the littered floor and were still.

Cop cars from the MPD, THP, and the SO began moaning and flashing into the drive, the men and women getting out, staring in disbelief at the wreckage that lay before them.

A Tennessee trooper looked at the huge refrigerator on the hood of the cop's unit, and then looked at the totally bewildered city cop. ''Did you get a little impatient for breakfast, Ralph?''

Eight

The stinking, rotting, headless corpses had vanished as mysteriously as they had arrived in the cafe.

All the patrons of the diner (except for three and the still unconscious truck driver) were talking at once, and no one was making any sense.

The naked man and woman had blankets wrapped around them and were sitting at a booth.

"Jimmy," a local cop walked up to Jim Deaton. "What the hell happened here?"

"My guess would be a freak tornado," Jim lied. "I can tell you this: it sure scared the hell out of all of us. The place just suddenly exploded."

"Uh-huh," the veteran cop said. He looked at Cole. "A friend of yours, Jimmy?"

"Old army buddy of mine. We were in 'Nam together. He's visiting from Louisiana. He just retired from the sheriff's office down there. Cole Younger."

"Cole Younger?" the cop said with a smile.

"My father had a weird sense of humor," Cole explained.

"You know what happened here, Mr. Younger?"

"Sure don't. But it happened real fast."

"Uh-huh," the cop said.

"Hi, Bob," Katti said. She knew the cop from her newspaper days. "Don't ask me what happened here. I was too scared to do anything but duck."

"Uh-huh," the streetwise cop said. "Right." He sensed all three of them were lying, but had no basis to pursue that hunch. But he wondered why the hell the three of them were at a diner before dawn. The Memphis cop also knew he wasn't about to get jack-crap out of Jim Deaton, and the retired cop with him looked tough as a tank. He also knew that Katti Baylor could be as stubborn as a mule.

"Any of you see these headless corpses these folks are babbling about?"

Cole, Katti, and Jim smiled and shook their heads.

"Uh-huh. Everybody else saw the bodies, but you three."

"We were under the table," Cole said.

"Right," the Memphis cop said drily. "Katti, a transformer blew in front of your house a few hours ago. It blew with such force, it took the top of the pole out."

"I know," Katti said. "Cole is staying at my house. We had just been awakened by a call from Jim. His office was broken into earlier. Jim and Cole are helping me with a book I'm writing, and we were going into the city at first light to see if any of the notes and material were missing after the break-in. We stopped in here for breakfast. Big mistake, I guess."

"Uh-huh." Pure bullshit, the cop thought. You're all lying. But why? "Did any of you see any sparkling lights on the way in?"

"Sparkling lights?" Cole asked. "What kind of sparkling lights?"

The Memphis cop shook his head. "Probably just kids pulling a stunt of some sort. But both the PD and the SO got flooded with a lot of frantic calls. What about this ghost music everybody heard here in the cafe? I guess you three didn't hear that, either."

"Oh, we heard that, all right," Jim took it. "It seemed to

be coming from outside. Somebody probably left their radio on." He smiled. "We all enjoyed the music."

"Uh-huh. Right. Did you report your break-in, Jimmy?"

"Sure did."

"Well, we'll probably be talking again about this . . . incident. Nice to meet you, Mr. Younger. See you, Jimmy, Katti." He walked off.

"He knows we're lying," Jim whispered.

"Sure, he does," Cole said. "But he can't prove anything. Come on. Let's get out of here."

Outside, standing by the vehicles, Katti asked, "What was all this show about, Cole?"

"Ol' Nick letting us know he's around, I'd guess. He was just having fun with us, that's all."

"Fun!" Katti blurted.

"Sure. The devil himself isn't going to hurt us. It's the people who worship him, those who have sold their souls to him that we have to look out for. But there is only one problem with that."

"Just one?" Jim asked sarcastically.

"Yeah. The old devil is pretty slick. We won't have any way of knowing who serves him and who doesn't." Cole opened the door for Katti, and she got in.

"Wonderful," Jim muttered.

The news media reported that freak and unexpected high winds caused the damage to the cafe, and those same strange high winds were responsible for the power outage. Local professors and other so-called experts suggested that the many reports of sparkling lights that same night were no more than a freak of nature (which meant they didn't know what the hell *really* caused the sparkling lights). Nothing was said about the two headless corpses that appeared in the cafe.

Jim Deaton's office was shut down for a few days, until carpenters could repair the damage done during the break-in.

And Cole and Katti made plans to return to the site where her brother had disappeared.

Chief Deputy Sheriff Win Bryan closed the door behind him and took a chair in front of Sheriff Pickens's desk. "You're not going to believe who just checked back into the motel."

"I bet I can guess," the sheriff said, leaning back with a sigh. "Ms. Baylor and Mr. Younger."

"You got part of it. This time they got three others with them. All P.I.'s out of Memphis. Jim Deaton's crew."

That straightened the sheriff's chair with a thump. "Jim with them?"

"You bet. Cole Younger and Jim Deaton are old army buddies. Friends for years."

"Shit!"

"I had a buddy with the ASP check out this Younger. He's a straight shooter, and no one to fool around with. He can be damn rough, and won't hesitate to drop a hammer on you. Retired a captain from a Louisiana SO. His background is damned impressive."

"Jim Deaton is no one to fool around with either," the sheriff said glumly. "How about the others?"

"Gary Markham and Beverly English."

"I know about Gary. He's tough. What about this English woman?"

"She was in here a short time back, posing as a land buyer and nosing around the county. She talked to a lot of people."

The sheriff was silent for a moment, thinking hard and fast. Al Pickens had been sheriff of this county for years, and he planned on remaining the sheriff. But lately he'd been suffering bouts of conscience about the ghost club. He knew that what he and the others were doing was wrong. Oddly enough, Sheriff Pickens was a very competent lawman and ran a good county. He had made only one terrible blunder in the past ten years, and that concerned his son, Albert. But blood is thicker than water and Sheriff Pickens wasn't yet ready to put his son in prison for his part in what happened to that school teacher, Tommy Baylor. Al Pickens had spent many a sleepless night over the years.

And as far as those . . . well, *things,* that popped up every now and then out at the old County Line . . . what was he supposed to do about *them?* Put a bunch of ghosts in jail? He had spoken with Sheriff Reno of the county just above his, and to Sheriff Paxton of the county just to the west. They both belonged to the club, so to speak, and they both knew some really weird events had taken place in their counties over the years. But damn it, they were events that no human had any control over. So how the hell could people blame them for something that had been done by . . . well, *spirits?* It just wasn't fair.

And it wasn't fair for these strangers to come in and start muddying up the waters, either.

No, sir. It wasn't.

It just by god wasn't.

Judge Roscoe Evans had decided to take his annual vacation. All of it, right now. This matter of the strangers coming in and poking around had unnerved him terribly. He could be ruined and possibly even sent to prison, if they poked around and scratched up enough dirt. Something had to be done. He made up his mind. He'd go see Victoria Staples. She would know what to do.

Victoria Staples was a tall, very handsome, very mannish-looking woman. A very forceful person. A person accustomed to getting her own way. Always. Her graying hair was cut short and brushed back. She did everything she could to appear masculine. In any woman's prison, Victoria would be referred to as a bull dyke. Victoria hated men. All men. She enjoyed humiliating them. Especially that fool judge, Roscoe Evans. She knew he was one of several weak links in this long human chain that she was a part of. Sheriff Paxton was another, and so was Elmo Douglas and Albert Pickens.

And now Judge Evans was coming to see her, running scared. Good. She thought for a moment. Yes. That was it. She'd dress him up in a bunny suit with big floppy ears, and they could spend the rest of the afternoon playing. After she fucked him.

While Victoria Staples was selecting her various sexual instruments to be used that afternoon, and laying out Roscoe's bunny suit, Warren Hayden and Jefferson Parks, the two federal judges who had long known of the existence of the ghost clubs, were meeting in the countryside with Arlene Simmons, wife of a very rich industrialist, and Curtis Wood, captain of highway patrol. They were meeting in a barn on the back acreage of a tract of land she owned. The land was lying idle this planting season. Which suited her just fine, since the government was paying her not to plant. Which, unless one is a farmer, makes no sense at all.

"There is no point in looking back at this matter," Arlene said. "The past is done and we can't change it. What we've got to do is find some way to cover our ass."

Judge Jeff Parks was thinking that he would very much like to cover Arlene's ass. But for some reason, she had never let him fuck her.

"An accident could be arranged," Judge Hayden said.

"It might have to come to that," Captain Wood said.

Arlene looked around her at the old barn. The place brought back a lot of memories. It was here she used to fuck her foreman. Right up there in that loft, in the hay. Until he got too demanding and kept wanting more and more money from her. No dick was worth what he finally demanded from her. Arlene hit him on the head with an axe one afternoon, and dumped his body into the St. Francis River some miles away. The body never was found. That had been a real mess. Caved in one side of the man's head. Brains all hanging out. Real icky. But that ol' boy could sure get in the saddle and ride, for a fact.

"Not until we have that tape and the dubs they're sure to have made in our hands," Arlene said. Great god, did she had to do all the thinking around here?

"My man tossed Deaton's office," Captain Wood said. "The tape was not there."

"I understand he made quite a mess of it," Jeff said.

"Oh, he didn't do that. That was done afterwards. And we all know who it was. Or *what* it was, I should say."

Arlene fixed her eyes on Captain Wood. "You take care of it, Curtis. Money is no object. Just take care of the situation and get it cleaned up. All right?"

"Consider it done."

Sheriff Paxton was meeting with state representative Maxwell Noble, US senator Charles Bergman, businessman Gerald Wilson, state judge Silas Parnell, and state senator Conrad Wright, just south of the Missouri line.

"If we had reported those damned . . . *creatures* when we first learned of them, none of this would be happening," Gerald said sourly.

"Yes, and if your aunt had balls, she'd be your uncle," Senator Bergman snapped at the man. "There is no point in dredging up the past. It's over. We can't change it. We've got to decide what to do about these people snooping around."

"Get rid of them," Silas suggested.

"Oh, my god!" Gerald moaned. "Now you're talking murder."

Silas pointed a finger at the man. "Now you get hold of yourself, Gerald. You, along with the rest of us, have known for years those hants in the honky-tonks have and are killing people. That's murder, Gerald. Any way you slice it up, it's still murder. And you're as much a part of it as the rest of us. You damn hypocrite," he sneered at the man. "Big worker in the church, that's you. You whiny son of bitch! You're drenched in innocent blood, just like all the rest of us. So get with the program, buddy. You're an accomplice to hundreds of murders.

Your name is on those tapes with the rest of us. Now stop your bitching and start adding something constructive to this meeting."

"How about all the rest of the names on those tapes?" Conrad asked. "They should be here, too."

"Oh, they're meeting," Silas said. "In various locations around the area. My god, we couldn't all get together in one place! Not even at Victoria's ranch. We can't ever do that again. Each group will have a spokesman. I'm it for this group. Victoria has already met with her group. The spokesmen will get together this evening and hash it out. But I suspect Arlene has already put the ball into play. Now listen to me, all of you. When this is over—and it will be over very soon—we don't meet again. Ever. The club is broken up. Do you all understand that? That's the way it has to be."

"No," Gerald said, standing up. "My part is over right now. I'm finished. Through. I'll say nothing. But I'm out of this. I will have no part in cold-blooded murder. We can't control the actions of those things in the old clubs. But we could prevent this. I don't ever want to see any of you again. Ever. Never. I'm going to go pray for forgiveness. Goodbye."

After the sounds of Gerald's car had faded into the afternoon's warm air, Senator Bergman said, "You think he'll talk?"

"No," Sheriff Paxton said. "He's too scared for that. But even if he had that in mind, he won't live long enough to do anything about it."

"What do you mean?" Conrad asked.

The sheriff pointed to a darkened corner of the old lodge. Heads turned.

The corner was filled with sparkling dots.

Nine

Cole, Katti, Jim, Bev, and Gary suddenly hit a stone wall of silence. Very few people would talk to them. Most doors were slammed in their faces. Nearly everyone they tried to interview turned away from them.

Acting on a hunch, Cole took Katti and went back to see the sisters, Idabelle and Clara Mae.

"You young people certainly stirred up a lot of folks around here," Idabelle said, passing around a plate of fresh home-baked sugar cookies.

"Yes," Clara Mae said. "Sheriff Pickens is all worked up about your asking questions about the old honky-tonks in this area."

"Do you know why that should be?" Katti asked the old lady.

"Oh, sure. Once a body starts covering things up, the cover-up process can't ever stop. And while Sheriff Pickens has been an adequate sheriff over the years, he has his flaws. Just like Sheriff Reno north of here, and Sheriff Paxton over to the west. Idabelle and me, why, we've known all those men since they were boys. Haven't we, dear?"

"We certainly have," Idabelle said. "And they were all

rounders in their youthful days. Not bad people, mind you, jus
a bit on the wild side. But they all outgrew it, and became
good men and responsible citizens. Our husbands, God res
their souls, knew quite a bit about their antics and would tel
us about them. Some of it very racy, indeed.''

''How about the people who were in office before them?'
Cole asked.

The sisters exchanged glances. Clara Mae said, ''That's anothe
story, young man. You're talking about the bad old days, back i
the forties and fifties and early sixties. Sheriff Speakman is lon
dead, and so is the man who was his chief deputy before A
Pickens got that job. And I doubt you'll get any of the peopl
who served with them to talk. If you could even find them.''

''We're not trying to deliberately smear anyone's reputa
tion,'' Katti said.

''Oh, we know that. You're interested in finding out the trut
about what happened to your brother, that's all. Billy Jorda
told you some of it, didn't he? And just look what happene
to poor Billy.''

''We heard from a cousin of ours that Ray Sharp is preparin
for his death,'' her sister picked it up. ''He's had his good blac
suit all cleaned and pressed, and made arrangements with th
undertaker in town. Mind you, he's not afraid to meet his Maker
Just getting ready.''

''Do you find that odd?'' Cole asked.

''Not really. Ray used to go over to Billy's house and si
and pray with him. Until Billy took a broom handle and ru
him off. Billy said he was washed in the blood of the lamb a
a child, and that was enough. He didn't need some damned ol
reprobate coming around and thumping on the Bible. He'd tak
his chances with the Lord when it came time.''

''The time came a bit sooner than he suspected, I think,'' Ida
belle said. She stood up with a visible effort. ''Let me make a phon
call. I'd see if I can arrange something for you young people.''

When the screen door had closed behind her, Katti asked
''Who is she calling?''

''Cousin Ray. She gets along well with him.'' Clara Ma

made a face. "Personally, I can't stand the damned old fart!"
She picked up the tray and held it out. "Have another cookie."

Cole concluded that Ray Sharp must have been hell on wheels
when he was younger. The man was about six and a half feet
tall, and anyone with eyes could see that at one time he had
been an enormously powerful man. He waved Cole and Katti
inside and to a sofa.

"I've been waiting for you," Ray told them. "I knew you'd
be back." He pointed to the cassette recorder in Katti's hands.
"Turn that machine on and get all this." He waited until the
tape was rolling. "I'll be dead come sundown today. They'll
kill me just like they killed Billy Jordan. I prayed for Billy."

"Who will kill you, Mr. Sharp?"

"Ray. Call me Ray. Oh, Steve Deal, Bobby Perkins, Eddie
Morgan, Ace Black, Sly Bailey. They're all dead, you see. But
they made a deal with the Devil. I wouldn't never do that. Even
when I was a bad one, I wouldn't never deal with Satan. When
I got out of prison, I hunted up every person I ever done a hurt
to, and I begged their forgiveness. Most of 'em forgave me,
too. And I prayed for them that didn't. I don't blame them for
not forgiving me, but I still prayed for them."

"You weren't there the night my brother was killed, were
you, Ray?" Katti asked.

"No, child. I had just been released from prison, and was
working in a halfway house in Little Rock. But I heard about
it. Dreadful thing. I found the Lord in prison, and started taking
Bible courses through the mail. I was ordained in prison by
the chaplain. Preached in there for five years. And the Lord
gave me seven good years on the outside preaching, before a
heart attack felled me, and then I had a stroke and that put me
into retirement." He smiled. "I heard about all that mess that
happened in Memphis. The sparkling lights. Tell me about it."

Cole did.

The old man laughed. "A stun gun. A darned stun gun. Well,
it don't make no sense to me, but if it works, that's all that

matters. But a word of caution here, boy, that was some of the newer dead you hit with that contraption. It might not work on the older crowd. Reason I know that is, 'cause I been going to a lot of those old places since I got back here. I've seen those old joints appear in the night, heard the terrible profanity, and seen the wickedness that takes place. And yes, I've seen people lured to their deaths. But what could I do about it? Nothing, that's what. I couldn't go to the authorities; around here, that's Sheriff Al Pickens. And he's into this up to his neck. Could I go to the state people? Not likely. Who would believe an ex-con? I served fifteen years for second-degree murder, people. Even though it was self-defense, and I wouldn't lie about that. Not being so close to death as I am this day.''

"You want to tell us about it?" Cole asked.

"Why not? Charles Bergman's brother . . ." He smiled. "Yeah, the brother of the US senator from the state just north of us. He'd just been elected. Well, his brother's wife had been giving me the eye for some time. She was trash. Still is. So was I, in those days. Anyway, he confronted me with a gun one night outside a joint up in Missouri. In the bootheel. We struggled for the gun, and it went off. The man shot himself right in the heart. And like a fool, I ran. The police caught me the next day. It was a very quick trial. I got fifteen years to life. End of story. So you see, I couldn't go to anyone with what I know about those ghost clubs."

"Tell us all about everyone who is involved," Katti said. "Living and . . . dead."

The once most famous barroom brawler in North Arkansas leaned back in his easy chair. "I hope you've got lots of tapes. It's a very long story. With no happy endings."

"It's dynamite stuff," Jim said, after listening to the hours' long tapes. "But——"

"Not admissible in court," Cole finished it. "But at least we now have a fairly complete list of names. Living and dead."

"And in this case," Bev said, "we have to fear both the living and the dead."

"You want me to take that tape back to Memphis and get some dubs?" Gary asked.

"Both of you go. I want someone riding shotgun."

Bev and Gary pulled out, heading south. Jim stood by the big window of the motel for a time, staring out, Cole and Katti sat on the small couch. Jim turned and looked at them. "I want to see this club come alive."

"I got a better idea," Cole said.

"Oh?"

"Let's go face-to-face with Sheriff Pickens."

The sheriff was not happy to see them. He sat in his chair and scowled at the trio. Finally, he said, "I don't have much use for P.I.'s. I could run you out of this county, Deaton."

"You could try," Jim said. "In the meantime, I'll just call the governor, and we'll have a little chat about how my office stopped that attempted kidnapping of his youngest child last year. Or maybe we'll chat about——"

Pickens held up a hand. "All right, Jim. All right. I get the message. Forget I said that." He looked at Cole. "What's your interest in this county, Mr. Younger?"

"I'm helping Ms. Baylor do research on her book."

"Yeah. Sure you are." He cut his eyes to Katti. "I remember you now. You were nearly a permanent fixture around here for a few weeks after your brother disappeared."

"You mean after my brother was murdered, don't you, Sheriff? Beaten, and then run over by a two-bit punk driving a pickup truck."

The sheriff didn't lose his composure. He'd had ten years to practice for this moment. "No one really knows what happened to your brother, Ms. Baylor."

"Sure they do, Sheriff," Cole said. "And you're one of them."

"That is a serious allegation, Mr. Younger. You have any proof of that?"

"I didn't go public with it, Sheriff. Not yet. But I will tell you this: Ray Sharp is convinced he's going to be killed tonight. Could you spare a couple of deputies to keep an old man alive?"

"No, I'm short-handed; besides, I spoke with Ray this morning. He told me about his fears and also that he was going to talk to you people when you came around. There is no basis for his fear of being killed, and I told him I didn't give a damn who he talked with."

"I've been in one of the ghost clubs, Sheriff," Cole spoke softly. "The date was October 1957. But I was there only a few months back. Along Highway 61, just south of here. It was the K & G Club. I witnessed a man being killed. He was hit in the back of the head with a cue stick, and his body was tossed outside in the parking lot."

The sheriff almost lost it. His face paled, and he silently struggled for a moment before recovering. "Prove it," he finally managed to say.

"Oh, I intend to, Sheriff. Believe that."

"That was almost forty years ago, Mr. Younger," Sheriff Pickens said. "If anyone is still alive who might have any interest, they're old men and women whose main concern is staying alive a few more years, not dredging up old murder cases. You really think anybody cares?"

"Let's put our cards on the table, Sheriff. Face up. Those ghost clubs exist, and you know it. So did Sheriff Speakman before you. You were his chief deputy during his last term in office. Sheriff Reno knows about them, as did the sheriff before him. And so does Sheriff Paxton, and the sheriff before him. So let's cut the crap. There have been several hundred people— at least that many—killed and tortured and raped over the past two decades, but most of them simply disappeared. Only God and the devil know for sure. It's past time for it to stop. Are you going to work with us, or against us?"

The sheriff stared at Cole for a moment, then spun his chair around, putting his back to the trio. He sat that way for a full minute, then slowly turned to face them. "I don't know what you're talking about, Mr. Younger. I don't believe in ghosts."

Cole sighed. "Well, at least my mind is satisfied with the knowledge that we tried."

"Leave it alone, people," Sheriff Pickens whispered, surprising them all. "For your safety, leave it alone. You don't know what you're getting into. These things can't be stopped."

"The public has to be warned," Katti said.

The sheriff laughed, but it was a laugh totally void of humor. "Don't you think I haven't thought of that? Good god, people! I made one damn mistake in nearly twenty-five years of law enforcement. It's my son we're talking about. Do you know what would happen to him, if he were put in prison? The son of a cop? Cole and Jim know. He'd be gang-raped and possibly killed. I've kept his feet to the fire and tried to keep him walking the straight and narrow since that night. I'm sorry about your brother, Ms. Baylor. I really am. But I can't bring him back."

"But we can put him to rest forever!" Katti blurted. "We can let him go . . . home, I guess is the word."

Sheriff Pickens held out his hands. "How? Sheriff Speakman tried to figure out a way to destroy those damn things, when they first popped out around here. We both tried to come up with something. Listen to me, I've been haunted about your brother's death for a decade. There isn't a day goes by that I don't think about that night. Every time I look at my son, I think about that night. I've laid in bed trying to come up with some plan to rid this county of those damn . . . *spirits* . . . whatever the hell you want to call them. It can't be done. It isn't me you have to fear. I don't want to hurt anybody. But there are some powerful and ruthless people involved in this matter. You have all the names. I know you do. Senators and federal judges and millionaires. You think they're going to allow themselves to be ruined by this thing? Think again. But you're right about one thing for sure: Ray Sharp is dead. And there is nothing or no one on the face of this earth that is going to prevent that. Because what's going to kill him is not of this earth. And if I tried to help you, I'd be dead. It's just that simple, people. That's the bottom line. Those of us who have knowledge of those ghosts are trapped just as surely as they are. And I don't know how to free myself of that trap."

"Would you, if you could?" Jim asked.

"If it would mean turning my son in?" The sheriff shook his head. "No. No, I won't do that. But I won't have to. I told you: it isn't *me* you have to fear. It's mainly the others. And I've got to go along with whatever they decide to do. If not, I'm a dead man. Period."

"You have to have a spark of good in you, Sheriff," Katti said. "Or you wouldn't be telling us this."

That remark got to the man. His face changed, and his eyes took on a haunted look. "A spark of good," he whispered. "God, I hope so. Ms. Baylor," he raised his eyes to hers, "most of us who belonged to that club are good people, I think. Well," he amended that, "*some* of us, anyway. We were wild as bucks in our youth, then we grew up and married and had families and careers and mortgages and all the rest of it. Gerald Wilson is a good man. So is Elmo Douglas and Jack King. Betty Harris is a good person. And there are others. But we got caught up in this . . . trap. When we finally figured out what was happening, it was just too late. We didn't know what to do, who to turn to. It was just too late for us all." He swiveled his chair and put his back to them. "I believe this interview is over, people. You've been warned. I simply can't do no more than that."

Cole, Jim, and Katti rose and left the office. At the door, Cole looked back. The sheriff was still sitting in his chair, his back to them.

Cole said, "We're going to expose this whole awful mess, Sheriff."

"You'll try," the sheriff said. "Just leave instructions with someone as to where you want the bodies sent."

Ten

"Jesus Christ Almighty," Jim Deaton whispered, as the sounds of rockabilly music suddenly filled the night.

The three of them were in Cole's Bronco, parked in a turn row in a field of soybeans across from the site of the old club.

A four-piece band was shaking the walls of the old joint with their rendition of the Carl Perkins's classic "Matchbox."

"I'd always heard how pure that music was," Katti said. "I never believed it. But that was real rock and roll back then. No gimmicks, just raw passion and sound."

"Oh, my god," Jim whispered, as the club began to materialize in the night, misty at first, then taking shape. The weeds in the parking lot were replaced with hard-packed gravel, as the cars and trucks began appearing. A neon sign flashed over the door, but to those across the blacktop, the sign was not a welcoming light in the night. It was evil. Blood red. An invitation to step through the gates of hell.

"No one comes outside," Katti observed after a few moments of watching.

"That we can see," Cole said.

Jim stirred in the back seat. "I feel bad about Ray Sharp refusing our offer to stay with him tonight."

"He was adamant about it," Cole said. "But I don't know the reasoning behind it."

"He wanted to face these things alone," Katti said. "They were his friends at one time."

"Still doesn't make any sense to me," Jim groused.

"Nothing has made any sense to me for several weeks," Cole said. "I spent nearly forty-five years scoffing at the very idea of ghosts." He pointed a finger at the honky-tonk across the road. "But there they are. I . . ." He paused as headlights cut the night.

A late model car drove past the lighted joint just as an old pickup truck in the drive revved up, backed out of the line, and began cutting doughnuts in the gravel, rocks and dirt flying in all directions from the spinning back wheels. Wild, mad laughter rang out from the cab of the truck. A huge cloud of dust hung over the road. The man and woman in the front seat did not turn their heads toward the club.

"They didn't even notice it," Katti said. She sniffed the air. "There is no odor of dust."

"None settling on us either," Cole said. He got out of the Bronco and ran his hand over a section of the hood. The hand came away clean.

Katti and Jim climbed out to stand in the darkness. The music from the club pounded the night air. The lyrics to an old Hank Williams song drifted around them: "Mind Your Own Business."

"I wonder if they're trying to tell us something?" Jim said drily.

Cole glanced at the luminous hands of his watch. It was nine-thirty.

Katti cut her eyes to him and said, "If you think I'm leaving here without seeing my brother, think again."

"Oh, I think those . . . things in the club over there want you to see him, Katti. I think they want you to become so angry, you'll do something stupid."

"Like what?"

"Like step through that door over there, maybe."

Katti remembered the touch of those terribly cold hands on her flesh, and she shuddered. "No way, Cole. No way."

The music from the club had softened, the band quietly playing and the singer singing a ballad: "Faded Love."

"That's an old Bob Wills song," Jim said. "My dad used to play his records."

The door to the night club suddenly slammed open, banging against the side of the building. A man stumbled out, his face bloody, the blood dripping down onto his white dress shirt. He fell to his hands and knees on the gravel and cried out in pain.

"Tommy!" Katti called, and started across the road.

Cole grabbed her. "Steady, Katti. Don't go over there. I told you, that's what they want. There is nothing you can do for him now. He's dead, honey. Dead. Just hang on."

She struggled briefly against his strong hands, then relaxed. "I'm all right now, Cole. I just lost it for a few seconds. I won't try to go over there."

Cole released his grip, but stood very close to her, ready for a grab, if she tried to cross the road.

That which was once Tommy Baylor struggled to his feet. Cole noticed that he was wearing penny loafers. He wondered if there was a penny in each shoe, like people used to do several decades past. He shook his head to clear it, wondering why he would think of such a trivial thing at a time like this.

A half dozen men and women stepped out of the club. One man balled a hand into a big fist and stuck Tommy, knocking him down. The others laughed.

"Sheriff Pickens's kid is not among the crowd," Jim said. "I saw a picture of him in the office today."

"Of course, he isn't," Cole said. "He's not dead."

"Yet," Katti said grimly. "But I'll see him dead before this is over. One way or the other."

Neither man doubted her words.

Tommy got to his feet and was knocked down again. He once more crawled to his feet, and again he was knocked down. By now, his face was a mask of blood.

Katti wanted to turn away from the brutal sight and bury her face against Cole's chest. But she held on for a few more seconds.

"Tommy never was a fighter." The words seemed to be forced out of her mouth. "Never was good at athletics. I don't think he ever had more than two fights in his entire life. Everybody liked him." She lowered her head from the sight and started crying.

Cole felt helpless. Hell, he *was* helpless. The scene before them had occurred a decade past. He put his arms around her and turned her away from the terrible sight.

"I wonder if he is experiencing any pain from this?" Katti asked, her voice muffled against his chest. Cole could feel the wetness of her tears through his shirt.

"I don't think so, Katti. How could that be? He's dead."

She pulled away from him and looked up, tears streaking her cheeks. "How can *any* of this be possible, Cole?"

He had no answer for that.

Across the road, Tommy had painfully crawled to his hands and knees and paused there for a moment, then he jumped to his feet and ran from the parking lot. When he reached the blacktop, he looked wildly in both directions, then started running toward town. He vanished.

"The Pickens punk is not here to run him down," Jim said. "This is as far as the story can go. It just keeps repeating itself up to this point."

The area suddenly became very dark and silent. The old club had vanished; no lights and no sound filled the night. The cars and trucks had disappeared. The parking lot was once more weed-grown and trash-littered.

"Where do they . . . go?" Katti whispered.

Neither man had an immediate reply to that. After a moment, Cole said, "I guess there are only two entities in the world who could answer that, Katti."

She looked up at him.

"God and the Devil."

*   *   *

The next morning, while Cole, Katti, and Jim were having breakfast, Sheriff Pickens walked into the cafe by the side of the motel and took a seat at their table.

"Just coffee," he called to the waitress. In a low tone, he said, "I just came from Ray Sharp's house. My men are out there now, picking up what is left of the old man."

"So when does all the killing stop, Sheriff?" Cole asked, as he buttered a biscuit.

Al Pickens waited until the waitress had filled his cup before replying. He sugared and creamed his coffee and then, without looking any of them in the eye, said, "When you people get the hell out of my county and let the dead alone."

"That's crap and you know it, Sheriff," Cole bluntly told him, but in a low tone. "Those . . . *things* have been killing for a quarter of a century, and they'll continue to kill until some way can be found to stop them."

"Can't you people understand that these things are dead?" the sheriff hissed. "You can't kill dead people, you hardheaded asshole." He cut his eyes to Katti. "My apologies for that language, Miss."

She nodded her head in acceptance.

"Just how interested are you in ridding this county of those ghosts, Sheriff?" Cole asked.

"Are you kidding? I'd jump at a way to free myself of those . . . devils. That's what they are, you know? Devils. Straight from Hell. I really believe that. I really do."

The cafe was rapidly clearing of the breakfast crowd, and the table where the four of them sat was in a corner, faraway from any customers who lingered over coffee before heading off to work.

"They haven't been to Hell yet," Cole said.

The sheriff's eyes widened.

"That's just one of the many points that Billy Jordan and Ray Sharp agree on."

"Go on," the sheriff urged.

"We all agree that those men and women who linger on after death are so damn mean and so utterly worthless, the devil doesn't want them in Hell. So to keep them out of his hair, so to speak, he allows them to remain behind after death."

The sheriff sat speechless for a moment, then he blurted, "That's the damnest theory I have ever heard."

"Oh, there's more," Katti said. "We also think that they act as recruiters for the devil."

Pickens stared at her for a moment. He shook his head as if to clear it of her words. "I beg your pardon, lady?"

"Some people, after having been subjected to the most hideous and painful of torture, would agree to anything, would they not?"

"I guess so. Sure. Sure, they would. That's why it's stupid for anyone to try and beat a confession out of a person. After a time, they'll admit to anything in order to get the pain to stop. So?"

"Think about it," Jim urged the lawman.

The sheriff looked down into the dark liquid in his cup. "Well, I'll just be damned!" he whispered after a few seconds. "Those *things* entice people in from the road, beat and torture them into renouncing Christ, and they get sent to Hell." He looked at the three. "You people figure this out all by yourselves?"

"No," Cole said. "Ray Sharp did, in prison. But it's just a theory. Personally, I don't think that's it."

"Neither do I. But Cole has found a way to fight these things," Katti said. "It's been effective, so far."

Sheriff Pickens looked at Cole.

Cole shook his head. "Not until I'm convinced what side you're on, Sheriff. Only then."

"That's fair. I don't blame you for that. I been thinking. It's been ten years since Tommy Baylor was run over by my son. Maybe I could work out a deal with the DA. Ahhh!" He shook his head. "What am I saying? Albert would never agree to it. And besides, those things out at the club would never let it go that far." He looked around the cafe. "They might be listening at this moment."

"Are you serious?" Katti asked.

"Just as serious as an iron lung." He sighed heavily. "All right. All right. I'll level with you. My god, people, some of us have tried to free ourselves from these monsters. Some packed up in the middle of the night and moved to New York City, Los Angeles, Seattle, New Orleans—all over the United States. Some even moved to Mexico. You know what happened to them? They're dead. Every one of them. Those goddamn *things* network with other *things*. They found you in Memphis, didn't they? You damn mighty right they did."

"Then those weren't, ah, spirits from around here?" Jim asked.

Sheriff Pickens shook his head. "No. I told you: they network with each other. But I don't know how they do it. And I don't know how to find out."

"We discussed that possibility," Cole said.

"It's more than a possibility, Cole. It's fact."

"Then you've just placed your life in danger," Katti said.

"Not necessarily," the sheriff replied. "Those of us in the club have discussed these spirits many, many times, and nothing has happened. It's only when members tried to run away or go public with what they know that they were killed."

"Have you done any background work on other old honky-tonks around the nation?" Cole asked.

"Oh, yes. A few sightings have been reported in spots around the nation. But for some reason, the majority of them are here in the South. I used to keep records of my findings. I stopped after the third time they disappeared from my safe."

"Disappeared?"

"Yeah. Vanished." The sheriff signaled for more coffee and waited until the waitress had left, before saying, "It was my men who tailed you two the other night." He smiled. "You're pretty good, Cole."

"Who tossed my office?" Jim asked.

"That wasn't me or any of my people," Pickens said quickly. "I think it was done on the orders of Captain Wood. He's in tight with Victoria Staples and Arlene Simmons, and those two are capable of doing anything. Both of them are vicious people.

I've long suspected that Arlene killed one of her lovers and dumped his body. I know that Victoria has lured enemies to some of these old clubs and . . . well, you know what happened. Federal judges Warren Hayden and Jefferson Parks are in tight with the women and with Captain Wood." He looked at Jim. "They could cause you a lot of trouble, Jim."

The P.I. smiled. "I've done a few favors over the years for some federal judges. Those two don't worry me."

"State judge Silas Parnell is another ruthless one. All of you be very wary of him."

"Why are you telling us all this, Al?" Cole asked.

The sheriff shook his head. "I don't know. To help ease my conscience, maybe. I've been a cop ever since I got out of the army. Hell, I was a cop in the army! I've always tried to do right. I haven't always succeeded, but I tried. When you're the sheriff, you can't always do what you know is right and just and moral. In every county in America there is a shadow government. You know that, Cole. People you give tickets to, and people you don't. Not if you want to stay in office. I've made only one real mistake in all my years behind a badge, and that concerned my son. I panicked that night. I knew I was doing wrong. Did it anyway. And it's preyed on my mind ever since. I thought I could set Albert's feet on the right course." He shook his head. "Didn't work out that way, though. He's no good. I finally forced myself to accept that a few days ago, sitting in my office. He's married to a wonderful girl, and runs around on her. Every night you'll find him at some goddamn honky-tonk, sloppin' up booze and lookin' for women. He was born with a bad seed in him. And he'll come to no good end. I've already accepted that in my mind. If he had just shown some remorse for what he did that night, some little spark of . . ." He sighed. "But he didn't. He didn't care then. Doesn't care now. So why should I worry about him?"

Katti's expression softened, and she put her hand on top of the sheriff's hand. "Because he is your son."

Al Pickens tried a smile. "I imagine you'd like to kill Albert, wouldn't you, Miss Baylor?"

Katti didn't hesitate in replying. "Yes, I would, sheriff."

"I couldn't blame you, if you did. Not really. But I'm as much to blame, or more, than he is."

"But you're filled with regret about it," she told him. "Genuine sorrow. And that makes you a better man."

Pickens was silent for a moment, then said, "You people watch yourselves around my chief deputy. Win's a bad one. He's a good investigator, but he's got a mean steak in him. We grew up together, went to school together. I know him. If it comes down to you or him, he won't hesitate to drop a hammer on you. Win knew about these ghost clubs long before I did. I was a little bit rowdy in my youth, on the fringes of it. But Win was all the way rowdy for a time. If he hadn't turned cop, he'd be in prison right now. You see, Miss Baylor, a lot of very good cops have just a touch of the rogue in them. And Cole will back me up on that."

Cole nodded his head in agreement. "Some of the best lawmen I ever knew were rowdy in their younger days." He smiled. "I wasn't exactly an angel myself."

Katti patted his hand and smiled sweetly. "Thank heavens for little favors, dear," she said, and those around the table broke up in laughter.

Eleven

Jim and Bev returned from Memphis, and the five of them sat in Cole's motel room and talked for a time.

"These things are nationwide?" Bev said. "Is that possible?"

"With the supernatural, anything is possible," Katti echoed the words they all had either uttered aloud or thought since becoming involved with the ghost clubs.

"But why are the ghost clubs found mainly in the South, along that old highway?" Gary asked.

"Questions on top of more questions," Jim said. "Hell, I don't know. I'm still having a very difficult time actually believing everything I've seen thus far. But I do think that Sheriff Pickens is on the level with us. Cole?"

"Oh, I do, too. I think basically the sheriff is a good, decent man."

"With a prick for a son," Katti said.

Bev laughed. "Well, at least the sheriff admits that now, right?"

"Says he does," Cole said. "And I think he means it. But that doesn't mean he's going to turn in his son, even if the punk would agree to it, which he will probably never do."

"So what do we do now?" Jim asked.

Cole spread his hands. "I'm out of ideas."

"Go back to the club," Katti suggested.

"Why?" Gary asked. "Why put yourself through that torture, Katti?"

"Because if we're going to unlock this mystery, that's where we'll find the key. I think."

"I have some questions," Bev said. "When does the . . . devil," she stumbled over the word, "contact the people he or she or it, has chosen to, ah, forfeit their soul? And how is contact made? The devil can't very well take out an ad in the local paper, or buy radio or TV time."

"Those are good questions," Cole said. "Unfortunately, I don't have the answers." He didn't think the devil had a thing to do with it, but he kept that to himself, for the time being.

"Let me do some guessing," Gary said. "Maybe the devil never makes personal contact. Maybe it's a gradual thing, over a period of years. Maybe the people don't even know what is happening, until they're dead."

"That's as good a theory as any," Cole admitted.

"Why don't we all just admit we're operating in the dark?" Jim said. "And none of us have the vaguest idea what we're doing."

Cole said nothing. He had a hunch about what was going on, but he had no idea how he was going to prove it—yet.

They were having supper in the cafe, when Jim looked toward the door and said, "It just keeps getting more and more complicated."

Cole cut his eyes to the door and sighed. The veteran cop from Memphis who had interviewed Cole, Katti, and Jim at the diner was standing there, smiling at them.

"Bob Jordan," Katti said. "I've known him for years. Now, what's *he* doing here?"

Jim waved the sergeant over to their table, and he sat. "Well, well," Bob smiled, picking up a menu. "What a happy little gathering. What's good on the menu?"

"Chicken fried steak," Gary said.

"My favorite." He waved to the waitress and ordered.

"Are you lost, Bob?" Jim asked.

"Oh, no. Not at all. I just had a lot of accrued time due me, and decided I'd better take it before I lost it."

"This is not exactly the garden spot of the state, Bob," Bev said.

"Actually, I'm from around here," the Memphis cop said. "Born in Hayti and raised up on a farm outside Kennett, Missouri." He smiled. "Forty-five years ago." He looked at Cole and then at Jim. "That makes us about the same age."

"Just about," Cole said.

"But I got me an older brother; he's older by fifteen years. He doesn't live around here anymore. Moved to Jackson years ago. He was quite a hell-raiser in his day. Used to tell me all sorts of wild stories about the roadhouses he used to hang around."

"Is that right?" Katti asked sweetly.

"Sure is. My brother now, he was a hard-drinkin', hard-ramblin' man in his time. I bet he made every joint between Cairo, Illinois and West Memphis in his day. But you know, he quit all that about twenty years ago. Just . . . quit one day. 'Course, we were all proud of him for doing that, but it surprised us all somethin' fierce when he did."

"Is there a moral or a point to this story, Bob?" Jim asked.

The Memphis cop smiled. "Oh, yeah. I'm getting to it. Day before yesterday, I drove down to Jackson to see my brother. I asked him some hard questions about this country, and why he moved away so abrupt-like. Now, my brother used to spin some wild yarns in his time. But what he told me was just about the wildest thing I ever heard of."

"And you're going to tell us about it, Bob?" Katti asked.

Bob chuckled. "Oh, I 'spect y'all know more about it than me. But I'll play your game for a while longer."

"What game, Bob?" Bev asked.

"Oh . . . how about ghosts?"

No one spoke as the waitress began setting their plates of

food in front of them. That was followed by a basket of fresh baked rolls and more iced tea.

''Y'all enjoy your supper now, you hear?'' the waitress said, and walked away.

''Ghosts, Bob?'' Jim said. ''Have you been hitting the bottle?''

Bob again smiled. ''I do enjoy a drink now and then. But not this day.'' He met each pair of eyes around the table. ''Katti, your brother vanished not five miles from this spot. Ten years ago. I had just made detective. You haven't been back here in years. I know. I checked. Then all of a sudden, you team up with the Outlaw here,'' he looked at Cole, ''and, yeah, I did some checking on you, too. You're 'bout rough as a cob when you want to be, aren't you?''

''I have been known to take a rocky road from time to time,'' Cole replied.

Bob nodded. He was a stocky man, with salt and pepper hair that had once been dark brown, and big hands and big wrists. He was barrel-chested and still maintained a trim waist. Jim, Gary, and Bev knew that Bob Jordan was not a man to play deadly games with.

''Then,'' Bob continued, ''Katti girl, you suddenly hire the services of Jim, here, and two of his top guns. I find that all very interesting.''

''I'm writing a book,'' she told him.

Bob tasted his chicken fried steak, smiled in approval, and chewed for a time. ''Sure, you are, Katti. I'm sure that much is the truth. And you're paying these high-priced private investigators to help you do research, right?''

''That's right, Bob.''

Bob smiled. ''You folks seen any old honky-tonks materialize out of the night yet? Any ghost music floating through the night air?''

''We have heard rumors about sightings over the years,'' Cole told him.

''Uh-huh,'' Bob said, after swallowing a mouthful of mashed potatoes and gravy. ''Me, too. So I decided to use that accrued leave time of mine and just poke around some. You never know what you'll find poking around.''

Jim lifted his eyes. ''I never knew you were interested in ghosts, Bob.''

''I'm more interested in files back in Memphis. A box filled with files about mostly unsolved disappearances that goes back twenty-five years. And I'm also interested in two old men from around here who were murdered recently, days apart. I'm sure you all are familiar with those murders.''

''We've heard about them,'' Katti said.

''I just bet you have,'' Bob replied, making no effort to keep the sarcasm out of his tone. ''When we're finished eating, we'll all just take a little walk to help this fine meal digest. And while we walk, we'll talk some. I don't trust motel rooms. Not since the chief deputy of this county almost had a heart attack when he spotted me gassing up about an hour ago. I've had more than one run-in with Win Bryant over the years. He's a really lousy cop.''

''What's your opinion of the sheriff?'' Cole asked.

''Al Pickens is all right. He was a good chief deputy.''

''And his son?'' Katti asked.

Bob stared at her for a couple of heartbeats. ''Albert is an asshole—spoiled and arrogant. Sheriff Pickens is not a poor man. He owns several thousand acres of good bottom land around here. And he married into money. Hell, he doesn't have to be sheriff. He just enjoys the job. He gave his son fifteen hundred acres of the best soybean and cotton land in the county, in an attempt to straighten the punk out. Didn't work. Personally, I never figured Albert would live this long. I gather none of you have met Albert?''

''Not yet,'' Jim said.

Bob took a sip of iced tea. ''I've met him three times, in Memphis, when his dad drove down to get him out of jail. Albert's runnin' buddy is a half-ass thug named Nick Pullen. He's a bad one. We think he killed a man in Memphis five years ago, outside a honky-tonk. Couldn't find a single witness to point the finger at him. You see, Albert's style is to pick a fight, and then give it to Nick to finish. Albert's really a coward. Nick is his bodyguard."

"Why is the name Nick Pullen familiar to me?" Gary asked.

"Star high school football player. Went on to the University and played there for two years. Both he and Albert were busted out because of grades. He would have gone pro, but he has a bad knee. He's Albert's foreman on the farm."

"How come you know so much about Albert and Nick?" Jim asked.

"Because I want that little bastard. And I want Nick Pullen. Both of them have caused a lot of trouble around Memphis. They can't get into the better clubs in the Memphis area. Barred. I want the satisfaction of being the person who slips the iron on both of them. Then, after talking with my brother, I figured this was as good a time as any to come up here. Here I am."

"You seen Jane lately?" Jim asked.

Bob shook his head. Like many cops, his marriage had collapsed. Being married to a dedicated cop is not easy. "She moved to Nashville. I see the kids every now and then. Hell, they're all grown up except for Cathy. And she's a junior in high school." He smiled. "Stop trying to get me off the subject, Jim. I'm here, and you people are stuck with me." He glanced at Cole. "You might be able to take Nick Pullen. You're sure big enough. You got a fighter's hands and a mean look in your eyes."

"I never much believed in this fair fight crap," Cole replied.

The Memphis cop grinned. "Me, neither!"

Victoria Staples stilled the ringing phone and listened for only a few seconds. She didn't have to ask who it was; she recognized the voice. "It goes down tonight."

"Fine," she said, then hung up. She smiled and looked down at Arlene Simmons, lying naked on the big bed. Arlene had three fingers jammed up her cunt. "Your man will take care of the problem tonight."

"Good," Arlene said. "Now you come here and take care of me."

"If this is not handled right, we could all end up in prison," Federal Judge Warren Hayden said.

Federal Judge Jefferson Parks nodded his head. "We were fools to ever get involved in that stupid club. And speaking quite frankly, Victoria and Arlene frighten me. Those are two of the most ruthless people I have ever encountered. And after twenty-five years on the bench, I have encountered some real dillies."

"All of us have," district judge Silas Parnell said. "The person who worries me the most is Roscoe. He's the weak link. And if his ... ah ... sexual habits were ever made public, anyone standing close to him would be tarred with the same brush."

"Victoria will keep him under control," state senator Conrad Wright spoke up. "Right, Maxwell?"

The state representative cut his eyes. "Maybe. But I've got a bad feeling about this whole thing. I think it's coming unraveled, and there isn't a damn thing we can do about it."

"It's being taken care of tonight!" Warren said. "I told you. Captain Wood is seeing to it." Warren Hayden picked up the ringing phone and listened for a moment. He slammed the receiver down and said, "Shit!"

"What's the matter?" Silas asked.

"A cop from the Memphis PD has checked in at the motel. He's having supper with the others as we speak. This is getting too complicated, people. If he's with them when Wood's people strike, we've got real problems on our hands. Killing a cop is bad business. Real ... bad ... business."

"Can it be stopped?" Judge Parks asked.

"No. It's too late. Everything is in motion. It's out of our hands now."

"Son of a bitch!" Conrad said.

"Just settle down," Warren told them all. "We've been playing poker on this night for years. Must be several hundred people know that." He put his hands together and moved them from side to side. "We play poker here, our wives play bridge there. We cook our meat, we drink our bourbon, we play cards. Tonight will be no different. Let's get to it, boys."

Sheriff Chuck Reno, Sheriff **Paxton,** Chief of Police Dick Austin, Chief of Police Paul **Mallory,** and chief deputies Win Bryan and Sam Rogers sat in the living area of the hunting camp and looked at one another. Sheriff Reno finally broke the silence.

"Al Pickens has gone turncoat on us. I'm pretty sure he's working with that Baylor bitch and her friends. No telling what all he's told them."

"Relax," Win Bryan said. "It'll be all over tonight. I met Arlene last evening out at the barn for a quick fuck, and she told me everything was taken care of." He smiled. "That's the horniest bitch I ever met in my life. And it don't make no difference where you stick it, any hole will do."

"I think it's disgusting," Chief of Police Austin said. "She's over at Victoria's right now, the two of them doing only god knows what." He shuddered. "I can't stand queers."

"Me, neither," Chief Deputy Rogers said.

Win laughed at them. "You mean you guys never had a man suck you off? When I was in high school, little Petey Watson used to polish my knob regular out behind the gym. Hell, if it feels good, do it, that's my philosophy."

"You're disgusting, too," Austin told him.

"Knock it off," Sheriff Paxton said. "We're not here to discuss personal sexual habits. I'm going to say this again: I don't like the idea of killing cops. It's wrong."

"It's too late to stop it," **Win** said, opening another can of beer. "It's in the works. Just like a blow job: lay back and enjoy it. In a few hours, it'll all be over and we can relax."

Chief Austin grimaced. "You know, Win, if someone were

to cut open your head and look inside, all they'd see is a bunch of little pussies working. That's all you can talk about.''

Win chuckled. ''I ain't never found nothin' better than sex, Dickie baby.'' Win picked at his nose and found a bugger. He inspected it as if he were looking at a cultured pearl. Then he flipped it against a wall.

Bob Jordan had walked with the group and listened to them intently. His mind just would not accept everything they had told him during their stroll.

They walked in silence for a few minutes. Standing outside the motel, Bob said, ''It's . . . well . . . Hell, I don't know what to say.''

''It takes some time to grasp it all,'' Bev told him. ''I'm not sure I have, as yet. I haven't seen those . . . things. I'm not sure I want to.''

''I do,'' Bob said. ''Tonight.'' He looked at Cole.

''All right,'' Cole said. ''Tonight.''

Twelve

It was full dark when the six of them pulled out, heading for the site of the old honky-tonk. Katti and Jim rode with Cole, Gary and Bev with Bob. There was no moon, and the sky was filled with low, moisture-heavy clouds, obscuring the stars. It was very humid; the car air conditioners were working on high.

Katti noticed immediately that Cole was tense and unusually silent. Before they left the city limits, she asked, "Other than the obvious, Cole, what's wrong?"

"I've got a bad feeling in my gut. It probably amounts to nothing, but it's there."

Katti turned in the seat to glance at Jim Deaton. "How do you feel?"

"Well, I'm a little nervous about confronting ghosts, but other than that, fine."

A couple of miles from where the old club once sat, Cole noticed county highway equipment parked on the side of the county road, but thought nothing of it. As soon as the two-car caravan had passed the highway trucks, several men ran out from behind the trucks and put detour signs up, closing the highway and rerouting any traffic to another road that led off to the north. A highway truck was backed into place, completely blocking the road. Miles ahead, another crew was doing the same. Cole and Katti and friends were now sealed in.

They didn't know about it.

Yet.

Captain Wood had made a lot of unsavory acquaintances over his years as a highway cop. He had deliberately overlooked some very major infractions of law over the years, in order to build up a large group of "you owe me" thugs. With a pocket full of money from Arlene and Victoria and some of the others in the club, setting up the ambush had been easy.

But Captain Wood either forgot he was sending his thugs and hoodlums and country boy punks against experienced cops, and grossly underestimated Cole and the others, or grossly overestimated the abilities of the men he had hired for this night's nefarious work.

Cole's radio crackled. "We've got three- and four-wheelers pacing us on either side," Gary radioed from behind.

Cole keyed his mike. "I spotted them a moment ago. They must be muffled down."

With hundreds and hundreds of radio frequencies to choose from, the odds of them being monitored were slim. Even if they were monitored, the transmissions would make no sense, because they were scrambled. It wasn't entirely legal on the part of Cole and Jim, but if that worried them, it wasn't evident. Sometimes one has to do what one has to do.

"What is it, Cole?" Katti asked.

"Ambush, I think. By a bunch of amateurs. And I'd rather deal with professionals. Amateurs can hurt you without meaning to."

"But in this case . . ." Jim let that tail off.

"Yeah," Cole said with a sigh. "I think push has finally come to shove. Someone has made up their minds to shut us up—permanently."

Riding with Bev and Gary, Bob Jordan said, "What the hell do those snake-heads out there in the fields want?"

"Us, probably," Bev told him, and unsnapped her 9 mm. "You carrying?"

"I got my pants on, don't I?" Bob replied.

"The last time I looked," Bev came right back at him.

"Oh, you've been looking me over, hey?" Bob said with a smile.

Bev smiled in the dim light from the dashboard. "Purely professional, I assure you."

Cole's voice sprang out of the radio. "When we get to the club site, stay on the left side of the road, Gary. Don't any of you even get close to the other side of the blacktop. You understand?"

"Ten-four," Gary responded.

"What's the big deal about the right side?" Bob asked.

"Things that go bump in the night," Bev told him. There was not the slightest trace of humor behind the words.

"And neither of you have seen these . . . things, right?"

"No," Gary said. "But Jim told me they scared the crap out of him."

"I knew Jim back in his Tennessee trooper days," Bob said. "I never saw him scared of anything."

Ahead of them, Cole's left-turn signal was flashing in the night. The two vehicles pulled off the road and onto the turn-row of the soybean field. As before, they were directly across from the site of the old honky-tonk.

The off-road vehicles were moving around them in a wide circle, as yet making no attempt to tighten the circle. The engines had been muffled down to a low purr.

They all heard the beat of the music gradually building in volume, coming from across the road. After a moment, they could make out the words in front of the music. "Whole Lot Of Shakin' Goin' On."

"I do not believe this," Bob Jordan muttered.

The sounds of many feet on a hardwood floor wafted through the night, all mixed in with music and laughter.

The three- and four-wheelers had stopped their circling. The riders were not visible.

Bob Jordan's head moved left and right, scanning the dark area across the road. The old club had not yet appeared out of the darkness.

The song had changed.

The music had increased in volume.

The singer was crooning a ballad: "There Stands The Glass."

When he got to the line about filling it up to the brim, Bob said, "I could use a drink myself."

And he wasn't kidding.

At first, it was only a very dim light that appeared across the road. Then, gradually, the outline of the club could be seen; the parking lot was filled with cars and trucks.

"Oh, my god," Bev whispered, her eyes riveted on the sight.

Katti glanced up at Cole. "You have a very strange expression on your face, Cole," she whispered.

"I'm wondering if those thugs who have circled us can see the club and hear the music." He shook his head. "I'm betting they can't."

"Are you saying that club appears only to people who *want* to see it?" Bob asked.

"I don't know. I don't know what I mean." He lowered his voice to a faint whisper. "I'm going to do something very rash. And I don't want any arguments. You people get down on the ground and stay put. If what I have in mind works out, whoever set up this little ambush just may not have considered all the possibilities. Not a word out of any of you, not a sound. Just watch."

Cole jumped up and ran across the blacktop, stopping in the center of the parking lot, crouching down behind a '55 Ford Crown Vic.

Katti managed to stifle a scream and remain silent. Her heart was beating so fast, she thought it might explode.

"What the hell is he doing?" Bev whispered.

"I don't know," Jim returned the low murmur. "But I saw him take some incredible chances in 'Nam. One of them earned him the Silver Star, and another got him put in for the Congressional Medal of Honor. He didn't get it, but he should have."

"One of them ran across the road!" the shout came out of the darkness. "Earl! You and Luddy take him out."

"Yeah," Jim muttered. "You and Luddy just try that. You're both gonna be stickin' your hands into a buzz saw, when you do."

"He's that rough?" Bob whispered.

"When he wants to be."

Across the road, Cole put his hand on the body of the Crown Vic. It was cool to the touch. So it was real—at least to him. He waited and watched.

Two four-wheelers suddenly came out of the night and crossed the road. Cole watched as the riders rode right through the shapes of cars and trucks.

Shit! Cole thought. Maybe my plan won't work after all.

The riders stopped, cut off their engines, and stood by their four-wheelers. "Where the hell did he go?" one asked.

"I don't know," his partner replied. "Son of a bitch has got to be around here somewheres."

"We can't let none of them get away, Luddy."

"I *know* that!"

"Well, where is he?"

Cole took a flat police slapper out of his back pocket and stood up. "Right here, assholes," he said, then swung the slapper. The leather-covered lead ball impacted against the head of one of the men, and dropped him like a rock. Cole popped the second man on the noggin, stuck the slapper back into his pocket, dragged the nearly unconscious man to the front door of the club, and then slapped him awake.

"How about going honky-tonking?" Cole said, when the man had opened his eyes.

"Huh?" Luddy asked, still dazed.

Cole opened the door to the club and shoved the man inside. He quickly closed the door and ran back into the center of the parking lot. From inside the old roadhouse, Luddy started screaming hysterically.

"Luddy?" the shout came from the field behind the club. "Earl? What's goin' on? Who's that screamin'?"

Interesting, Cole thought. He dragged Earl to the door,

opened it, and shoved him inside. But before he could close the door, a man appeared, holding the door open. The music stopped. The man smiled down at Cole.

"You're playin' a game you can't win, buddy," the man said.

"Maybe," Cole told the man, and felt rather strange doing it. He hadn't had much experience talking to people from the other side.

"No one from out yonder's ever won it yet. But you got guts, I'll give you that."

"What's your name?"

"Dutch Morrison."

Behind him, either Luddy or Earl started wailing. It was a sound of pure anguish.

"I'll see you again," Dutch said. "Bet on that."

One of the men Cole had shoved into the ghost club was shouting and cursing. "I seen you dead, George Bailey! I went to your funeral. Tom Matthews shot you dead out huntin'. This ain't real! Get your fuckin' hands off me! You stink, man. Get away from me!" Then he started screaming.

Dutch Morrison smiled down at Cole. "See you around, partner." He closed the door.

"Luddy? Earl?" the shout was closer than before. "What the hell is goin' on? Who's screamin'?"

Cole crouched down and waited.

The screams from inside the club had reached a new intensity. They brought chill bumps on Cole's bare arms. They sounded much like the screams that Cole had heard in 'Nam, after a napalm drop on VC positions.

"I'm gone, man!" another voice shouted. "I don't know what's goin' on. But I don't like it worth a shit!"

"You stay put, Vic."

"Fuck you, Neely. I'm outta here."

The sounds of several off-road vehicles drifted to Cole. He stayed put, kneeling on the gravel of the parking lot. His knees were beginning to ache from the pressure on the sharp stones.

"Dick's right, Neely," yet another voice sprang out of the fields. "This thing's all fucked up. Let's get out of here."

The screaming had ended. It was now more of an inhuman, bubbling moan of pain from inside the club. Cole could not imagine what was being done to the men. He really didn't want to know.

"We can't leave Earl and Luddy."

"I think they're beyond help," another voice called out in a drawl. "Me . . . I'm outta here."

"Okay, okay," Neely said. "Let's go."

More off-roaders cranked up and pulled out. Cole ran back across the road and crouched down beside the others. "Dutch Morrison and George Bailey. Remember those names."

"What happened over there?" Bob asked, his voice shaky.

"I think I just shoved a couple of guys into Hell."

"You can't be serious?" Bob said.

"Oh, God!" the wail came from across the road. "Oh, God, help me. Please, God, help me!"

The cars and trucks in the parking lot began to fade as the club turned misty. For a brief second, the mist was filled with sparkling dots. Then . . . only darkness.

"I saw it, I heard it, but I don't believe it," Bob said. "I just . . . can't." Then he shook his head, cleared his throat, and shouted, "What in the name of God is going on around here? What happened to those two punks? Where the hell is the club!" He pointed. "The goddamn thing was right there. I saw it; heard the music."

"Calm down, Bob," Jim told him. "Just take some deep breaths and calm down."

"Has anybody got a cigarette?" Cole asked, slapping his pockets out of habit.

Katti looked up at him. "I thought you told me you quit?"

"I did. I just started back again."

Bob gave him a smoke, and they both lit up. Bob held the lighter, and his hands were shaking.

"Who is this Dutch Morrison you mentioned?" Gary asked.

"The dead guy who was talking to me over there."

Bob had just taken a deep drag from his smoke and started coughing at that remark. When he had caught his breath, he looked at Cole and shouted, ''The dead guy you were *talking* to?''

''I told you this whole thing was weird, didn't I?'' Jim said to the astonished Memphis cop.

Bob did not reply. He turned away and slowly walked to the car, getting in the back seat and closing the door. He rolled down the window for ventilation and stared straight ahead.

Cole suddenly snapped his fingers and said, ''Well, I'll just be damned!''

''What is it?'' Bev asked.

''It just came to me. Dutch Morrison was wearing my ball cap. You know, Katti. The one that sailed off my head the other day, when we were out here.''

''In-fucking-credible!'' Bob muttered from the back seat of the car.

''You mean he was the one, or one of them, who felt me up the other day?''

''It's possible.''

''I wish I had been over there with you. I'd have kicked him in the balls.''

''Kick a ghost in the balls,'' Bob muttered, but loudly enough so all could hear him in the very still and muggy night. ''Sure. Well, you have no one to blame but yourself, Jordan. You just had to come up here. You could be eyeballing the girls down on the beach in Biloxi. But no. No. You had to come stick your nose right in the middle of all this weirdness. You just never learn, do you?''

''Katti?'' the voice sprang out of the night, startling them all.

''Who said that?'' Bob asked, jumping out of the car and looking all around him.

''Katti?'' the voice came again.

''Tommy?'' Katti called to the darkness.

''*Tommy?*'' Bob asked, moving closer to the others. ''You mean, ah, like in Tommy Baylor?''

''Yes,'' Cole told him.

''Oh, my god!'' Bob said.

"Sis?" the voice again spoke. It seemed to be close, but had a faraway sound to it. A hollow quality.

"This is not happening," Bob whispered.

"It's happening," Cole said.

"Get out of here, Sis," Tommy's voice warned them. "Take your friends and leave. This is not what it seems. You're on the wrong track."

"Tommy," Katti called. There were tears running out of her eyes. "Tommy, what do you mean? We came here to free you from . . . wherever you are. And we will."

But there was no reply.

Katti called out again.

Silence greeted her words.

"This is most unusual," Gary said.

Everyone turned toward him.

"I've been doing some reading on the subject of ghosts, the afterlife, things of that nature. There have been thousands of sightings of ghosts, but almost never does a spirit communicate vocally."

Bob opened his mouth to speak, then closed it. He wasn't sure he could speak.

"Let's get out of here," Cole suggested. "I could use a drink."

"You can sure say that again," Bob muttered.

"We'll be back, Tommy," Katti called. "I promise you, we'll free you from this terrible place."

A breeze suddenly began blowing; the air was damp, filled with moisture.

Bob shivered despite the nearly oppressive heat of the summer night and the high humidity. His eyes opened wide, and he pointed a finger across the road. "What the hell is *that?*" he asked.

Heads turned. Dozens of sparkling shapes had appeared where the old club had stood. They were bobbing up and down, moving from side to side.

"They're dancing," Katti was the first to speak. "Dancing to music only they can hear."

The night was suddenly shattered by the sounds of "Good Rockin' Tonight."

Then the music stopped.

The sparkling dots faded into nothing.

The night became silent.

A light rain began to fall.

"It's over for tonight," Cole said. "Let's head on back to the motel."

"Y'all excuse me for a minute," Bob said, heading out into the soybean field. "I got to go to the bathroom—real bad!"

Thirteen

Sheriff Pickens was waiting for them at the motel. He got out of his car and walked over to the group. "I figured you had all gone out to the old club. I don't go out there anymore. Let's go sit over there by the pool and talk. I don't trust motel rooms. Too easy to bug."

"I'll get a bottle, some glasses, and ice," Katti said.

"I'll help you," Bev volunteered.

"And some Coke," Sheriff Pickens said. "I'm a country boy. I like my bourbon with Coke."

Drinks fixed and every one comfortable, Cole told the sheriff all that had transpired that night. The sheriff cussed softly. "Wood set that up. At the direction of someone in the club. Bet on that. Someone is running scared."

"Al, who is Dutch Morrison?"

The sheriff frowned. Shook his head. "I don't know the name. There are some Morrisons live 'way to hell and gone out in the county. But I never heard of one called Dutch. Why?"

"Because I talked to a dead man who said his name was Dutch Morrison."

Bob sighed heavily.

Al Pickens's eyes widened, but he said nothing.

"And when I shoved those punks inside the club, one of them shouted something about a man named George Bailey. Seems he was shot dead by a man called Tom Matthews."

"That's right. Ten years or so ago. Tom was fooling around with George's wife, Susan. A months after that so-called hunting accident, Tom and Susan were married. They live in town."

"Still married?"

"In a way. They fight all the time. Both of them are trash. City cops are always having to go over to their house to break up fights."

"You don't seem surprised to learn that George was out at the club."

"Nothing surprises me about that goddamn place. As far as I'm concerned, it's a part of Hell. When I was younger, it used to be fun to go out there and stand across the road and listen to the old music and so forth. Until I realized what it really was. I haven't been out there in several years."

"Never?" Cole asked.

"Oh, I have to drive past the damned place every now and then. I never look in that direction. Place spooks me."

Cole waited, sensing something else besides ghosts was on the sheriff's mind.

Sheriff Pickens took a healthy slug of his drink and said, "I spoke to my son a few hours ago. Told him I could make a deal with the DA—which I can. Turn himself in, go public with this whole sorry business, and let's see what we could do about putting those . . . *things* out there at that old club to rest." He expelled breath and shook his head. "Albert laughed at me. Called me a fool. That didn't come as any shock; I was expecting something like that. What did surprise me was the viciousness behind the words. I think my son has made a . . . well, a deal with those creatures out there. He didn't say as much, but . . ." The sheriff's voice trailed off for a few seconds. "My wife has been wanting to go on a cruise for some time now. Bunch of women around here have talked about that for several years. When I got back home, I suggested she start packing. She needs a vacation, a long one. She and several of her friends are leaving day after tomorrow. Be gone about three or four weeks. It's some sort of European/Scandinavian cruise. While she's gone, we're going to get this whole sorry mess all straightened out around here. And if my son has to take a hard fall for his part in it, so be it. So I'm in with you people . . . but if I'm dead in the morning, don't be surprised."

"We'll just prowl around the area, until your wife is gone," Cole said. "We'll stay away from the club. What about Luddy and Earl?"

"Who?" the sheriff asked. "Oh! The two 'necks you shoved through the door. Yeah. That would probably be Luddy Post and Earl Wilson. I'm guessing now. Sometimes we find the bodies, but mostly they just disappear." He sighed. "I've got a lot of sins to atone for, people. I don't even know where to start."

"You've already started, Sheriff," Katti told him. "Let me ask you something: other than the chiefs of police and sheriffs that we know about through Billy Jordan and Ray Sharp, how many others know about the clubs in their jurisdictions?"

"Well, it would be purely a guess on my part, but I'd say none of them. Reason I say that is, because over the years, some of them would have surely gone public with it. They wouldn't all be like me and Sheriff Reno and Captain Wood and Dick Austin and Paul Mallory and Sheriff Paxton and the few others." He shook his head. "No, I don't think there are any other conspirators among the law enforcement community. But I know there are many, many files about missing persons in other agencies. I've spoken with sheriff's investigators and police detectives and state police from several states. Hundreds of people have vanished along this stretch over the long years. Three or four years ago, it started leaving a bad taste in my mouth to lie about it." He paused, a strange expression on his face.

"What's wrong?" Gary asked.

"If those . . . *things* . . ." Like the others, Sheriff Al Pickens had a difficult time vocalizing the word ghosts. ". . . know so damn much, how come they didn't see I was getting more and more reluctant about shielding them and do something with *me?*''

"You mean, perhaps they are not all-seeing and all-knowing?" Jim asked.

"Yeah. That's exactly what I mean."

"Somebody is feeding them information?" Bev asked.

"That has to be it. They can travel only a few miles from that old club site, then they begin to lose . . . something, I don't know what to call it, and change into those sparkling dots that people see."

"And it's only when they materialize that they are vulnerable," Cole said.

"Yeah." The sheriff smiled for the first time that evening. "To that souped-up stun gun of yours. Who the hell would have thought that? Where the hell did you get those things?"

"At a police supply place in Memphis. I just did a little bit of work on them. I've got a case of them."

"I want one."

"You've got it."

"Will they kill a man?"

"I . . ." Cole hesitated. "Well, they might. If a person was not in good health. They might stop a human heart."

"Umm," was all the sheriff had to say about that.

"You fucked it all up," Arlene told Captain Wood.

"I underestimated the abilities of Younger and the others, and overestimated the abilities of the men I hired to do the job." Wood admitted that much. "I can bring some professionals. But it's going to be very expensive if we go that route."

"Are they good?"

"It's what they do for a living," Wood said drily. "One of the men has over thirty whacks to his credit, and has never even been a suspect in any of them. He's a mob favorite."

"How much?" Victoria asked.

"For a job this size?" Captain Wood thought for a moment.

"About a quarter of a million dollars, plus expenses. We're talking about killing a half dozen people, at least. The man I'm thinking about will have to bring two or three others in with him. And it can't be done over any long period of time. It has to be done all at once."

"We'll think about it," Victoria said, standing up. "That's a lot of money. Right now, you fuck her," she pointed to Arlene. "I want to watch."

Cole had said nothing to Sheriff Pickens about Tommy's warning that they were looking in the wrong direction. He had suspected that for several days, and had said nothing about it to Katti or the others. He had no proof—just a hunch. But that hunch was growing stronger.

Without telling the others, Cole used a pay phone and called a man he knew down in New Orleans, a man who for years had walked both sides of the law and order line. Only recently had he straightened up his act and gone legitimate.

Cole talked for about fifteen minutes, and when he hung up the phone, he was smiling. Sitting in his Bronco, he muttered, "How bizarre. But where do the ghosts tie in? What the hell is the connection? And who is really behind it all?"

He slipped the Bronco into gear and pulled out. "Time to do a little police work," he said.

Fifteen hundred miles away, John Costa hung up the phone and sat in his study for a time. When he had told Captain Wood his price, that double-dealing, rogue cop son of a bitch had not hesitated. So that meant there was real big money behind this hit.

John walked into the kitchen and fixed a pot of coffee. He had a lot of thinking to do. He still wasn't sure he wanted to take this job. Killing cops was bad business. He knew that for a fact, for John used to be a cop. It was a big family, with thousands of relatives. A brotherhood. And if he took the deal, he couldn't use just muscle, the men would have to be intelligent, as well. And that combination did not often go hand in hand.

Costa fixed his coffee, carefully mixing in sugar and cream, and walked back into his study. He sat down and went over the list of possibles in his mind, rejecting most of the men and women immediately. He really didn't want to use city boys and girls in the country. They stood out like a hammered thumb.

After an hour, he had chosen three people: Weber, Collins, and Ginny Hammond. All three were experienced, and they were smart. Costa packed an overnight bag, locked up his house, and drove into the city. He checked into a small but expensive downtown hotel, and began contacting the two men and the woman. It took most of that night and all of the next day to set up meets and firm up the deal. He met Weber at a restaurant down on 1st Avenue, Collins at Grand Central Station, and Ginny up at the Cloisters, laying out the deal . . . at least as much as he knew about it. He held back nothing.

The next morning they began their flights into Memphis, Little Rock, and St. Louis. Costa and Ginny linked up in Memphis, Collins went into Little Rock, and Weber into St. Louis. They rented cars and headed for northwest Arkansas. Costa had told Wood what they would need, and the rogue cop had said supplying it would be no problem. They checked into motels at Blytheville and Osceola, Arkansas. The next night they would shift to motels in Dyersburg, Tennessee and Sikeston, Missouri, the third night they would move to motels in Kennett, Missouri and Piggott, Arkansas. On the evening of the fourth day, they would make their touch and be gone. At least that was the way Costa had it worked out, if all went well.

Sheriff Al Pickens saw his wife and her companions off at the airport in Memphis, and was back in his county an hour and a half later. His chief deputy, Win Bryan, had asked for his vacation time and Al had okayed it. Al sensed that everything was coming down to the wire, and the whole mess was more than likely about to explode. In whose face was the question.

Al sat behind his desk at the office, the office door closed, wondering who in his department he could really trust. He knew that most of the older deputies were solidly behind Win. They knew nothing firm about the ghost clubs, only that there were dozens of rumors about strange sightings in and around the area, but those had been circulating for years. Al concluded that there was only one deputy he could really trust. A young man who had only been wearing a badge for a couple of years—Frank Bruce. Al had known Frank all his young life; had coached him in Little League. Frank was six foot three, about two hundred and twenty pounds, solid as an oak tree, literally did not know his own strength, and he was totally loyal to Al.

Al walked out of his office, through the front door, and spotted Frank just pulling up in his unit. He walked over to the young deputy. "Meet me at the south gate of Fletcher Farms in an hour, Frank. Don't tell anybody where you're going. No one. Understood?"

"Yes, sir, Sheriff. One hour. I'll be there."

Using the phone in his car, Al called the number of Cole's mobile phone, which Cole always took into the motel room with him. An hour later, all the players on one side of the issue were gathered in the timber, by a little creek on the south side of Fletcher Farms. Al introduced Frank all around. There were a dozen questions in the young deputy's eyes, but he kept his silence.

"Everyone seems to have taken their vacations at the same time," Al told the group. "My chief deputy, Judge Evans, Chief Deputy Sam Rogers, Sheriff Paxton, Judge Silas Parnell, Captain Curtis Wood. Something is about to pop. And I got a dirty feeling that it's gonna be us, if we let it." He turned to Frank. "Frank, sit down on that stump over there, boy. Believe me, you don't want to be standing when you get a head full of what we're about to tell you."

"Yes, sir." Frank sat.

Two minutes later, the young deputy's eyes were bugging out, and his mouth had dropped open.

And that was only the beginning.

Fourteen

A badly shaken young deputy sat on the stump in silence for a few moments, trying to make some sense out of what he'd just heard. Frank Bruce was a deeply religious young man, a member of the local Baptist church who taught Sunday School whenever his work schedule permitted it. He was religious, but not prudish. A *truly* prudish cop is a rare thing.

"The devil? Ghosts?" Frank finally found his voice. "The rumors about that old roadhouse are *true?* Come on!" He tried a smile. "You guys are putting me on, right?"

He met the eyes of the group. He saw no humor in any of them. Frank's smile slowly faded. "You guys are serious, aren't you? I mean . . . you . . . Oh, my God!"

"The devil has nothing to with it," Cole said, after a moment had passed. "Or at the least, very little. I finally figured out what Tommy was trying to tell you the other night, Katti. Or I think I have."

"Let me call in to see if I have any messages," Al said. "I want to hear this." He returned in just a moment. "Everything is quiet. You ready with this theory of yours, Cole?"

"Yes. Gary, you said you'd been doing a lot of reading about the supernatural, as have most of us. Have you ever found a single incident where a ghost actually killed anyone?''

Gary shook his head. ''No. Never. A ghost can certainly make a person hurt themselves. And a poltergeist can make noise and throw things around—or whatever they do to make objects move. But a ghost can't kill anyone.''

''That's right. Billy Jordan and Ray Sharp were right in a lot of their beliefs, but way off base as far as the rest of it goes.'' He looked at Katti and Jim. ''You recall how bright those sparkling dots were out at Katti's house? We had to avert our eyes to maintain vision. They were almost blinding in intensity. I don't doubt those sparkling beings appeared at Billy and Ray's houses, but someone else did the killing, while the old men were nearly blinded by the lights. Someone very human.''

''But how about the years of assaults and rapes all up and down the highway?'' Katti asked. ''I *felt* hands on me. I know that!''

''Ghosts can't rape anyone. You certainly felt something cold,'' Cole said. ''But what you were experiencing was the touch of the grave.''

Katti was not alone in shuddering at that thought.

''So you're saying these ghosts are real, but harmless?'' Sheriff Pickens asked.

''Not harmless. Just unable to kill. What they do is entice people into the clubs, then somehow, I don't know how, hold them there until a living being comes for them. Perhaps just the sight of these things cause most people to faint, or become so scared and disoriented that they can't get away, can't find their way out of that old roadhouse.''

''Then what happens?'' Bob asked.

''Well . . . my theory gets awfully iffy at this point. I don't know how these things communicate with the living, but somehow they do. That's when those people who were unfortunate enough to wander into that roadhouse are seized and used by *real* people.''

''But what is the point of it all, Cole?'' Jim asked. ''Is this some sort of weird, kinky sex club?''

"I can believe that," Sheriff Pickens said. "Roscoe Evans is damn sure kinky. And so, from what I've heard, are Arlene and Victoria. And Captain Wood, to a degree. Maybe a few of the others. But there's more, isn't there, Cole?"

"Yes. I spoke with a man who was on the wrong side of the law for years. He lives down in New Orleans. For years he was heavily involved in the pornography business. But he drew the line at snuff films. He testified before a federal grand jury and helped put a number of people behind bars. I asked him if the snuff film business was still going on. He said it was—big time. Maybe stronger than ever before. With new slants to it. And he said of late he'd been hearing that the films were being shipped out of Memphis. But not shot there. He said he heard they were being filmed somewhere out in the country . . . in North Arkansas."

"Son of a bitch!" Al Pickens blurted. "Things are beginning to fall into place now."

"Please excuse my ignorance," Deputy Bruce said. "But what is a snuff film?"

"A porno film where one or more of the participants is killed during or at the end of the sex act," Bob Jordan told the young man.

"That's disgusting!" the deputy said.

"You bet it is," Cole said. "But there is more. My man in New Orleans says this part of the country is fast becoming known—in certain circles—as not just the snuff film center, but also the kiddie porn capital of the United States. There is big money behind it, and big money being made from it."

Bob looked at Cole. "Mob money?"

Cole shrugged his shoulders. "Maybe. I didn't ask about that."

"How young are the kids being used?" Frank asked, his face tight with anger.

"All ages, my man said."

"People who use children in deviant acts should be killed," the young deputy said. "No trial, just killed on the spot."

"I damn sure agree with that," the Memphis cop said.

"Victoria Staples is a mean bitch," Sheriff Pickens said. "She's a man-hater, and most people know that, too. If y'all know what I mean. But she's worth millions. One of the richest people in the state, if not *the* richest. Old, old money. Her family settled here back in the early 1800's. Arlene Simmons had buckets of money, when she married into more money. And in her own way, she's just as mean as Victoria. I often wondered why those two women would want to keep company with the likes of Win Bryan, Nick Pullen, and Sid Ballard. Those three are abnormal in the sex department, if you ladies will excuse my language———"

"Heavy hung ol' boys," Bev said.

The sheriff flushed and cleared his throat. "That's right."

Deputy Frank Bruce went red in the face and refused to look at Katti and Bev.

"Well," Cole said, breaking into the silent embarrassment, "there is something we're going to have to do, and like it or not, it has to be done."

"Get ahold of some snuff films and view them," Bob said, then spat on the ground.

"That's right. Bob, can you access your Memphis files and get pictures of the people reported missing in this area?"

"Sure. I get you. We cross-check the people in the snuff films against the pictures on file."

"Right."

Katti said, "Cole? How are you going to get your hands on some snuff films? I mean, you can't just walk into a video store and rent them!"

"The guy in New Orleans is sending me a box of them. They should be here tomorrow."

"I have a wide screen TV at my house," Al said. "We can view the goddamn things there."

"I think I'm going to be sick," Deputy Bruce said.

"The distributor is screaming for more films," Win Bryan told the gathering. "He wants more rape and torture scenes."

"Let's grab these people who are nosing around, and use them," it was suggested.

"No!" Victoria quickly nixed that. "That would be too risky. Someone would be sure to recognize one of them and link it to this area, then to us. It's a good idea, and it would be fun watching, but no."

Albert Pickens stirred restlessly in his chair. He needed some pussy bad. He knew he could always screw Arlene, but that cunt was old and tired. Albert wanted a young girl, twelve or so. Albert liked firm and hot young flesh beneath him; he liked the way they screamed when he rammed the meat to them. He rubbed his crotch. Damn! He was getting a boner just thinking about it.

"That's not all," Win said. "The distributor wants more black on white rape scenes. Big niggers and young white girls. There is a hell of a market for those."

"We don't do anything until this present mess is taken care of," Victoria said. "And that will be over in seventy-two hours." She paused and looked at each man and woman gathered in her den. "But we have another problem. Gerald Wilson."

"That little goody-two-shoes, tight-assed prick," Arlene said. "I have an idea how we can shut him up without killing."

"Oh?" Victoria cut her eyes to the woman.

"Yes," Arlene said with a smile. Then began to outline her plan.

Cole picked up the phone in the motel room. "Cole. Al Pickens. Luddy Post and Earl Wilson just showed up. They're over at the hospital now. Frank Bruce is with them. They're babbling about being kidnapped by ghosts and seeing the devil and all sorts of crap. A farmer was driving by the old club site, when those two men suddenly materialized out of the air. Both of them naked as jaybirds. Like to have scared the shit out of that old farmer. He's hospitalized, too, heart palpitations."

"Well, now. The ghosts spit them out. That is interesting."

"Spit them out?"

"In a manner of speaking. Tossed them back. They weren't keepers."

The sheriff was silent for a few seconds. "This is getting weird, Cole."

"Hang in there, Al. It's going to get a lot weirder. UPS just delivered the package from New Orleans. I'll see you at your house this evening."

"I can't say I'm looking forward to this."

"None of us are, Al."

Members of the strike force of federal officers from various government enforcement agencies were meeting in a motel suite in Memphis. The suite was electronically "swept" every day, as were the rooms on either side and the room above it. Two portable radios had been placed against the glass of the window in the rear of the suite, the radios playing rock and roll music. The slight vibration of the glass would distort the sound of their voices and help prevent them from being overheard by long-range shotgun or parabolic mites.

"It appears that all activity has stopped in that area," a postal inspector opened up the meeting.

"Except for a bunch of damned amateurs running around muddying the water," an ATF man said.

"I wouldn't exactly call Cole Younger, Bob Jordan, and Jim Deaton amateurs," another voice was heard. "Between them they've got about a hundred years of law enforcement experience."

"Hick town cops and deputies," a Bureau man said, scorn evident in his voice. But he was young and full of himself, thinking himself ten feet tall and bullet-proof. All that would soon be knocked out of him. By the most unlikely of persons and events. "What the hell do they know about anything?"

"Knock it off, Steckler," another Bureau man said. "You tangle with any of those three, and they'll clean your plow before you can blink. And that gold badge won't mean a goddamn thing to any of them."

"I doubt that!" the young FBI man said hotly.

The older men in the room sighed, all of them thinking the same thing: George Steckler was a horse's ass. The only person who didn't know he was a horse's ass was George. George thought himself to be the perfect FBI agent. He spent so much money on clothes, he had to eat most of his meals at MacDonalds or Burger King. To say that George Steckler was overcome with his own importance would be a classic understatement.

However, George was soon to discover that he was quite human after all.

For the strike force, this had been a particularly frustrating, year-long investigation. Wire taps, mail intercepts, and bugged rooms at a dozen homes had produced nothing they could take to court. The members of the strike force knew that Victoria Staples and Arlene Simmons were up to their asses in snuff films (among other very odious and illegal activities), as were about a dozen other members of that so-called club. They just couldn't prove it.

For all their expertise, all their resources, all the equipment at beck and call, occasionally the Bureau will overlook the obvious. As they did in this case. But that was all right. It was about to come to their attention.

The strike force leader answered the ringing of a rather complicated phone in a large briefcase. He listened for a moment. "Are you serious, sir?" he finally said. "Oh. Yes. I see. Of course, sir. We'll . . . ah, get right on it." He set the phone back into the recessed cradle with a grimace and a slow shake of his head.

"We'll get right on what?" the postal inspector asked.

"Not we, Paul. Us. The Bureau. Everybody else can go home. The investigation has been sidetracked for a time. Somebody put some pressure on. And we all know what judge that was."

"Everybody's favorite, good ol' Warren Hayden," an agent said.

"You got it. No more taps, no more bugs, no more mail intercepts. But I can assign two people to stay with it. Softly."

He looked at an older agent, a man with almost twenty years experience in the Bureau. Scott Frey. "Scott, you stick with this one. But don't step on anybody's toes. Okay?"

"Right. You said two men?"

"Take George with you."

"Shit!" Scott muttered.

"I heard that!" George complained.

Scott ignored him. "What was it that we'll get right on?"

"Ghosts."

Scott blinked. "I beg your pardon?"

"You heard me. Ghosts. Somebody wrote the Bureau a long and rambling letter about ghosts being responsible for all the disappearances in that area over the years."

"Are you fucking *serious?*" Scott blurted.

"I wish you wouldn't curse so much," George admonished the older man. "It isn't becoming to a federal officer."

Scott looked at the younger man for a moment. He sighed. "George, why don't you take a Roto-Rooter and stick it up your ass?"

"I won't even dignify that with a reply," George replied. He looked at the strike force leader. "Ghosts, sir?"

"Ghosts. The letter is being faxed to us. Soon as it gets here, you two pack and get gone. Don't step on any toes up there."

"Yeah, and be careful around those ghosts," another agent said with a grin.

"Fuck you, Foster," Scott said.

George sighed and looked very pained.

Fifteen

"I have to go to a meeting this evening, dear," Gerald Wilson told his wife. "It's political. I'll be late."

"Yes, dear," his wife said, and gave her husband a peck on the cheek. "I won't wait up."

Gerald was ecstatic; couldn't believe the governor actually wanted to meet with him on the QT. He was sure the gov was going to ask him to accept some very important job in the new administration. What a feather in his cap that would be!

Gerald drove to the motel in Blytheville, as instructed, and knocked on the motel room door. He straightened his tie while he waited. The door was opened and Gerald stood there for a moment, not believing his eyes. Win Bryan and Nick Pullen stood there, grinning at him. Gerald realized that he'd been set up. He opened his mouth to holler. But Nick jerked him into the room and slapped tape over his mouth, before he could shout his alarm. He was thrown on the bed; his jacket was pulled off and his shirtsleeve jerked up. Gerald felt the sting of a needle in his arm. A few moments later, he felt all cares leave him. He felt wonderful. Better than he'd ever felt in his life. He grinned foolishly at the two men.

"Now the fun starts," Nick said.

Win grinned and nodded his head. "I'm goin' to enjoy this."

They got Gerald to his feet and walked him drunkenly out to his car. Nick got behind the wheel. Win would follow in his own car. "I'll be right behind you."

Nick nodded and pulled out, heading for Victoria's.

Frank Bruce had to leave the room two minutes into the first snuff film. He vomited into the commode, washed his face with cold water, took several deep breaths, and walked back into the den, taking his seat.

Katti was a couple of minutes behind Frank in losing her supper, and she was followed by Bev. Cole, Bob, Al, Jim, and Gary had worked too many wrecks and had seen too much blood and gore, had swept up from the highway too many brains, teeth, hair, and eyeballs, to be sickened by what was taking place on the screen. The scenes disgusted them, made them angry, but did not physically sicken them. They were long past that point.

"There's one of the kids that vanished!" Bob almost shouted the words. "Stop the film."

"Gladly," Al muttered.

The lights were clicked on, and the two pictures compared.

"Sally Oldham," Bev said. "Twelve years old when she disappeared."

The tape rolled on, the young girl being raped repeatedly. At the culmination of the scene, she was slowly strangled to death by what looked like a silken cord.

Frank Bruce again hit the toilet with the dry heaves.

The next tape showed Sally's older brother Brian, fourteen years old, being sodomized. His screaming was difficult for all to take. And like his sister, Brian was strangled to death by a silken cord just as the last rapist was climaxing.

"Jesus God in Heaven!" Frank whispered the words. "What awful, perverted, evil people."

"That's Doc Drake," Al said, hitting the remote pause button, stilling the tape and pointing to the wide screen TV. "I recognize that scar on his back. Farming accident when he was a kid. He's not a doctor. That's just a nickname.''

''Have you picked out any others?'' Bob asked.

The sheriff shook his head. ''Not yet. But it's just a matter of time.'' He punched out the tape and stuck another one into the VCR. ''Here we go again.''

Gerald Wilson was naked, stretched out on a big bed. The injectable Valium he'd been hit with had produced a throbbing erection. He grinned stupidly at all the lights around the bed. He licked his dry lips as a young girl, twelve years old, crawled onto the bed with him. Her eyes were glazed from the drugs in her system. She was naked.

The cameras were rolling.

The girl fondled his erect penis, slowly masturbating him. She kissed his belly and moved her mouth to his balls. Gerald hunched on the bed. The young girl then took him into her mouth. Gerald groaned in heated pleasure, his face distorted by primal lust. As the girl mounted him, taking him into her wet tightness, crying out as he filled her, Nick Pullen crawled onto the bed, being careful to keep his back to the cameras. He stuck his dick into Gerald's willing mouth. A silken cord was tossed onto the big bed.

From that point on, it was all downhill for the three of them. Especially for the girl.

''This is ridiculous!'' George Steckler groused, tossing his suitcase onto the bed in the motel room. ''We are reduced to chasing ghosts!''

''That's not the reason we're here, George,'' Scott said patiently.

''Oh?''

''That's just an excuse for us to continue the original investigation.''

George sat down on the bed and thought about that. His face brightened. "By golly, Scott. You're right."

"Thank you," the older agent said.

"You're welcome."

Scott glanced at George and shook his head. Then he grinned "However, we do have to check out that letter. And that's your job."

George's smile vanished. "Gee, Scott. Do I have to?"

"Yes. You have to. First thing in the morning. Now, I'm going to get something to eat. You ready?"

"Not yet. I want to change my shirt. I feel a bit rumpled. I've had this one on all day."

Scott sighed. "Fine. I'll be in my room. I need a drink."

"You shouldn't drink even when we're *not* on the job, Scott. Someone might smell the liquor on your breath. That would not make a good impression on the public. After all, we are FBI agents."

Scott paused at the door. "George?"

"Yes, Scott?"

"Fuck you!"

The group just could not watch any more of the tapes. To a person, they had seen all their minds could take for one night. The perversion, the degradation, the pain, and the killing. Cole suggested they get something to eat. Katti gave him a look that was guaranteed to melt titanium.

"It was just a thought," Cole said.

"A bad one," Bev said.

"So what now?" Gary asked.

"Nothing," Cole said, and cut his eyes to Bob, who nodded his head in agreement. "We might be able to prove this Doc Drake was a part of it, but he's small fry. We want to chop off the head of the snake. We think we know who they are, but so far, we don't have any proof. We'll just have to view all these films and any others we might be able to get our hands on.

And hope that somebody made a mistake, maybe we'll catch a glimpse of a face."

Al Pickens was deep in thought when Cole turned to him. "What's on your mind, Al?"

"That girl who was killed just before you folks showed up. She wasn't strangled. She was beaten to death."

"I know. That one is a puzzle. Unless the death is not related to what we're working on. You know the sheriff over in that county?"

"Oh, sure—French—he's a good man. And he is not now nor has he ever been a member of our . . . club," he said the last with distaste.

"How many sighting over in his country?"

"Not many. But that was always a very quiet county. Only one roadhouse in the entire county. It was bulldozed some years back." He said the last with a smile, and Cole remembered what the old man had told him while watching him pump gas. "French doesn't believe in ghosts," he added.

"What puzzles me," Jim said, returning from the kitchen with a can of beer, "is why the Feds haven't been in here on this snuff film business. Unless they have, and you didn't know it, Al."

"This is a rural county, Jim. I would have known it if they spent any time at all here. Strangers asking questions gets back to me in a hurry."

"But they could have come in and set up some wire taps," Cole said. "That doesn't even have to be done here. They could have bugged some houses. There are voice-activated bugs now no larger than a dime, that transmit for miles. And if the Feds had even a modicum of evidence on anyone in this area, they would be doing mail intercepts. They can duplicate an envelope in a matter of seconds."

"It would make my job so much easier, if I had only a tiny fraction of all that high-tech equipment," Al said wistfully.

"Dream on," Bob said, a sour note to the words. "I quit hoping for some of that fancy equipment years ago."

Al reached over and stilled the ringing telephone. He listened for a moment, thanked the party on the other end, and hung up. "Two guys just checked into the motel about an hour or so ago. Both of them wearing guns. High-ride holsters."

"Bureau," Cole said. "How were they dressed?"

"Nicely. The younger one especially." He glanced at Jim and smiled. "See what I mean about rural people letting me know things." He rose from the chair. "Cole, you want to come with me? The rest of you folks, make yourselves to home. I'm the high sheriff of this county. Folks come in here carrying guns, I have a right to brace them and find out what's going on."

Cole stood up and smiled. "If they are Bureau, they are not going to like this."

"Good," Al replied, and headed for the door. He paused and turned around. "Oh, by the way. Stop by the office in the morning and sign your commission cards and give my secretary some money to cover your state bonds. Get your pictures taken and pick up your badges. You're all being deputized. I want this legal."

"Even me?" Katti asked.

"Even you, Katti. Come on, Cole. Let's go see the FBI."

At the motel, Al asked the desk clerk the number of the older man's room. Cole nodded his approval. Al Pickens was a good and cautious lawman. At the door, Al rapped softly, Cole standing to one side, ready to back him up if necessary. Scott Frey cracked the door.

"Sheriff Pickens," Al announced, putting a cowboy boot between the door and the jamb. "Keep your hands in sight and back up."

"I'm FBI, Sheriff," Scott said, backing up. "Come on in. My partner is in the room next door. To your right."

Al looked at Scott's ID, and all three men relaxed. Scott waved them to chairs and pointed at the bottle of bourbon on the dresser.

"Don't mind if I do," Al said. "This has been a long day for us. You want to call your partner in on this conversation?"

"I'd rather not. Steckler's an asshole."

Cole chuckled, liking the Bureau man almost instantly. Scott was about forty; maybe a couple of years over that. And he was the type of man who could get lost in a crowd of two.

Drinks fixed, Al said, "Can you tell us why you're here, Scott?"

"In a manner of speaking. We've cleared you in this investigation. And you, Mr. Younger. Is that enough for the moment?"

"Cole. Call me Cole. Yeah. That will do."

The Bureau man nodded and took a sip of his drink. "A Mrs. Doggett wrote the Bureau a letter concerning all the disappearances that have occurred in this area over the years."

"Alma Doggett," Al said.

"That's right."

"Did she tell you that ghosts were responsible?"

The Bureau man smiled. "Ah, as a matter of fact, yes, she did."

Al nodded his head. "Well, she's right."

Scott Frey sat on the edge of the bed and stared at the county sheriff. For the first time in many years as an FBI agent, he was, momentarily, at a complete loss for words.

"How'd my dick taste, Gerald?" Nick Pullen asked. "You were gobblin' at it like a pup to a tit."

A now fully lucid Gerald had viewed the film and had promptly vomited all over himself. He had been taken to a bathroom, took a long and hot shower, and now sat in a chair, fully clothed, and said nothing. He looked at the people in the room. Victoria Staples, Arlene Simmons, Captain Wood, Win Bryan, Nick Pullen, and Albert Pickens. Several others he did not know. The people who had been operating the cameras were gone.

But he was relieved that he had not killed the young girl with the silken cord. Nick Pullen had done that, while sodomizing the child. Her screaming had been hideous. Gerald was sure he would never forget that sound.

He found his voice. "What happened to the girl?"

"We feed them to the hogs," Albert said with a smile. "Hog'll eat anything . . . almost."

"Did you like that tight little pussy, Gerald?" Arlene asked with an evil smirk. "I bet you never had any that good."

Gerald did not reply.

"Now, Gerald," Victoria said. "You're going to cooperate with us. Or that film you just saw gets circulated. And as a further incentive, you have a daughter who just turned thirteen. She's a nice little piece. Very pretty. How would you like for her to star in some of our films? Can you just imagine Nick shoving the meat to her? Who knows, she might like it."

"Leave Vivian out of this. I'll do whatever you ask."

"That's a boy. We don't want you to do anything, Gerald. Except keep your fucking mouth shut. Can you do that?"

"Yes," Gerald whispered.

"You can go home now, Gerald. Back to your wife and your pretty little daughter. Just go on with business as usual, Gerald. But always bear in mind that you are now an accessory to murder, crimes against nature, rape, carnal knowledge of a juvenile, and a willing participant in illegal pornography. Show the man out, Nick."

"Come on, sweetie-pie," Nick said with a nasty chuckle. "Let's go be alone for a time."

Scott finally found his voice. "You're not serious!"

"Oh, yes, we're serious," Al assured him. "And we also know about the snuff film industry in this area. My chief deputy is probably up to his ass in that dirty business."

"Jesus!" Scott blurted. He swallowed half his drink.

"Cole here put most of it together."

Scott cut his eyes to Cole. "You struck a federal officer some years back."

"I damn sure did," Cole replied. "And I would have struck him several more times, had not some of my deputies pulled me off."

Scott Frey was by nature an easygoing and good-humored man. He could not contain a chuckle. "Believe it or not, Cole, a lot of people with the Bureau were delighted to hear about you jacking his jaw. Steerman was not a well-liked man. He got himself fired a few years after that, ah, incident."

"Good."

Scott's grin faded. "Let's get serious about these ghosts, people. I mean, you are putting me on, right?"

Before either man could reply, the adjoining room door burst open and George Steckler stood there, .40 caliber autoloader held out in front of him just like he was taught at the academy. He would have appeared a lot more threatening had he not been standing there in his underwear.

"Freeze!" he shouted. "Federal officer. FBI. Don't move. What's going on here?"

Scott sighed. "George, will you put that gun away and go put on your pants. You look like a goddamned idiot!"

Sixteen

Cole and Al left the motel room shortly after George made his appearance. While George was in his own room, putting on his pants, Scott conferred with Cole and Al and all three decided the wisest thing to do was not to tell George yet, about the possibility that the ghosts might actually exist.

"Not a possibility," Al told the senior Bureau man. "They exist."

"I've got to see them to believe it."

"How about tomorrow tonight?" Cole asked.

"Fine with me."

"And bring George," Al said. "I want to see his reaction."

That brought a wide and genuine smile to Scott's face. "It might be worth the price of admission. But I still think you two are putting me on."

"I wouldn't joke about anything connected to snuff films," Cole told him.

That wiped the smile away. "No," Scott said soberly. "I guess you wouldn't, at that."

"We won't say anything about your being in town," Al told him. "And we came over in one of Jim Deaton's cars tonight.

I'll tell the desk clerk to keep his mouth shut. He will. See you tomorrow.''

Al drove over to the hospital to check on Earl and Luddy. The two were being held under guard and incommunicado. Under guard because of their assault upon Cole, and kept away from other people to keep them alive, for both Cole and the sheriff believed an attempt on their lives was possible.

But when they arrived at the hospital, both hired thugs were asleep and heavily sedated.

A doctor was just finishing up his evening rounds, and Al stopped him. "What's the word on Earl Wilson and Luddy Post?"

"Not good, Al. Oh, physically, they're all right, except for some bruises and some rather strange burns on the soles of their feet. Deep burns. They won't be doing any walking for quite some time. It's their mental condition that's got us all worried. I'm a medical doctor, not a psychiatrist, but in my most unprofessional opinion, they're both basket cases—sometimes lucid, sometimes raving lunatics. Other times they're almost comatose. When they come out of their comatose states, they always come out screaming. Shouting about being in Hell, seeing Satan. Being manhandled by men and women, who've been dead for years. They swear they were both in a nightclub outside of town. I'm not from this area, as you know, so I don't know what club they're referring to. I didn't know we had any clubs out in the country.''

"We don't," Al said. "Not in years. Did you do a blood alcohol on them?"

"Oh, sure. They were both clean. But that's something else."

"Oh?"

"Yes. They both claim to have been forced to drink heavily over the past couple of nights. They have no recollection of the daylight hours during the time they were missing, just the night. Quite frankly, it's the strangest thing I have ever seen. I'd have to say it borderlines on the paranormal.''

"When can we see them?"

"Oh, in the morning. But don't expect to get much sense out of either of them."

"Thank you, Doctor."

Cole walked with Al down the corridor to the room where Luddy and Earl were being held. He faced a deputy, his nose about an inch from the man's face. "If anything happens to either of those men in there, Starr, I'll have your ass on a platter. You understand that?"

"Yes, sir!"

"You'll be relieved at five o'clock in the morning. Don't even think about nodding off or taking a catnap."

"Yes, sir! Ah, Sheriff?"

"What?"

"I'm on your side in this thing, Sheriff."

"What do you mean, Starr?"

"I don't like Win Bryan and never have. I lost a cousin five years ago, if you'll remember. He was last seen out there where the old County Line club used to be."

"I remember, Tom," the sheriff softened his tone. "Sorry I snapped at you. It's been sort of a tense time for me."

Tom Starr nodded his head. "Sheriff? I've seen that Tommy Baylor fellow. Twice over the years, on patrol. I never said anything about it, because . . . well, you know why."

"I understand." Al put his hand on the deputy's arm. "Tom, I've got a dirty department . . ."

"I know that better than you, Sheriff," Tom interrupted. "You just don't know how dirty."

"And you do?"

"Yes, sir. It's more than dirty. It's . . . evil."

"Why didn't you come to me with this knowledge?"

"Well, sir. Ah . . . well, I always figured you were a part of it. Your, ah, son is."

"Shit!" Sheriff Al Pickens said softly. "I knew it. I guess in my heart I knew it all along. How many can I trust, Tom?"

"Me and Frank Bruce. That's it, sir."

"Damn! The women in the office? Cynthia, Maggie?"

"Dirty. I'd swear on the Bible to that. I can't prove it. But I know it's true. They both are, well, screwin' Win and some others. I've seen their cars out to the Staples' mansion more'un once. A lot more'un once."

Al Pickens did some pretty fancy cussing for a moment, then turned to Cole. "Cole, get Jim on the horn. Use that hall phone over there. Tell him to get his people in from Memphis to guard these two nut cases. Around the clock. If the county balks at paying for them, I'll pay them out of my own pocket. But I've got to free Tom here to help us."

Cole nodded and walked to the phone. He was back in a moment. "They'll be here in two hours. Four of them."

"Good. Stay until they arrive, Tom. Then get some rest. Meet me in the office at eight in the morning."

"Yes, sir. And . . . Sheriff?"

Al turned to face him.

"Thanks for trusting me. I won't let you down. Ah, you can ask Frank. Me and him have talked about this."

"Glad to have you with us, Tom. Stay on your toes until those P.I.'s get here."

"I will, Sheriff."

Al Pickens had everybody legally deputized and sworn in. Scott Frey sent George Steckler out to get a lengthy interview with Mrs. Doggett.

"He'll be gone all morning," Scott told the team once they had gathered outside the motel. "George is very thorough . . . to the point of driving you crazy. He can be a pompous asshole and a pain in the neck, but he's a good agent."

"Let's head for the country," Al suggested. "We've got to make some plans."

"This is going to be the damnest field report I have ever turned in," Scott muttered.

"Providing any of us live to write a report," Al said grimly.

Book Two

All that we see or seem
Is but a dream within a dream.

—Edgar Allen Poe

One

Cole and Katti stopped at a MacDonalds and bought a sack full of breakfast sandwiches and coffee to go, then headed out into the country, soon catching up with the others. Scott Frey was riding with Sheriff Pickens, Tom Starr with Frank Bruce, Bob Jordan with Jim Deaton, and Gary and Bev were together.

"We won't fool people for long," Al said, when the group was all gathered under the shade of a huge old oak, munching on breakfast biscuits and sipping coffee. "By this evening, those people we're looking at will be looking right back at us and be busy covering any tracks that aren't already covered."

"We know this Victoria Stables is a wealthy women," Scott said. "Richest person in the state. So why would she get involved in something as slimy as child porn and snuff films?"

"She's sick," Al said. "I've known Victoria since childhood. We went to school together grades one through six. Then her parents sent her East to school. She was a weird kid, very cruel to everything and everybody around her. Arlene was and is the same way."

"Clue me in on this Nick Pullen. All we've got is the Memphis PD's arrest reports. Not that that isn't a lot of interesting reading, for it is.''

"Nick is a punk. Just like my son, Albert. But I'm beginning to believe that my son is the more dangerous of the two . . . in his own sneaky little shitty way. Nick is bigger and tougher than Albert, but not nearly as smart. Albert is a schemer, and I think he is a coward.''

"Who can we trust, Al?" the Bureau man asked.

The sheriff put out a hand, palm up, indicating the group.

"That's it?"

"That's it."

"Are you going to call in for help?" Katti asked Scott.

He shook his head. "Not just yet." He looked at the sheriff. "Have you ever tried to videotape these, ah, well, the ghosts?"

"No. I don't think that's possible."

Cole elaborated on his own experiences with the ghosts at the club.

Scott clearly did not believe any of it. He shook his head. "You crouched behind a car that Luddy and Earl could not see? The vehicle hid you, but they walked right through it. Oh, now, come on, people! Give me a break.''

"You'll see. Tonight.''

"I think I am going to wait until the last minute to tell George what we're doing," Scott said. "His reaction should be one for the book.''

Deputy Tom Starr answered the phone in Al's car. "It's the hospital, Sheriff. Both Luddy Post and Earl Wilson are awake and lucid, if you want to talk to them.''

"That I do. I'll see you folks later on. You comin' with me, Scott?''

"Yeah. I want to hear this.''

"We was in Hell, Sheriff," Luddy said. "I mean it. I know it sounds stupid. But we was in Hell.''

"We damn shore was," Earl spoke from the other bed in the

semiprivate room. "I seen the devil. I seen him. Up close. I know he's real. I seen him. It's church for me from now on. I'm a changed man."

"Me, too," Luddy said.

"Who paid you to attack Mr. Younger and the others?"

"Huh?" Earl said.

"What?" Luddy echoed. "Who's Mr. Younger?"

"What others?" Earl asked.

Al questioned the pair closely, then Scott took it. It became obvious to both lawmen that the pair had absolutely no memory of why they were out at the club that night.

"Do you know Captain Wood of the state police?" Al asked.

"Oh, sure," Luddy replied. "He's hepped me out of several jams." He frowned. "But for the life of me, I don't know why he did. And I can't recall what it was I got into trouble about."

"Me, neither," Luddy said. "The last thing I remember, Neely come to see us at the trailer. You see, me and Earl bunk together. But . . . I don't know what it was he come to see us about. I'm not lyin' to you guys. I swear to God I ain't lyin.' I'm just drawin' a blank."

"I wish I knew how come my feet was burned so bad," Earl said. "It's like I been walkin' through far."

"Maybe we did walk through the fars of hale," Luddy said. "I want to see me a preacher. I want to re-pent. Can you arrange for a preacher to come see us, Sheriff?"

"Yes. I can do that. You boys rest for a while. We'll talk more later."

Standing outside the room, a few feet away from a rather tough-looking P.I. from Deaton's Little Rock office, Scott said, "I believe them. I think they're telling the truth."

"So do I. Certain memories have been wiped from their minds."

"Well . . . I prefer to think they are suffering from some sort of temporary amnesia."

Al grinned. "Tonight is going to be a real eye-opener for you, Scott."

"I'm going to have to see it to believe it."

*   *   *

"They're FBI," Captain Wood told Victoria. "Not local. Out of Washington. This complicates matters. Listen to me, ladies: You don't want to kill a fed. That is bad news spelled with capital letters."

Arlene stirred nervously and stared at him from her position on the couch. "Can you call off your people?"

"Oh, yes."

"Do it," Victoria commanded in a harsh voice. "Right now." She pointed to a phone. "Use the scrambler phone."

Wood opened a drawer and took out a portable phone, and then consulted a list of numbers that had been previously used. With over sixty thousand combinations, the phone was virtually tap-proof. Wood looked at a card in his pocket with Costa's schedule on it, and punched in first the code combination and then the number. Costa did not pick up on the other end. The briefcase containing another scrambler phone had been stolen out of his car the night before.

"No answer," Wood said, clicking off the scrambler phone and unplugging it from the standard home handset. "No problem. I know where they're staying. I'll use the phone in my car." He walked outside and dialed the motel number on his cellular phone.

"I'm sorry, sir," the motel operator said. "Your party has checked out."

Wood hung up and said, "Shit!" He went back into the house and told the women the news.

"I don't like this," Arlene said.

"Me, neither," Victoria echoed.

"No problem," the highway cop said. "I have their schedule. I'll get in touch with Costa this evening and call everything off."

"Just make damn sure you do," Victoria told him, real menace in her voice. "Now then. What about Luddy and Earl?"

"They can't remember anything, and couldn't tell it if they

lid. My contact at the hospital told me not an hour ago those wo are babbling idiots. Both of them are certifiably crazy as oons. Pickens and one of the feds went to see them this morning. They got nothing."

"Where is the other FBI man?" Arlene asked.

"He interviewed that old bag Doggett woman. Spent all morning with her. But she can't give him any hard proof. She doesn't have any to give. All we've got to do is keep our heads down, until this blows over."

"You just make damn sure you call off your dogs," Victoria said. "And don't follow these people anymore. Call everybody off. They can't find anything, for there is nothing out there to find. Just let them blunder around. Understood?"

Wood nodded his head and left.

Gerald Wilson took a few days off from work. Told his wife he wasn't feeling well and just wanted to rest. That really wasn't a lie. Physically, he was in good health. Mentally, he was very, very shaky—bordering on insanity. The events of the night before had just about pushed him over the line. Before he was driven back to his motel, Nick had forced him into oral sex with him and Albert Pickens. It was disgusting. All during that ordeal, Nick had talked about screwing Gerald's daughter, Vivian; had gone into great detail about what he'd like to do to her. It was perverted, disgusting, and evil. The more he thought about what had happened, the further into mental illness he sank. By nightfall, Gerald Wilson had slipped all the way over the line. He dressed in jeans, lace-up hunting boots, and a long sleeve shirt. He walked through the house. It was quiet and empty. His wife and Vivian had gone out to eat. His oldest son was going to summer school at the university. Gerald opened his gun cabinet and took out a Remington 7600 slide action rifle in .308 caliber. He loaded it up and stuffed his pockets full of cartridges. He opened another drawer in the expensive gun cabinet and picked up a pistol. A Colt government model autoloader, .45 caliber. He filled three extra clips and took a full box of .45's, putting those in his back pocket. He was just about ready. Gerald had some shooting to do. But first . . .

He went to his desk and took out a sheet of good bond paper. He picked up a pen and wrote: *My darling: This is something I must do, for you, and for our children. There is just too much evil in this county. I must do my part to erase that evil. Just remember that I love you.*

He read it over, signed it, and left it on the desk. He stood up, shoved the pistol behind his waistband, picked up the rifle, and went out to his pickup truck. He drove away into the night.

"I don't believe this!" Special Agent George Steckler said. "I cannot believe we are actually taking part in this nonsense!"

"Well, we are. Whether you believe it or not," Scott told him. "What don't you put on some jeans and a sport shirt. Get comfortable. We're going out into the boondocks, George. Not having dinner at the Ritz."

"A good agent should be presentable at all times."

Scott sighed and walked out of the motel room. "Come on, George. We've got an appointment to see some ghosts."

"Ridiculous!" George snorted. He straightened his expensive tie, slipped into his tailored summer weight jacket, and stepped out into the humid north Arkansas summer night. "Do you want me to drive?"

"No. You just sit."

"You never let me do anything, Scott."

"I let you interview Mrs. Doggett, didn't I?"

"That woman is mentally unbalanced, Scott. She's a fruit-cake."

"Then you two found a lot in common," Scott muttered.

"What was that, Scott?"

"Nothing, George. Nothing at all. Get in the car."

"Shouldn't we get our shotguns out of the trunk, Scott?"

Scott cranked the engine into life. "We're going to see some ghosts, George. What the hell are you going to do, shoot a ghost?"

"This is no such thing as a ghost, Scott."

"George?"

"What, Scott?"

"Shut the damned door."

Two

Gerald drove out into the country, out past Victoria Staples's mansion. About a mile past the sprawling grounds and the huge house, he pulled onto a dirt road, drove for a few hundred yards, and then drove the pickup into some brush and left it, taking only a blanket. He would no longer be needing the truck.

At a convenience store, Gerald had bought several containers of bottled water and some snacks. He worked his way deeper into the woods, until he found a huge pile of brush. He walked off a few yards and urinated, then poked around in the brush to scare off any snakes. Gerald crawled in amid the bramble and made himself as comfortable as possible.

He had been out to Victoria's house enough times to know that she had a very elaborate security system that she turned on at night. But she turned it off during the day. Her servants kept kicking the alarms on. But unless she was planning a party, she had no servants at night, and none on the weekend. And tomorrow was Saturday. Nearly all of the field workers would be off, and then Gerald could make his move.

He went to sleep smiling, thinking about killing Victoria Staples.

*   *   *

Captain Wood slowly turned off the phone in his car. Now he was really worried. Due to a reservation mix-up, Costa was not at the motel. No. They didn't know where he was. But they did feel really really bad about the mix-up.

"Not half as bad as I feel," Wood muttered, breaking the connection.

He had to find Costa. Costa was the only one who could call this off. And to make matters worse, Costa was under no obligation to stick with his timetable. If he saw a chance to make the hit sooner, that was his option.

"Shit!" Wood said.

Gerald's wife found the note and immediately called the sheriff's office.

"I'm sorry, ma'am," the deputy told her. "But we've got to wait for twenty-four hours. If he isn't back by then, we can put a BOLO out for him."

"A what?"

"Be On The Lookout. And all-points bulletin, if you like."

"I . . . see."

"Sorry, ma'am. But he'll probably show up. They usually do."

"He's been under a great deal of stress lately."

"Yes, ma'am. Maybe he just went out for a weekend toot. You know."

"Well . . . thank you."

"You're welcome, ma'am."

A few minutes later, Win called in from his house. "Anything happening, Larry?"

"Quiet as a church, Win. Oh. Mrs. Wilson did call. Seems her husband took off. Left some sort of ramblin' note about evil and so forth."

Win was silent for a moment. "Have you logged it?"

"Not yet."

"Don't. Just forget you got it, Larry. And don't tell anyone about her calling."

"I gotcha, Chief."

Win sat still for a moment after hanging up, deep in thought. So Gerald had flipped out and taken off. Win believed the first part, but not the second. Gerald had killing on his mind; he was sure of that. He slipped on a shirt and went out to his car. He had some people to see this night. And if possible, one man to stop.

Win drove first to Albert Pickens's house. He told them about Gerald, and warned Albert and Nick to be careful. Then he drove out to Victoria's. She was not in a real peachy mood.

"You idiot!" she shouted at him. "That was stupid, telling your dispatcher not to log the call. Call him and tell him to log the goddamn thing in. If anything happens—and it's going to, bet on that—she'll tell the sheriff she called it in. There has to be a record."

"Ah . . . sure, Victoria. Anything you say."

Then Captain Wood showed up, telling his sad story of being unable to reach John Costa.

"Oh, wonderful," Victoria said acidly.

"We'd better do something about those tapes down in the basement rooms," Win said.

"Only a handful of people even know about those rooms. Those rooms were dug more than a hundred years ago. My grandfather had them renovated, then my father did more work on them with a crew he brought in from out of state. That was fifty years ago. After father and mother died, I brought in a crew from Chicago to finish the work to my specifications. That was twenty-five years ago. That company has been out of business for years. Forget the basement rooms. Only a few of us know they even exist."

"You mean you had the work done after you *killed* your parents, don't you?" Captain Wood reminded the woman that he had enough on her to put her in the electric chair.

She glared daggers at him. "Don't push me too far, Curtis," she warned. "That would be very unwise on your part."

"We're in this together, Vicky," Wood said, calling her by her nickname, which he knew she despised. "Don't you forget that."

"Oh, I won't, Curtis. I assure you of that."

As they had done before, Cole and the others parked in the turn-row across the county road from where the roadhouse used to sit. Scott had warned George to cool his bitching and just play along with the game. George was introduced all around. No one on either side was terribly impressed with the other. The group stood around for a few minutes, exchanging glances.

"Any time now," Sheriff Pickens said.

"Nonsense!" George muttered.

Then, very faintly, as full darkness began settling over the land, music drifted to the group. George and Scott looked all around them, doing a slow three hundred and sixty.

"Kids parked somewhere with their radio turned up very loud," George remarked.

"Kids playing music from the 1950's?" Cole asked. "I doubt it. I've done some research on oldies tunes. That one is called 'The Fool.' Sanford Clark had a big hit with it."

"My dad used to sing that," Scott said. "Drove my mother up the wall. Dad couldn't carry a tune in a bucket."

Faint laughter reached the group.

Again, the Bureau men did a slow circle, looking all around them.

"Look across the road," Katti told the FBI agents. "It's appearing."

Scott and George stopped and stared. At first it was a misty, sparkly non-shape . . .

"My god!" Scott breathed.

. . . that slowly began taking on a firm outline. Then . . .

"It's some sort of illusion," George said.

. . . the weeds and grass in the parking lot disappeared and hard-packed gravel took its place . . .

"This is impossible," Scott whispered.

. . . Cars and trucks began appearing in the parking lot . . .

"Look at those old vehicles," George said. "They're thirty and forty years old!" He rubbed his eyes in disbelief.

. . . The music changed and grew louder. The guitarist was playing the old Duane Eddy hit: "Forty Miles of Bad Road" . . .

"Incredible!" Scott said.

. . . The neon light above the front door to the roadhouse was the first to take firm shape. It blinked off and on in bright red . . .

. . . The music stopped for a moment. Laughter filled the warm night air. A honky-tonk piano began playing, and a male voice began singing the Fats Domino hit: "Blueberry Hill" . . .

"Still think it's some sort of illusion, George?" Sheriff Pickens asked.

George opened his mouth, but no words came out. He was mesmerized by the scene in front of him.

. . . The music changed, a hard-driving rockabilly version of the old Hank Williams hit: "My Bucket's Got A Hole In It," the drummer really pushing the beat . . .

Without realizing it, Scott began tapping the toe of one shoe on the ground, in time with the music.

No one noticed when George Steckler, who had been standing off to one side in the darkness, left the group and began walking across the road. Cole was the first to spot him.

"No, George!" he shouted. "Don't go over there."

George kept walking.

. . . The music abruptly changed, a female with a country twang to her voice was singing: "Come on-a My House" . . .

"Goddamnit, George!" Scott shouted. "Get your ass back over here."

George stepped onto the parking lot of the old roadhouse. He touched a '49 Mercury on the trunk. It was real. He looked at his hand in disbelief.

. . . The music again changed. A male voice sang: "Endless Sleep" . . .

George put one foot on the first step leading to the front door of the roadhouse.

"Shit!" Cole said, and ran across the road, Scott right behind him. "The rest of you stay put!" Cole shouted.

... The music changed. The singer was doing a pretty good job of the old country classic: "Hello, Walls" ...

George put one hand on the doorknob.

"George, don't do it!" Cole shouted.

... The music changed again, fast as a heartbeat. The Ivory Joe Hunter hit: "I Almost Lost My Mind" ...

George turned the doorknob.

"Goddamnit, George!" Scott shouted. "Step back from that door. That's an order, you hard-headed dipshit!"

... The music changed again: "I Hear You Knockin' " ...

George pushed open the door. The smell of death was very nearly overpowering. He stepped back, a grimace on his face as the odor of death hit him full blast. The smell of rotting flesh assaulted his nostrils. George stepped back further, both feet now off the steps.

... A man appeared in the brightly lighted doorway. He wore jeans, a shirt with pearl snaps, cowboy boots and hat. Inside the club, the singer began a country version of the Brook Benton hit: "It's Just A Matter Of Time" ...

Cole and Scott had come to a sliding stop in the gravel, a few yards behind George.

... A woman shoved the cowboy out of the way and stood in the doorway to the roadhouse. She smiled lewdly at George. "Hi, there, big boy. Come on in, baby. We're havin' a real good time."

"You are not real," George said firmly. "This is some sort of trick."

... The woman, dressed in tight jeans, put one hand down to her crotch and rubbed it. "You like to fuck, baby?"

George straightened up and said very indignantly, "Madam, I am a federal officer on official business."

... She laughed at him ...

"Oh, shit!" Scott said. "He's hopeless."

The music became wilder and louder. The band hammering

out the Jerry Lee Lewis hit: "Whole Lot of Shakin' Goin' On."

. . . The woman hunched her hips at George . . .

. . . The cowboy rudely shoved her out of the way, and his bulk filled the doorway. The smell of death had softened somewhat, becoming bearable . . .

Across the road, Bev had lifted a minicam and was filming the scene taking place. At least, she hoped she was filming it.

. . . The cowboy stepped out of the doorway and down the steps. He was smiling . . .

George flashed his ID. "Let me see some identification."

"Oh, good lord!" Scott said.

. . . The cowboy laughed at George. His breath stank of the grave. He stepped closer to George . . .

George stood his ground.

. . . The cowboy suddenly reached out and grabbed George's tie . . .

George slugged the cowboy. It was like hitting a solid block of ice.

. . . The cowboy laughed at him . . .

George tried to break the grip on his tie. "Turn loose of my tie, you redneck apparition!"

. . . The cowboy began dragging George toward the doorway to the roadhouse. The tie came loose and was tossed to the woman . . .

Cole moved swiftly, his souped-up stun gun in hand. He hit the cowboy with the stun gun, just under the chin. The head exploded into thousands of sparkling dots. A hideous scream cut the night. The music stopped. The dead hand released its grip on George's tie. Off balance, George fell over backward, landing on his butt on the gravel.

Headless, the cowboy began running wildly in the parking lot, slamming into cars and trucks. Cole ran after him, the stun gun cracking wickedly. He hit the cowboy in the center of his back, and the torso exploded into another mass of thousands of sparkling dots. The legs ran on, stumbling and smashing into parked cars and trucks.

George was sitting up, on the gravel, his disbelieving eyes watching the strange pursuit. Scott seemed frozen where he stood.

The sparkling dots began popping and cracking; with each pop and crack, several would disappear, leaving gaps in the night.

. . . Inside the club, the band cranked up again. But every instrument was badly out of tune. The drummer off the beat. The words out of the singer's mouth were all jumbled . . .

The now sparkling and running legs in the parking lot seemed to falter and stumble. The dots began to pop and explode, the sparkle leaving the legs as the dots died.

The music stopped. The laughter died. The cars and trucks in the parking lot began to fade. The roadhouse became misty. The neon light over the door blinked rapidly several times and then winked out, plunging the area into darkness. What was left of the running legs fell to the now weed-grown and grassy parking lot. A stinking and rotting corpse slowly began to materialize. The fifties-style suit hung in tatters. Bits of rotting flesh and tufts of hair clung to the skull of the dead man. The smell of the grave grew stronger.

"What the hell . . .?" Scott muttered.

The roadhouse was no longer visible. Only the old and cracked concrete slab could be seen in the dim light.

"I can't believe it," George mumbled, still sitting on the ground. "I saw it. I hit the guy. I heard the music. But I just can't believe it." He put his hand to his shirt. "That . . . thing, whatever it was, stole my tie. I paid thirty dollars for that tie!"

"Better your tie than your ass, George," Scott told him. "Didn't you hear me yelling at you?"

"Sort of," George replied, getting to his feet and brushing himself off.

"Sort of, George?" his partner said. "What the hell kind of answer is that?"

"There was a roaring in my head. I can't explain it. I've

ever experienced anything like it in my life. It was as if something was pulling me across that road. Some . . . force, I guess you'd have to call it."

Scott looked around at the others gathered in the grassy parking lot. He shrugged his shoulders. "What can I say? I have no answers."

"Maybe it was because George was such a nonbeliever," Katti suggested. "Maybe the ghosts wanted to show him up close and personal."

"Well, they certainly did that!" George unbuttoned the top button of his shirt and began rubbing his sore neck. He abruptly stopped his rubbing and stood quite still for a moment. "What am I saying? Good lord, what am I saying? There are no such things as ghosts!"

Scott pointed to the stinking, stiffened, and rotting corpse, lying in the weeds only a few feet away. "Then how do you explain that, George?"

George opened his mouth, then closed it, and shook his head, refusing to speak.

Sheriff Pickens knelt down beside the body and put the beam from his flashlight on the corpse. "Paul Hensley. Died in a car crash years and years ago. I was just a kid. He was drunk and running from the highway patrol. Left the road at about a hundred miles an hour, and slammed into a tree."

"But he was dressed like a cowboy, when he appeared in the doorway," Scott said. "Now he's wearing a suit."

"I know." Al stood up and clicked off his flashlight. "Don't ask me to explain it."

"What are we going to do with the body?" Bob asked.

"What do you mean?" Scott said. "We don't have a choice, do we?"

"Look," Cole said, facing Scott and George. "We show up in town with this corpse. Say we found it alongside the road. The family wants it re-buried. They go out to the grave site and the grave is undisturbed. Questions. The grave is opened and the casket exhumed. It's empty. More questions. As soon as that hits the press, there'll be thousands of curious people flooding into this area, with thousands more behind them. You'll be polygraphed, and the examiner will detect you're lying about where the body was found. Then what? Will you tell them about the ghosts you saw?"

Scott sighed and looked at George. The younger agent shuffled his feet on the grass. "Whatever you decide to do, Scott, is all right with me," he said softly.

"Shit!" Scott said. "I've got to call in on this thing. I won't make this decision on my own." He grinned. "That's called passing the buck."

"What about the body for the time being?" Gary asked.

"Toss a tarp over it," Al said. He looked over at Tom Starr and Frank Bruce. Both of them appeared to be in a mild state of shock. "You two stick close. Make sure nothing happens to this body. But you can sit in your units across the road."

Both men looked very relieved at that.

George cut his eyes to Scott. "Do you know what you're going to say about this?"

"No. Not yet. But I'll think of something."

"Better you than me," the younger agent muttered.

Three

Scott talked to his superiors for a long time. A very long time. He was sweating when he finally hung up the phone in Al's den.

"Well?" the sheriff asked.

"Can you trust the local mortician?"

"Yes. That much I know for certain."

"Does he have facilities for storing the body?"

"Yes."

"All right. Have him go out there and pick up the body. Stash it away for the time being. Say nothing to anyone. I've got people coming in here. They don't believe me about the ghosts."

"I can't blame them for that."

"Incredible," George mumbled. "Bizarre."

Cole patted him on the shoulder. "I do know the feeling, George."

Bev came into the room, a frown on her face. "The tape I shot was blank. Except for Cole, Scott, and George. George looks like he's doing some sort of strange dance."

Sitting off by himself, George grimaced at the thought.

"Nothing else showed up?" Scott said. "The cars, the club?"

She shook her head. "Nothing."

"Damn!"

"I am not looking forward to being interviewed by our people," George said. "It's going to be very unpleasant."

"Oh, maybe not, George," his partner told him. "We do have witnesses to back our story."

"This could well mean the end of our careers," George said mournfully.

Scott had to laugh at the expression on the man's face. "It's not that bad, George."

The sheriff's home was in the country, the nearest neighbor more than a mile away. The house sat well back from the road in a stand of timber, with several acres cleared around the house. Clouds had begun rolling in and the air was heavy, the clouds just beginning to dribble out sprinkles of rain.

John Costa had moved the timetable for the hit. He had come very close to calling off the whole damn thing; he felt his luck had turned sour. First the briefcase holding the scramble phone was stolen, then the ball-up with the room reservations made them all nervous. But the money was too good to pass up, so John had hit the button for the green light and assembled his people. When he saw that everyone involved had gathered at the sheriff's house in the country, it was just too good an opportunity to let slide. John didn't know who the two new people were, and he really didn't care. Over the years, John had killed several politicians, local and national, politician's girlfriends, cops, heads of industry, and everything in between. He once killed a mentally retarded six-year-old girl—the parents of the kid had paid him for that one. They said they had grown tired of seeing the brat slobber all the time.

It really didn't make any difference to John who or what he killed, just as long as he got paid for it.

Costa was at the front of the sheriff's house, Weber at the rear, Collins on one side, and Ginny Hammond on the other. They were all dressed in dark clothing and wore ski masks. They were armed with automatic weapons and ready to go. There would be little finesse to this touch. It would be quick and bloody and very final. It is very difficult to really silence an automatic weapon, at least for any length of time, but these were silenced as effectively as present technology allowed.

Lightning began ripping through the sky, and thunder rumbled all around. Costa glanced up at the sky and smiled. The weather would soon be perfect. They would wait until the full fury of the summer thunderstorm hit, before they launched their strike. Sound would not carry far in this weather.

A vicious slash of lightning briefly illuminated the land just as Katti was looking out the kitchen window, where she was standing by the sink, rinsing out the coffeepot, preparing to brew another pot. She caught just a split-second glimpse of what seemed to be a man standing by a huge old tree. Lightning cut the sky again, and the man was gone.

Katti blinked her eyes and stared. She shook her head, was thoughtful for a moment, then left the sink, and walked into the den. "Cole? It's probably just my imagination, but I swear I saw a man standing out by that big tree just a moment ago. He seemed to be holding something. I don't know what. It looked like a big T-shaped thing."

"A golf tee?" George asked.

"No. The down slash was shorter than the upper part."

"Like a banana clip in a rifle, maybe?" Gary said softly.

Sheriff Pickens leaped for the gun cabinet and threw it open. "Help yourself, people," he said. "Ammo in the bottom drawer." A minute later, with everyone holding a rifle or shotgun, he hit the light switches and plunged the room into darkness.

"Get on the floor, Katti!" Cole said. "Right now! Do it! Get next to a wall and belly down."

"Shit!" Costa said, as he watched the house go dark. "We've been spotted. Now!" he shouted. "Go, go, go!"

"We should advise them that we are federal officers," George's voice came out of the darkness. "Assaulting a federal officer is a serious matter. I think——"

"George," Scott said, very patiently.

"I know, Scott. I know. Shut up."

"Right."

Then there was no more time for talk as four sub-machine guns opened up from out of the suddenly rainy night. The windows were blown out, and the slugs shredded drapes and curtains, tore into furniture, shattered lamps, knocked out chunks of paneling, destroyed the china cabinet and all the dishes in it, punched holes in the refrigerator, the microwave, the dishwasher, the coffeepot, the stove and oven, raised hell with the flatware, and tore the doors off many of the cabinets.

While the thirty- and forty-round magazines were being emptied, those inside the house were unable to do anything except stay low and pray they didn't get hit.

When the assassins paused for a few seconds to change magazines, Cole slipped through the darkened and bullet-shattered home and out the back door, while the others opened up with hunting rifles and pistols.

No skill was involved in Cole taking out Weber. The two men ran into each other in the stormy night. But Cole's reaction time was faster, and he clubbed the assassin on the side of the head with the butt of his rifle. Weber dropped unconscious to the wet ground.

Returning fire from inside the house tore a huge chunk of bark from an oak tree, and the bark slammed into the face of Ginny Hammond, drawing blood and momentarily blinding the woman. Collins had a leg knocked out from under him by a slug from a .30–30 rifle and hit the ground hard, dropping his sub-machine gun, both hands going to his bleeding leg.

By this time, George and Scott had left the house, circled around, and got behind Costa.

"Give it up!" Scott yelled over the crash of thunder. "FBI. Drop your weapon. Right now!"

"FBI?" Costa said, then dropped his assault rifle. "No one said anything about the FBI being here," he muttered. "Damn!"

George put Costa on the ground and cuffed his hands behind

his back, while Tom Starr and Frank Bruce rounded up the others. Al called in for an ambulance.

"You could get me out of this damn rain," Collins bitched to Sheriff Pickens. "I'd be drier and a whole lot more comfortable."

"I could also shoot you in the head," Al responded. "Then you could be dry and comfortable forever."

Collins wisely decided to shut his mouth.

Al walked over to Scott. "Since I can't be sure who to trust in this area, you take over here. Normally, I don't have much use for the Feds, but you and George seem like all right people."

Scott smiled, while the warm summer rain plastered his hair to his head. "I guess I'll take that as a compliment, Sheriff. In a left-handed way."

George took offense at the sheriff's remark. He opened his mouth to speak, but Scott beat him to it. "Shut up, George."

"But I haven't said anything yet!"

"You were about to. Just cool it. Go call this in. Tell our people to get here ASAP."

"Well, gee whiz!" George said, and walked off.

Victoria slammed down the phone in a rage, stilling the voice of Capt. Curtis Wood. She didn't believe that crap about Costa not talking. If a good enough deal could be cut between prosecution and defense, Costa would blab. And if Curtis Wood went down, he would take everybody with him.

Victoria calmed herself, then sat quietly for a moment, deep in thought. She smiled and rose from the chair, walking over to a wall safe. She removed several stacks of bills, put the money into her purse, and then went out to the garage and got into her car. She drove straight to the home of Nick Pullen. She found him home and surprised to see her.

"What's up, Ms. Victoria?" Nick asked, after showing her to a chair.

Victoria opened her purse and tossed the money onto a coffee table. "I want you to kill a man, Nick. That's half the payment. You get the other half when the job is done. I want it done tonight."

Nick didn't hesitate. "Who's the man?"

Victoria told him.

Nick smiled. "Well, I'll be damned."

"And burn his house down around him, just in case he's got something on paper about us."

"No problem."

"You'll have to kill his wife, too."

"No problem."

"Don't tell Albert anything about this. He's weak."

"I know that. Don't worry. This is between us."

Victoria rose from the chair. "Come see me in the morning."

"I'll sure be there."

Victoria walked out into the stormy night. She felt better. Nick would do the job, and do it right. She knew that for a fact. She'd used him before. But this would be his last job for her. Tomorrow, when he came to the house, she'd take care of Nick.

A team of Bureau people was in the area within the hour. Ginny and Collins were taken to the local hospital for treatment and placed under heavy guard. Jim Deaton's people, who were guarding Earl and Luddy, and the FBI, guarding Collins and Ginny, spent the rest of the night staring at each other in the hallway of the hospital. Not all of the stares were friendly.

Sheriff Al Pickens decided to stay at his house. The guest room had not been touched by the gunfire. But the rest of the house was sure a mess.

Costa and Weber were placed in the local jail and guarded by FBI agents. No one else was allowed to get near them.

Win Bryan sat in his chair at his house, having been unsuccessful in finding Gerald Wilson, and shook his head at the news he'd just heard from a deputy. Everything seemed to be coming apart. He figured all along that Curtis Wood would crew everything up, since, in Win's opinion, most highway cops were overcome with their own importance.

But he just didn't know what to do about the situation.

The residents of northeast Arkansas and southeast Missouri were shocked the next morning, when they heard the news about the attack on Sheriff Pickens's home and the deaths of Highway Patrol Capt. Curtis Wood and his wife; they had died when their home exploded due to a faulty gas water heater. The coroner's initial report was that they had been overcome with the gas and died in bed, before the house blew up and caught fire. There were no signs of foul play. An investigation was under way, but the bodies were so badly mangled that if foul play *was* involved—other than a gunshot or a stabbing— it was going to be very difficult to determine.

Gerald Wilson had spent a wet night in the brush, but he hadn't paid any attention to the weather. His thoughts were solely of revenge. And now it was time to take that revenge.

Gerald emerged from the brush just as Nick Pullen was driving up to the Staples mansion. He smiled. "Good," he muttered. "Now if that weasel Albert would just show up, everything would be perfect. I could rid the world of three evils in one day." He consoled himself with the knowledge that two out of three wasn't bad.

Staying low, Gerald ran along a carefully trimmed hedgerow that grew left and right from the house, starting about ten feet from each side of the mansion and set back about thirty feet from the porch. He made it to the north side of the house without being spotted. There he paused to kneel down and catch his breath. He had been watching the house all morning, had seen no one come or go, and guessed that Victoria was alone. The huge old mansion had been built of stone shipped in from some damn place by her great-grandfather. Gerald had never liked the house. The place had always given him the creeps.

Then he remembered his most recent visit to this house and

the humiliation he had suffered at the hands of Victoria and the others, and in his mind rage grew as large as his madness.

Gerald moved to the rear of the mansion and entered the house through one of the back doors.

Gerald was fully prepared to die this day, and that knowledge did not frighten or alarm him . . . not as long as he could take some of this evil with him.

The sound of voices in heated argument drifted to him as he moved closer to the front of the great house. Two voices— Victoria and Nick.

Gerald moved closer, his boots silent on the polished floor, his rifle at the ready.

The quarreling voices grew louder. Gerald could not make out what they were quarreling about, but he was somehow pleased the two were quarreling. It meant something was wrong, and that was satisfying to him.

He came to a closed door and stood for a moment, listening to the angry voices. He could tell the two were in the next room. How to do this? Gerald wanted the moment to last for a time. He wanted to savor the sight of fear on their evil faces, and the scent of dread as they faced death . . . by his hand.

Gerald pushed open the door and stepped into the den of the mansion. Victoria and Nick stood facing each other, a few feet separating them. They stopped their quarreling and slowly turned to face him.

Gerald knew that while Nick was the younger, bigger, and stronger of the two, Victoria was by far the most dangerous. She was ruthless and cruel. He would kill her first.

But there was no fear in the woman. "Put that rifle down, Gerald!" Victoria commanded, her voice calm and strong. "Don't be a fool."

"Shut up, Victoria," Gerald said. "Just shut your ugly mouth."

Nick shifted his feet, and Gerald moved the muzzle of the .308 in his direction. That stopped the two-bit thug cold. Gerald could sense his fear, and he relished the moment. "Both of you, strip! Right now. Take it all off."

"Gerald, boy," Nick said. "Just take it easy with that rifle. You got a right to be mad, but think about this."

"Shut up your goddamn mouth!" Gerald screamed at him, spittle spraying from his lips. "And do what I tell you to do. Right now." He raised the rifle, and the man and woman began hastily removing their clothing.

In a moment, they stood naked before him. Even at fifty years of age, Victoria had a magnificent body. Gerald knew she worked hard to maintain her youthful appearance. He smiled. "You like to humiliate people, Victoria. You like to inflict pain on people. Now you're going to see how it feels."

For the first time, Gerald could see real fear on the woman's face. He laughed at her. "Get down on your hands and knees, Victoria." He looked at Nick. Despite the situation, the man was getting an erection. "Now get behind her, Nick. In position, you might say. I think you know what to do."

"No!" Victoria screamed. "He's too large. He'll hurt me."

"That's the general idea, Vicky baby," Gerald said. He lifted the rifle and took aim at Nick's privates. "Do it or lose it, Nick."

A few seconds later, Victoria started screaming. Gerald sat down to enjoy the show.

Four

Win Bryan figured it was the damnest sight and situation he'd seen and got caught up in in many a day.

He'd gone looking for Nick. When he couldn't find him, he went looking for Albert. Couldn't find him either. On a hunch, he drove out to the Staples Mansion and pulled in when he spotted Nick's pickup truck. First thing he heard when he stepped onto the porch of the mansion was someone hollerin' and squallin' loud enough to raise the dead.

Win knew that Victoria didn't have servants on the weekend, unless she was having a big party (it was on the weekends they usually made most of their snuff films), so Win figured it was Victoria entertaining that fool Judge Evans.

But no, he thought, pausing at the door, that was a woman screaming. And that was no scream of pleasure, that was someone in real pain. Someone was hurtin' real bad.

Win pulled out his pistol and stepped into the mansion. The screaming was much louder inside the big house. He followed the sound, and for a few seconds stood mesmerized by the sight before him. Gerald had backed up into a corner and was out of Win's line of sight.

There was the haughty and snooty Victoria, naked on the

floor, on her hands and knees, with Nick behind her, also naked, and he was pumping the meat to her butt. Victoria's face was a twisted mask of pain and fury. Win figured Nick was skinnin' up his dick some, too, judging by the expression on his face. Win holstered his pistol and stepped further into the room.

"Look out, Win!" Nick hollered, the instant he spotted the chief deputy.

"Kill the son of a bitch!" Victoria screamed at Win.

"Kill Nick?" Win asked.

"No, you stupid bastard!" Victoria hollered. "Gerald!"

Win looked around, spotted Gerald just as the man was raising his rifle, and said, "Oh, shit!" The chief deputy was on the way to the floor just a split second before Gerald's rifle boomed. The slug passed so close to him, he could feel the heat from the round as it passed about two inches from his head. The lead slammed into the wall.

"Get off me!" Victoria squalled at Nick.

Gerald pumped in another round and pulled the trigger just as Nick rolled off of Victoria and hit the floor, both of them yelling, for different reasons.

Gerald jerked out his .45 and emptied a clip into the room, insuring that everybody kept their heads down while he exited the house.

Win jumped up and ran after Gerald, but at the back door, a .308 round near his head, which sent wood splinters into his face, convinced him to give up the chase.

A highway patrolman, driving out to pick up a license plate from a fellow who lived several miles up the road, heard the shooting from the road and whipped into the drive. He jumped out and ran into the mansion, through the open front door. He could smell the gunsmoke from the front porch.

The highway patrolman pulled up short at the sight before him. "Good god!" he said, looking at the naked Victoria and Nick, and at Win, who was bleeding from the face where the wood splinters had buried deep into his skin.

"I'm hurtin' real bad," Nick said, holding his erection with one hand.

"Are you shot?" the highway cop asked.

"No. I got to cum."

"What?" the cop asked.

"I got the stone aches, man."

The Arkansas highway cop had visions of his captain reading this report and then thumbtacking it up on the bulletin board so everybody at the Troop could read it and have a good laugh—at his expense. He looked at Win. "You want to tell me what's going on?"

"It's a long story."

"Beats pullin' license plates, I suppose."

"Call me an ambulance!" Victoria shrieked from the floor.

"Where are you hurt?" the patrolman asked.

"My asshole, you asshole!" Victoria screamed at him.

The highway cop took off his sunglasses and rubbed his eyes. "Why me?" he said, looking heavenward.

Sheriff Pickens answered the one phone left in the house that still worked after the attack. He listened for a moment and then asked, "You had to put stitches in her *what?*" A few seconds later, after the doctor switched from medical jargon to plain English, Al said, "Good god!"

He picked up the suitcase he'd just packed and headed for the door, having hired a crew to come in and clean up the mess. He went first to the motel, where he checked in, then drove over to the hospital.

Al rounded up a doctor. "She's resting now. She's still groggy from the surgery. That is an extremely profane woman, Sheriff. I don't like her very much. Excuse me, I have patients to see."

The highway cop strolled up. "You want to tell me what in the hell is going on in your county, Sheriff?" the patrolman asked.

"It's a long story."

"That's the second time today a cop has told me that. I'm sorry I asked the first time."

"We're investigating a series of murders that we think were probably committed by ghosts," Al said straight-faced.

The highway cop stared at the sheriff for a moment, then closed his aluminum report case and tucked it under one arm. "I'm outta here."

He walked away without looking back, the heels of his boots clacking on the polished tile of the corridor. He was still muttering under his breath and shaking his head as he got into his unit and drove away.

"So Victoria got a taste of her own medicine," Bev said, as the group gathered for lunch in the dining room.

"She sure did," Al said, sugaring his iced tea. "But we've got a heavily armed and very dangerous nut running around the county. We've got to find Gerald. Maybe he can be brought around and be lucid enough to give evidence against the people he's trying to kill."

"I wouldn't count on that," Scott Frey said. "I think Gerald has gone completely around the bend."

Al nodded his head. "I sweated that deputy who took the call from Mrs. Wilson. He admitted that, at first, Win ordered him not to log it. I just fired Win. I figured Win would kick up a fuss about it, but he didn't say a word. The look he gave me said it all. I put Tom Starr in as chief deputy. He's in the process of cleaning house. Most of the deputies will be gone by this time tomorrow. I'll have a clean crew, but they'll be mostly young and inexperienced. However, they will be men and women I can trust." He looked at Scott. "What happened to all the Bureau people? A few hours ago, you couldn't walk down the street without running into one."

"Something came up," Scott said, and would say no more.

Cole and Gary had discussed the sudden disappearance of the agents and reached the conclusion that someone very high-placed had decided the Bureau had no business in the ghost-chasing business.

"But George and me are still assigned to this area," Scott added.

"Did your superiors believe you about seeing the roadhouse and the ghosts?" Katti asked.

"Not really," George answered that one. "But who could blame them? I still have difficulty believing it myself."

Cole looked at first Scott, then at George. "Are you guys sort of, ah, out of the loop, so to speak?"

Scott smiled. "That's one way of putting it, yes. I have this suspicion that one day soon I will be sent to some small office in, say, oh, Montana, and there I will spend the rest of my time until I get my twenty in. Which, thankfully, isn't that far off."

"And I will be sent only God knows where," George said.

Cole leaned forward, put his elbows on the table, and said in low tones, "But there just might be a way for you two to come out of this as heroes, with your pick of assignments and/or stations."

"Oh?" George immediately perked up.

"I'm listening," Scott said.

"Break this snuff and kiddie porn film racket that we know is right here in this area, and solve the many disappearances in this area. And I think we can do it, if we all work together and are open and honest with each other."

Scott looked at George, and he received a nod of approval. "You got it, Cole. I can get some things done in a heartbeat from friends within the Bureau, that might take Al weeks to get done, if at all."

"Good. Let's finish lunch and get to work."

With Capt. Curtis Wood now dead, John Costa openly admitted that he had been the one who hired him to kill Sheriff Pickens. He did not know that any FBI agents were in the area. Had he known the agents were in the house, he would not have fired upon the people. As to why he had been hired to kill the sheriff, Costa said he figured it was about a woman . . . it usually was.

Since the sheriff had been the primary target, the government quietly backed out of the picture, for the moment at least, and let the county DA handle it.

"Chicken shits," Frank Bruce said.

Scott Frey shook his head. "The government is working out a deal with John Costa's attorneys. He'll go into the witness protection program, and all charges brought by your people," he glanced at Sheriff Pickens, "will be dropped for his cooperation and testimony in other matters. You can bet your paycheck on it."

"I just might kick up a fuss about that," Al replied.

"Don't. For it won't do you a bit of good."

"How about the others with Costa?"

"They'll go with him. Just let it slide, Sheriff. You are absolutely powerless to do anything about it."

Al shook his head in disgust. "This government of ours is just too damn big and too damn powerful."

"And arrogant," Cole added.

The day after George and Scott agreed to work with the ghost-chasing group, the county DA ordered Sheriff Al Pickens to turn over the prisoners to federal marshals.

"Son of a bitch!" Al cussed.

"Told you," Scott said.

Victoria was released from the hospital and sent home. Arlene immediately rushed over to take care of her.

Albert Pickens and Nick Pullen settled down to work the farm, and stopped going to roadhouses and beer joints, or anywhere else, for that matter. It was obvious to all that Victoria had put out the word to settle down and stay down and wait it out.

"What a nice pair of boys," Sheriff Pickens remarked, the sarcasm in his voice as thick as sorghum molasses. "Next time we look up, they'll be going to church and leading the choir in song."

"Any word from your wife?" Katti asked, trying to hide her smile at the expression on Al's face.

"Oh, yeah. She and that bunch she went over with love it so much, they've decided to spend the summer touring Europe. Hopefully, we'll have this thing wrapped up long before she gets back."

A week had gone by since the federal marshals had spirited away John Costa and his cohorts.

"And no one has spotted Gerald Wilson?" George asked.

"Not that's been reported to my department." He glanced at the two FBI men. "Anything out of your office?"

Scott shook his head. "No. It's as if they're trying to forget George and me exist . . . which is probably what they'd like to do."

"And it was suggested, quite strongly," George added, "that we make no further reference about ghosts and roadhouses that appear out of the night. I told the SAC in Memphis about my tie, and he gave me thirty dollars and told me to go buy a new one and to shut up about it."

"What's a SAC?" Katti asked.

"Special Agent in Charge," Scott told her.

"That was a wonderfully colored and patterned tie," George mused. "You could wear it with almost anything."

"George——" Scott said wearily.

"I know, I know," George said. "Shut up."

"Right."

Al's new secretary buzzed him. "Line four, Sheriff."

Al picked up the phone and listened for a few moments, saying only an occasional "Yeah," or "Right." Finally he said, "Okay, Buster. We'll get on it. Yeah. I'll get back to you ASAP. See you."

Al hung up the phone and turned to the group. "That was Buster Perkins. Sheriff up in the bootheel of Missouri. He's got two missing girls. Been gone for forty-eight hours. Thirteen and fourteen years old. They were riding the bus down to Memphis to visit their aunt and do some shopping and so forth.

Bus driver remembers them. Said they got off along the way, to get a soft drink or use the john or something, and didn't get back on. He reported it to dispatch, and waited as long as he could before pulling out."

"Where'd they get off?" Scott asked.

"About ten miles north of here. Pretty girls—blonde and petite."

"I'll bet you a hundred dollars they're out at the Staples mansion," Tom Starr said.

"We'll never get a search warrant from any judge around here," Al told them.

"If they were grabbed forty-eight hours ago," Cole said flatly, "they've been used and are dead. But what the hell happened to all the bodies over the years? Very few have ever shown up."

"Thousands of acres of woods around here," Al said. "Plus dozens of old privy pits dating back a hundred and fifty years or more. They could weight them down with concrete blocks and dump them in the river. All kinds of ways to get rid of a body."

"I've had Bert McClusky under surveillance for a week," Tom said. "He hasn't been near the Staples mansion."

"Black on white rape and snuff films," Scott said. "Lots of kinkos like to watch that."

"Disgusting!" George said.

Cole cut his eyes to Scott. "Would you people have a listing of all black actors making porn films?"

Scott's smile was fast in coming and going. "Unofficially we might be able to help you."

"Your security index files?" Jim asked.

"Some people might call it that," Scott replied, his eyes studying the ceiling. "I don't recall ever hearing that particular phrase."

Cole smiled. "The file the Bureau keeps on American citizens who have broken no laws."

"Your words, not mine," Scott said.

George was very busy, completely absorbed in the close scrutiny of his fingernails.

"You mean the FBI keeps files on citizens who have broken no laws?" Katti said hotly. "Isn't that illegal?"

"I sure wish I could find another tie like the one that redneck stole," George said.

"Somebody better answer me!" Katti said.

"What was the question?" Scott asked, smiling at her.

Cole held up a hand. "Can you get the information I asked for, Scott?"

"I don't recall exactly what it was you asked for, but I just remembered I have to make a call to a friend of mine in Washington. Please excuse me for a moment."

"Isn't keeping files on Americans who have broken no laws illegal?" Katti was asking as Scott left the room, closing the door behind him.

"Ask George," Cole said.

"I have to go to the bathroom," George said, quickly standing up and heading for the door. "And I don't know anything about any files on law-abiding citizens."

"Liar, liar, pants on fire!" Katti called after him.

Five

The two young men were scared. Nothing like this was supposed to have happened. The sisters had willingly gone with them at the bus station; nobody had forced anybody to do anything. Well, at first, anyway. The girls looked like they were seventeen and eighteen years old. Then, after the girls had refused to give up some pussy, the young men had beat them up, raped them, and shortly after that, going through their purses, discovered they were both minors. Then the older one had tried to make a run for it. Jason had grabbed her and thrown her to the floor of the old hunting camp. He threw her too hard. She hit her head and died a few hours later. Then the younger one went ballistic and started fighting and biting and scratching them. That's when Dean had hit her . . . and hit her. When he stopped hitting her, she was unconscious. The next morning, she was dead.

Now the two cousins didn't know what to do with the bodies.

And to further complicate matters, the girls were all swole up and really starting to smell bad. They been driving around with them in the trunk of their car for nearly two days, and the cousins were afraid someone was going to smell them.

Jason turned down the heavy metal music that was roaring

through the speakers and vibrating even the seats in the car, and snapped his fingers. "Hey, I know! We can dump them out where we used to poach deer—remember?"

"Yeah! All right! That old bitch that lives in the mansion never goes out there, and neither does anyone else. If they're ever found, it'll be months away, and this summer heat will have turned them into mush and slop. Great idea, Jas."

The cousins headed for the Staples mansion. They felt better already. Besides, it wasn't really their fault the sisters were dead. No one forced the girls to go with them. They did that all on their own. And it wouldn't have hurt them none to give up some of that pussy. They didn't have to kick up such a fuss about it. That was real stupid on their part. I mean, the girls would still be alive right now, if they hadn't-a been so snotty about a simple little friendly fuck. You know, man? Everybody does it. What's the big deal?

Twenty minutes later, the cousins had dumped the bodies in woods about two miles from Victoria's mansion, and were on their way back to town. They'd maybe get a case of beer and celebrate tonight. Hell, they might even get lucky and score with some pussy. You just never knew.

"His name is Carlos Washington," Scott said, laying the fax on the sheriff's desk. "His screen name is Brother Long Dong. He always seems to have plenty of money, but works only occasionally. I just spoke with Bob Jordan, and he checked with the Memphis PD. They have nothing on the man."

"Did Bob say where he's been the past week?" Cole asked.

"Just said he's been chasing leads of his own that didn't pan out."

"You know Bob is from this part of the country?"

"We know everything there is to know about all of you," Scott said. "We knew before we came in here. Sheriff, let's get the group together and take a ride out into the country. I just don't trust closed rooms."

Bob checked back into his old room at the motel and met

im Deaton in the parking lot. "Sheriff wants a meeting out
n the country. Come on, you can ride with me. Where have
ou been, Bob? You missed all the shooting."

"So I heard. I wasn't far away. There used to be some
oadhouses up in the bootheel of Missouri I wanted to check
ut. I spent a night—or at least a part of the night—at several
f them. Nothing happened at any of the old sites. I got some
erie feelings, but that's probably due to an overactive imagina-
on."

The caravan of lawmen, FBI agents, ex-lawmen, private
nvestigators, and one civilian drove out past the Staples man-
ion and turned down a gravel road. They drove for a couple
f miles, and then pulled off to the left and stopped. Everybody
ot out.

"The old home place," Sheriff Pickens said. "The house
sed to stand right there." He pointed. "Everything across the
oad for as far as you can see belongs to Victoria Staples.
Victoria and I used to play together as kids. Hell, we were the
nly kids out here for miles around." The sheriff looked in the
lirection of the mansion, several miles away. He shook his
ead. "There is something in the back of my mind about that
nansion that I think might be important. But I can't bring it
o the surface. Maybe it'll come to me." He turned to Scott.
"You wanted this meeting, Scott. What's on your mind?"

"We got a break, finally," the Bureau man said. "Some
enator's grandkid got all doped up at a party, and later that
night she was used in a porn film Back East. The next day she
vent running to her granddad, and he blew his top. The girl
vas fourteen years old. So now kiddie porn and snuff films get
igh priority with us." The wind shifted directions, and Scott
vrinkled his nose at a very foul odor. The breeze died down
nd the odor was gone. "This Carlos Washington just might
e the key to opening up this nasty can of worms."

The wind again shifted, bringing the terrible odor with it.
This time, they all smelled it.

"Phew!" Bev and Katti said, waving their hands in front of
heir noses.

"That's something dead," Cole said. "I've smelled it too many times not to know that odor."

The wind abruptly died down to nothing, and the smell was gone.

"So, since the missing sisters crossed state lines, you people have been assigned to the case, right?" Al questioned the Bureau men.

"That's it. But the SAC in Memphis says he does not want to see anything more about ghosts or ghost clubs in my reports."

"Even though they might have something to do with this case?" Bob asked.

"He does *not* want to read about ghosts," Scott said firmly. "He . . ." Scott trailed that off, his eyes following Cole as he walked to the clearing and looked up into the sky.

"Vultures," Cole said, pointing. "Something is definitely down over there."

"Let's check it out," George said.

"Wait a minute," Al said, holding up a hand. "That's private property, and it's posted. Let's don't do anything that might screw up any case we might build against Victoria." He looked at his chief deputy. "Tom, you go call Kliner with Wildlife and Fisheries. Those guys can go any damn place they want to go, and they don't need a warrant."

Roy Kliner was on the scene in half an hour. "Let's go," he told the group. "You're assisting me, and no warrant is required."

"Victoria is not going to like this," Al said.

"Fuck Victoria," the Wildlife and Fisheries man said. "Excuse my language, ladies," he quickly added. "I ain't never had any use for that woman, and never will. She's cruel to animals, and I can't abide anybody who is cruel to animals."

Two of Victoria's hired hands were on the scene before the group had walked five hundred yards. "You're trespassing," one of them told Roy.

"Fuck you, Lucas," Kliner said. "Now get out of my way or go to jail. The choice is yours."

"I'm going to fetch Miss Victoria," Lucas said.

"Fine. You do that," Kliner told him. Then he grinned wickedly. "Is she able to hop around, since gettin' pronged in the ass?"

Lucas and his partner hotfooted it toward the mansion and the group walked on, the smell getting worse with every step.

"That's no animal," Cole said.

"You mighty right about that, boy," the older man said. "My eyesight might not be what it used to be, but there ain't nothin' wrong with my nose. That's rotting human flesh."

Katti stopped. "I think I'll stay right here."

"Stay with her," Jim told Gary.

The group walked on.

The sounds of grunting came to them.

"Hogs workin' at whatever it is," Kliner said. "Hog'll eat damn near anything."

George turned a little green around the mouth.

"Bes' way in the world to get rid of a body, is toss it in a hog pen," Kliner added.

"I may never eat bacon again," George muttered.

"You eat chicken, don't you?" Kliner asked, without breaking step.

"Of course, I do. It's good for you," George replied.

"Chicken'll shit, then turn around and eat it," Kliner told him. "Toss a body into a river, and the fish and turtles will gnaw on it. You eat fish and turtle soup, don't you?"

"I may never eat *anything* again," George said.

"Crabs will dine on a body," Kliner wouldn't let up. "You ever eat crabs?"

"If you don't mind!" George said.

Kliner chuckled and walked on. He paused to pick up a large stick from the ground.

"What's that for?" George asked.

"To beat off the hogs. Might have to shoot one, if he's a tusker. Hog can hurt you bad. I had a pet hog, when I was a little boy. Followed me around like a dog. Nobody would mess with me, when Norman was around."

"You had a pet hog named Norman?" George asked.

"Sure did. Big boar. I used to play hide-and-seek with him. He was smart. Lived a long time. Whoa!" the older man drew up short. "There it is, Al. Two bodies. But the hogs has been workin' at 'em. Let's shoo 'em off."

"Go get the tape, Frank," Al said. "Secure this area."

The group looked at the bodies of the two girls. Al lifted his walkie-talkie and keyed it. "Marge," he called into dispatch. "Get hold of Sheriff Buster Perkins. Tell him we probably found his missing girls. They're both 10–7."

Victoria came rolling and bounced up in a golf cart, sitting on a pillow. "What the hell are you doing on my property!" she shouted. She spotted the dead bodies and said, "Oh, shit! Who are they?"

"You don't know?" Al asked.

"How the hell would *I* know them?"

"You tell me."

"Get them off my property immediately," Victoria commanded. "They smell."

"Go on back to your house, Victoria," Al told her. "Right now. And don't open your mouth again. Just do what I tell you to do without argument."

Victoria looked at the sheriff, much like a queen would look at a peasant. "*You*, Al Pickens, do not give *me* orders on my own property."

Scott held up his ID. "This is a federal matter, Miss Staples. And I warn you, if you and your hired hands do not vacate this area within fifteen seconds, I will place all of you under arrest for obstruction of justice. Is that clear enough?"

Victoria glared hate at him. But she knew better than to push it any further. She turned her golf cart around and headed back to her mansion. She twisted around in the seat one time, to give the group the middle finger. "Fuck you!" she said, just loud enough for all to hear.

"I wouldn't fuck you with the Ayatollah's dick, Victoria," Kliner called after her.

That got the group two middle fingers from Victoria.

''Well!'' George said, and before he could stop himself, he gave her one right back.

Scott smiled at his partner; George was loosening up. His smile faded as he turned back to the bodies of the young girls. Kliner was helping string the CRIME SCENE—DO NOT CROSS tape.

''I'll bet you both a month's pay Victoria had nothing to do with this,'' Cole said to the Bureau man, speaking in low tones.

Both Scott and George nodded their heads in agreement, George saying, ''I agree. They wouldn't slip up this badly, after making as many of those disgusting movies as we think they've made.''

Scott said, ''George, call this in. We need some forensic people here ASAP.''

''Right.''

''Here's a purse, Al,'' Gary called, pointing. ''And here's another one.''

Scott acknowledged that with a nod and a wave, and said, ''We need evidence bags, too, George.''

''Right.'' George turned to go, paused to look at the bodies, and knelt down beside the dead girls. With the tip of a pen, he pointed to a stain on the back of the older girl's jeans. ''Look here. I bet you that's motor oil.'' He moved the pen over a few inches. ''And that, folks, is the very faint imprint of a tire tread.''

Katti had walked up, tired of being left out of things. She was pale at the sight of the dead and bloated girls, but held her food down. ''You think the girl was run over?''

George shook his head. ''No. The tread isn't that clearly outlined. I think they were being transported in the trunk of a car.''

When George had walked back to the cars, Cole said, ''He's a good cop, Scott.''

''Yes, he is. And I think being around you people has helped turn him into a fairly likeable person.''

''I think he's cute,'' Bev said. ''He's got a great-looking tush.''

''Oh, lord!'' Scott said, but it was softened with a grin.

* * *

By lunchtime the place was filled with FBI agents from the Memphis and Little Rock offices, and two top guns were coming in from Washington. Al was more than happy to turn the whole shebang over to the Bureau and back out of the investigation.

Jim Deaton and his people decided to nose around a bit, Katti went back to the motel to rest, Bob Jordan hung around with Scott and George, and Cole and the sheriff headed out to see Luddy and Earl, who had been released from the hospital and were once more living out in the country in their trailer.

Earl and Luddy were reading the Bible, when Al and Cole showed up at the trailer. Both of them limped badly, due to the soles of their feet having been burned raw during their experience in the old roadhouse. Cole and the sheriff could see that both men were changed for the better, and it was not a temporary conversion. That was obvious. The interior of the trailer was spotless, the men were clean-shaven with fresh haircuts, their clothing recently washed and ironed. They offered Cole and Al iced tea.

"We don't drink no more," Luddy explained. "And me and Earl signed up at the local Vo-Tech for classes this fall. We got to make something out of ourselves."

"Something good, for a change," Earl added.

Seated, with glasses of iced tea in front of them on the coffee table, Al asked, "Either of you boys remember anything else about your, ah, experience?"

The men exchanged glances. Luddy said, "Yeah, but you're gonna think we're crazy. I mean, ever'body else does. Why should you be different?"

"Try me and see."

Earl nodded his head. "First of all, I want to level with you. I told this to the preacher, and he said we have to come clean. So okay. I will, and take whatever the law hands out. It come to me a few days ago, why Neely was out here to see us. He hired us to work you people over. Not kill you, mind you. Just hammer on you some." His eyes took in Cole's solid bulk, big nuckle-scarred hands, and thick wrists. "Although now I'm eal glad we didn't try that. I think we'd-a come out on the hort end of the stick."

"Neely doesn't have that kind of money. He works for Victo-ia Staples."

"That's right. I can't prove this, but me and Luddy here both believe it was Victoria, who really put up the money for us to mbush y'all."

"Why would she do that?" Cole questioned.

Luddy shook his head. "That, we don't know. But, Sheriff, here's been strange goings-on out to the mansion for years."

"Such as?"

"Well, you 'member an ol' boy used to work around here named Floyd Mason?"

"Yeah. He's been gone for some time now." Al had punched on a small tape recorder. "Any objections?"

"No," Luddy said. "I want to clear my mind. Floyd's been gone three years now. Well, 'fore he left, he come to see me. I wore me to silence forever, 'bout what he had to say. Well, we're cousins on mama's side of the family, and blood is thicker han water. So I tole him to go ahead on with his story. He was scared, Sheriff. Real scared. He told me and Earl the damnest story you ever heard. Said Win Bryan come to see him one day, and told him that Miss Victoria wanted to see him. So Win took him out to the mansion. Miss Victoria told him to strip. I mean, right down to the buff. There was a big nigger there, too. Said his name was Carlos something or nother. Well, when Floyd was buckassed nekkid, Miss Victo-ia, she just reached out and hefted Floyd's pecker. Floyd said he jumped like he'd been hit with a cattle prod—startled him. I mean, she felt him up like she was inspectin' a side of beef. Floyd, he had him a pretty good-sized pecker, for a man who wasn't no bigger than a popcorn fart. Miss Victoria said that he would do, and would he like to make some real good money. Course, Floyd said he would. Floyd said that for a couple of years or so after that, he made movies. He said it come to a point where he just couldn't take no more of it. Now, Sheriff, you know that Floyd was a bad one. He's stole, and he's kilt more'un one man and he's tooken some pussy when the women din wanna give him none. But he tole me he couldn't hep harm no more younguns. He tole me he done some terrible things out to Miss Victoria's mansion. Awful pre-verted things. To both girls and boys. Children was all they was, he said. I asked him what he'd done that was so terrible, but he wouldn't tell me. Said I was better off not knowin'. Now you know what I know, and I feel better for it.''

"Where is Floyd now?"

Luddy shook his head. "I don't know. I ain't seen him to this day. His mama grieved some for him for a time. But I guess she finally 'cepted that he wasn't comin' back. But he showed me a wad of money, Sheriff. Fifties and hundreds in a tote bag. Stuffed full. Must have been twenty thousand dollars in there. Made my eyes bug out, it did.''

"This black fellow," Cole said. "Was his nickname Long Dong?"

"That's it! Shore enuff. That's it. Floyd said he was a bad one. And, Sheriff? Floyd said your boy Albert was all mixed up in whatever was goin' on. Albert, Nick Pullen, Bert McClusky, Doc Drake, and Win Bryan, too. And them women deputies work for you, Maggie and Cynthia? They made dirty movies, too. Floyd said they was a few big, powerful people involved also. But he wouldn't tell me no names. Well, he did tell me that he wasn't ever in no danger of doin' no more hard time, long as he worked for Miss Victoria. Said she had some judges in her pocket.''

Al tapped the tape recorder. "If I get this transcribed and typed up, will you sign it?"

"I shore will."

Cole took a drink of iced tea. "Luddy? Earl? What did you fellows see in that old roadhouse?"

"We seen the devil, Mister," Earl said. "Close up and real. And there ain't no way to describe the sight. It changes at the blink of an eye. It's . . . terrible.''

Luddy nodded his head in agreement. "Sheriff? There was

e more name that Cousin Floyd mentioned. Said he was all
ixed up in the terrible doin's at the mansion. Capt. Curtis
ood. Said Captain Wood had something on Victoria. Some-
ing about her parents. But he didn't know what.''

Al had always had a very strong suspicion about the deaths
Victoria's parents. But the sheriff before him would not
scuss it. "And you have no idea where Floyd is now?"

"No, sir. But I 'spect he changed his name and appearance
s' he could. Said he was goin' to try to forget the bad things
'd done out to the mansion. But he reckoned that was near'-
uts impossible. Said he'd just have to live with it."

Al and Cole thanked the men and stood up. Luddy's voice
rned them around in the yard. "Sheriff? Y'all watch it, if
u go out to that ol' roadhouse again. You can't beat the devil.
on't never get sucked in that front door. I don't know why
e and Earl was spared. I'm just glad we was."

On the drive back to the office to have the statement typed
, Al said, "Do you really think those men saw the devil?"

Cole nodded his head. "Yeah. I really think they did."

Al Pickens could not contain a shudder. "Gives me the
eeps."

"The experience sure changed those two back at the trailer."

"This tape we got isn't worth a shit in a court of law," Al
ruptly changed the subject.

"No. But it's another step in the right direction. What do
u say we go lean on this Neely person?"

"I'd rather go lean on Win Bryan. But he's tough as a boot.
e won't break. You're right. Let's go see Neely."

"You know him?"

Al smiled. "He's my wife's second cousin. But she doesn't
aim him."

Six

"What do you want?" Neely asked, standing in the door of his house.

"Some conversation," Al told him.

"I ain't got a damn thing to say to you!"

Al grabbed his wife's second cousin by the front of his shirt, jerked him out of the door, and threw him off the porch. Neely landed hard on his belly, knocking the wind from him.

"Sometimes you just have to get their attention," Al said, stepping off the porch.

Neely groaned and caught his breath, then grabbed Al around the leg and tried to bite him. Al stomped on the man's hand with the heel of a boot. Neely howled and turned loose.

"You're stupid, Neely. But, hell, you've always been stupid. You were a stupid kid, and now you're a stupid man. Why should anything change?"

Neely lay on the ground and cussed him.

"When you get done cussing me, cousin-in-law, we'll talk. Anytime you're ready. I got all day."

Neely stopped his cussing and lay still and quiet for a moment. "What is it you want to know?" he finally asked.

"That's better, Cousin. Who paid you to hassle those folks out in the country the other night?"

"I don't know what you're talkin' about."

Al sighed. "I guess you want to do this the hard way, Cousin. Okay. You're under arrest for murder."

"I'm *what*?"

"You have the right to remain silent . . ."

"I ain't kilt nobody, Sheriff . . ."

"If you give up that right . . ."

"Wait a damn minute here . . ."

". . . Anything you say can and will be used against you in a . . ."

"Hold on!"

". . . court of law."

"Wait a damn minute!"

"You have the right to have an attorney present . . ."

"Goddammit, Sheriff!"

". . . during questioning. If you cannot afford . . ."

"I ain't kilt nobody, goddammit!"

". . . an attorney, one will be appointed. Do you understand your rights?"

"Win Bryan!"

"Win Bryan what?"

"Win paid us to ambush them folks out to where that old roadhouse used to be."

"Now why would Win want to go and do a damn fool thing like that?"

"I don't know."

"You want to stand up so I can put these cuffs on you? Or do you want to answer my question?"

"Aw, Sheriff!"

"Get up and put your hands behind your back."

" 'Cause Miss Victoria tole him to have us ambush them folks, that's why!" Neely shouted. "I ain't kilt nobody, Sheriff."

"Why would Victoria want to harm these folks, Neely?"

"I don't know," Neely mumbled.

"You're lying, Neely."

"Sheriff, I just work for her in the fields. I done some work for Captain Wood ever' now and then, too. I don't know what goes on in that big house."

"Did Curtis Wood tell Win to hire you boys to rough up these folks?"

Neely sighed. "Yeah. Captain Wood pretty much run things on the rough side. For a long time. Ever' since I been workin' for her anyways."

"You ever go to, ah, parties in the big house, Neely?"

"Parties? Me? Hell, no! I never even been in that mansion."

"But you've heard talk about what goes on in that house." It was not posed in question form, and the sheriff's tone warned Neely he'd better tell the truth.

"Yeah," Neely said with another sigh. "I've heard all sorts of wild talk. But I swear to you, I don't know for a fact that any of it's true. I don't."

"What kind of talk, Neely?"

"Aw, shit, Sheriff! It's just talk amongst the hands."

"Get up and face me, Neely. Get up and look me in the eyes, boy. Do it! Get up, goddammit, or I'll kick you to your feet."

Neely's defiance was gone. Cole could see that in the way the man got to his booted feet. His shoulders slumped, and there was defeat in his face and in his eyes. Neely had come from the white underclass, and had never risen above it—had never made any real attempt. Cole had been dealing with the Neelys of this world for years, and while Al's method of getting information from the man might violate every big city police policy, that was the way it worked out in the country.

"Now we're going to go into your house and have us a nice long talk, aren't we, Neely?"

"If you say so, Sheriff."

"I say so. Move."

Cole got the tape recorder from the car, and the three of them went into the house. It was going to be a long and very productive afternoon.

* * *

The two FBI top guns from Washington were Harry Fremont and Charles Burton. They were waiting in Al's office, when he and Cole returned from interviewing Neely. Al called for a fresh pot of coffee, and the men all relaxed and sat down and eyeballed each other for a moment. Burton shifted his gaze to Cole.

"Cole Younger. I bet you take some kidding over that name."

"Some."

Fremont took it. "You and Ms. Baylor stirred up a hornet's nest around here, didn't you?"

"We did our best."

Fremont nodded in agreement, while Burton said, "Sheriff? You think Victoria Staples had anything to do with the killing of those two girls?"

"No. Nothing at all to do with it."

"Tell me all you can about this Gerald Wilson person," Burton said.

Fremont clicked on a small, but very expensive cassette recorder.

Al leaned forward and started from the beginning, way back when he first learned of the ghosts at the old roadhouses up and down the highway. Neither Burton nor Fremont ever changed expression during the entire relating. He told about the loosely knit club of people, of his suspicions about what was going on out at the Staples mansion, of the involvement of many prominent people, about the videotapes they had all viewed, about Gerald Wilson being basically a good person that had been, probably, pushed over the line. By whom? He could only guess. He told of his own son's involvement, of his son coming to him the night he killed Katti's brother, his own part in covering it up. He left nothing out.

When he finished, Fremont said, "Are you fully aware of just how much Victoria Staples is worth?"

"Millions."

"Something like half a *billion* dollars. Why would a woman worth that much money get involved in some crappy little two-bit porn operation?"

Al shrugged his shoulders. "You want a guess?" He tapped the side of his head with a finger. "Because she's crazy. She's evil and cruel to the bone. I've known her all my life. Played with her as a kid." He pointed to the recorder. "Turn that thing off, please."

Fremont clicked off the recorder without hesitation.

"I know where this is going," Al said. "I can see the writing on the wall. You're not going to nail Victoria for anything. Now or ever. You won't, and I won't. She's got too many people in her pocket. I know that. Judges—local, state, and federal. Senators and representatives—state and federal level. Oh, we'll get the little people sooner or later. We'll break up the snuff film business. But we won't touch Victoria Staples. Equal justice is for everybody in this country—everybody who can afford to hire an expensive lawyer, that is. All Victoria has to do is pick up a phone and Spence, Belqi, Bailey, and a dozen more top gun, million-dollar attorneys in thousand-dollar suits and hand-sewn Italian shoes would be in here on the next flight. There are no bodies, no witnesses to tie her in with any killing. Bail would have to be set. So it's set at five million. Big deal. That's pocket change to her. And even if we could produce a witness, by the time she finally came to trial, perhaps a year or so, or longer, down the line, that witness would suddenly have an acute loss of memory. Hell, boys, I've been a cop all my adult life. I know exactly how the system works. In a word, it *sucks!* I broke a man today. Cole was there. He's done the same thing in his time. Took me about five minutes to break him down to nothing. I can't tell you how proud that makes me feel. I feel like I want to go home and take a long hot soapy bath and then get drunk. The man wasn't much good, but he was a human being." Al spat into his wastebasket. "I got a real bad taste in my mouth."

"Try some Listerine," Burton suggested coldly.

Al stared at the Bureau people for a long moment. When he spoke, the heat behind his words surprised Cole. "Get the fuck out of my office!"

The group gathered in a far corner of the restaurant for supper. Burton and Fremont sat across the room, occasionally glancing over at them, but unable to hear anything that was said.

To their credit, the Bureau was working fast on the kidnapping and deaths of the sisters. They produced a couple of witnesses, who had seen the girls get into a car with two young men. The car, which witnesses described perfectly, had Arkansas plates. One of the witnesses remembered the first part of the plate. Working with Arkansas DMV, the Bureau began a search.

It appeared that Scott Frey and George Steckler had been welcomed back into the fold . . . after their brief transgression into the world of the afterlife. Which the other agents tactfully did not mention.

The girls' parents had driven down and identified the bodies. Both the mother and the father had to be briefly hospitalized after that ordeal.

After a long lull in the suppertime conversation, Katti broke the silence. "Does anyone have any ideas on how we can free my brother and let him . . . well, you know?"

"I've had a few thoughts about that ever since I saw those . . . things out in the country," Bob Jordan said. "But I don't think any of you will like it."

"Try us," Cole urged.

"Get some experts on the afterlife in on this. Let's face it: we're in over our heads on this thing."

"Who?" Katti asked. "How do we get in touch with them?"

"I can contact one," Bob said. "We've used this team before to help us locate, or try to locate missing persons, find bodies, so forth." He grimaced. "We, ah, don't generally go public with that information."

"Do they, I mean . . ." Cole asked. "Are they effective?"

"About fifty percent of the time, yes. I used to think it was
ure blind luck on their part. Now," he said with a sigh and a
ow shake of his head, "now, I just don't know. Those . . .
ings out there in the country, well, they've shaken up my
liefs on the afterlife."

"It might not be a bad idea to bring some religious person
on this," Al said.

"I've given that some thought, too," Bob admitted. "But
m not especially religious. I mean, well, hell, you know what
mean. I don't go to church. Not after the wife and I split and
e took the kids and moved away."

"I haven't been to church in years," Cole said.

Jim shrugged his shoulders. "Me neither."

"I go occasionally," Bev said. "I was raised in the Episcopal
urch."

"Are you friends with your preacher, priest, whatever they're
lled?" Jim asked her.

"Oh, yeah." She smiled. "Hank Milam is, ah, sort of a
aracter. His wife died some months back, and he stepped
own from the pulpit for a time to get his life back in order.
e's about ready to go back, but I think he'd help us. He's got
few weeks before he resumes a full-time ministry."

"Will you call him in the morning?"

"Oh, I'll call him right now. He can be here in ninety minutes,
he's interested. We can go out to the club tonight."

"You said he was a character," Katti said. "What did you
ean by that?"

Bev smiled. "Oh, you'll see." She pushed her chair back
d stood up. "I'll go call him now. If he'll come, he'll be
re before it gets dark."

Bob looked at the sheriff. "What about the body of that . . .
ell, *thing* that appeared out at the club? Paul something-or-
other."

"Hensley," Al said. "He's still in storage. Hell, I don't know
hat to do with it . . . him."

"How about these, uh, psychics you mentioned, Bob?" Jim
sked.

The Memphis cop nodded his head. "I'll go give them call right now. But they live in Nashville. Actually, just outside of the city. And they may not be home. They travel a lot."

"Assisting police around the country?" Gary asked.

"Yeah," the cop admitted reluctantly. "That's what they do." He left the table.

"Fremont and Burton are sure interested in us," Katti observed, stealing another look at the pair of FBI agents. "Why? You'd think they'd be out in the field with the others."

"Not those two," Cole told her. "I've got a strong suspicion they were sent here just to keep an eye on us."

"Why?" Katti insisted.

"I don't know. Maybe to see that we don't interfere in the Bureau's business."

"Maybe Victoria has more stroke than we give her credit for?" Al suggested.

Cole arched an eyebrow. "That's something to think about. But if she's got enough stroke to stop an FBI investigation, she is one powerful woman." He shook his head. "No. No, I don't think she has that much power." He paused for a moment. "Still no word on Gerald Wilson?"

The sheriff shook his head. "The man has simply dropped out of sight. I've had people out with dogs. I've done aerial searches. But I can't tie up my entire department looking for Gerald."

Al didn't put it into words, but those around the table got the strong impression that he wished Gerald had succeeded in killing Nick and Victoria. If that were true, his feelings matched what the others felt.

Conversation stopped, as the waitress cleared the table and then poured them coffee. Cole cut his eyes to the two Bureau men. They were also having an after-dinner cup of coffee. Waiting. And watching.

A smile suddenly creased Cole's face.

"You find something amusing about all this?" Al asked him.

"Maybe." He pushed back his chair. "Excuse me for

moment." Cole walked over to Fremont and Burton and sat down.

"Please join us," Fremont said.

"Thank you. I believe I will. Are you guys going to follow us around when we leave here?"

"Now, why in the world would we want to do that?" Burton asked.

"I don't know. But if you are, there are a few things you both need to know."

"Oh?" Fremont asked.

"We're waiting here for a fellow from Memphis to show up. When—or if—he shows, then we're going to drive out to the old roadhouse site. If you're going to tag along behind us, let me give you some advice—some friendly advice."

"About ghosts?" Burton asked, the sarcasm thick in his voice.

"Yes. About ghosts."

"This is going to be good," Fremont said.

"I can hardly wait," his partner said, struggling to hide a smile.

Cole studied them both for a moment, then shook his head. "No. No, I don't think I will. If you want to be smart-asses about it, I can play that game too."

"Mr. Younger," Fremont said. "Just calm down. We're not your enemy."

"Oh? I suppose you're here to help us?"

"In a manner of speaking, yes," Burton said.

Cole smiled. "You ever heard that old joke about the biggest lies in the world?"

Both men looked blank.

"I'm from the government and I'm here to help you, and the check's in the mail."

"Very amusing, I'm sure," Fremont said.

"I'll be sure and remember that one," Burton said, with about as much enthusiasm as a visitor to a proctologist . . . with fat fingers.

"All right. I can't let you go out there without some warning. When the club materializes, don't cross that road. I mean that. Stay out of that parking lot."

"This is getting ridiculous!" Fremont said.

"Absurd," Burton said.

"Suit yourselves," Cole told them, then pushed back his chair and returned to his table. Smiling, he sat down and let the others in on what he'd said to the men.

"Why the smile?" Al said. "You've got something up your sleeve, Cole. Give."

"I saw George and Scott return from the field, just as I was sitting down over there. I think they—especially George— would just love to see those two hotshots get some comeuppance. What do you think?"

Katti put a hand to her mouth to stifle a giggle. She didn't quite make it. Tom Starr chuckled, and so did Bob. "Cole, you're awful!" Katti said. "But those two might get hurt."

"We can prevent that," Bob said. "We'll keep an eye on them."

"Al?" Cole asked the sheriff.

"I think you have a truly dirty little devious mind." Al smiled. "But I love it. Let's go find George."

Seven

"Horseshit!" the Episcopal priest said, after listening intently to the story about the ghosts in the roadhouse that materialized along the old country road.

Cole blinked. "I beg your pardon, Hank?"

"I told you he was a character," Bev said.

"I said horseshit," Hank repeated. "I don't believe in ghosts. I came up here as a favor to Beverly. But don't insult me with wild tales of out-of-date music, spooky ghosts, and other things that go bump in the night."

"Will you at least ride out there with us?" Al asked. "I've got you a room here at the motel. Everything is paid for. Just ride out there with us, and then make up your mind."

The priest slowly nodded his head. "All right. I can do that. Sure. Why not? I need a good laugh."

"It's full dark out," Cole said. "Let's go."

"Waste of time," Hank muttered, getting to his feet.

The others smiled.

The last car to pull out of the motel parking lot was one driven by Scott; George was in the passenger seat. They were following Burton and Fremont, who were talking about this wild ghost chase, and about how silly this was, grown people actually believing in ghosts.

Burton and Fremont did not park across the road from the concrete slab. They parked in the old weed-grown parking lot.

"I'm sure that's Scott and George behind us," Burton said. "They've pulled over about a hundred yards or so back."

Cole had been right about Burton and Fremont being from another division of the Bureau. They were from Internal Affairs. And they were here to observe and work up a report on George Steckler and Scott Frey.

They both agreed it was going to be a very interesting report on the two agents who turned in field reports about seeing ghosts. A very interesting report.

Damn sure was.

Very interesting indeed.

Of the two men, Burton had a sense of humor. Fremont didn't. It was said of Fremont that he had been born with a serious expression on his face. It was also rumored around the Bureau that Fremont was an insufferable prick.

"They were warned not to park over there," Cole said to the group.

"Well, you can't hardly blame them for thinking this is some sort of joke," Bob said. "But they could have taken it just a little bit more seriously."

Al nodded his head in the darkness of the summer night. "George said Fremont is a horse's ass. He added that he ought to know, 'cause up until a few weeks ago, *he* was the world's biggest horse's ass."

"That's them parked a hundred yards or so down there," Jim said, pointing. "They're in a turn row."

"George said they both were bringing night binoculars," Cole reported with a grin. "Scott said he wouldn't miss this for a month's paid vacation."

Across the road from the group, Fremont was bitching to Burton. "This is ridiculous, Charles. They're playing games with us. That's all this is. They're sitting over there drinking beer or something, and laughing at us."

They weren't laughing yet. But they soon would be. They would laugh until the situation started turning deadly on the two IAD men. And that wouldn't take long.

"They didn't act like it was a joke, Harry. I didn't see anyone laughing."

"Don't tell me you're starting to believe their cock-and-bull tales?"

"I didn't say that. But I don't think they would go to all the trouble to bring an Episcopal priest in from Memphis, just to play a joke on us."

They had run Hank's license plate as soon as he made contact with the group.

"If the club is going to appear," Sheriff Pickens said, "it'll be any moment now."

"Turn off the radio, Charles," Harry said.

Burton looked at him. "The radio isn't on, Harry."

Fremont looked at the dash. The radio dial was dark except for the numbers denoting the time—9:30.

Then Charles heard the music, very faint. "Singing The Blues." "What the hell . . .?"

Fremont sat and stared as old model cars and trucks began materializing all around them. The music grew louder. The roadhouse began to take shape. The neon sign over the door began flashing.

"This is a trick of some sort," Fremont said.

"I don't think so," Burton replied.

"Just one great big elaborate hoax," Fremont insisted.

"I wish I had gone to the bathroom before we came out here," Burton said.

A male singer, backed by a country band, began singing "Tom Dooley."

Laughter sprang from out of the club.

Both men nearly jumped out of their shoes when someone tapped on the glass, Fremont's side. They looked. A man stood there, smiling at them. Both men wrinkled their noses at the musty smell that surrounded the man. The man lifted a hand, made a fist, then extended his middle finger. "Fuck you," he said.

Then he vanished.

Disappeared before their eyes.

Only the musty odor remained.

In the dark and close confines of the car, Harry Fremont and Charles Burton looked at one another, both of them too shocked to speak for several heartbeats.

"Now, by God, I won't put up with that," Fremont said. He started to open his door.

"Don't do it!" Burton said sharply. "Stay in the car, Harry. Stay in the damn car!"

Fremont pulled his hand away from the door. He stared at his partner.

"I don't believe any of this," Hank Milan muttered, staring at the old club from across the blacktop. "This is impossible."

The front door to the club opened, and a woman dressed in a tight-fitting, red dress stood there. She hunched her hips suggestively at the two IAD men and smiled at them.

The sounds of the Chuck Berry hit, "Maybellene," rammed through the night. The building was vibrating from the impact of many shoes and boots on the dance floor.

A pickup truck suddenly materialized behind the car where Burton and Fremont were sitting, blocking them in . . . or so the agents thought.

"I am beginning not to like this," Fremont said.

"Ghosts can't hurt you," Burton said.

"There is no such thing as a ghost, damn it!"

"Then where the hell did all this come from?"

"I don't know. It's . . . some sort of trick."

"No. They're ghosts, Harry."

"There is no such thing as a ghost!"

Another tap came on the glass, Fremont's side of the car. A man dressed in cowboy clothes stood there. The same musty odor clung to him. Fremont stared at the man.

"Hey, asshole!" the cowboy said. "Yeah, you. The snooty-

ookin' one. Why don't you carry your asses on away from
ere, 'fore I take a notion to jerk you outta that car and kick
our fancy butt all over this parkin' lot?"

FBI agents are not accustomed to being spoken to in such
manner.

His temper flared and Harry opened the door; the interior
ight flashed on.

"No!" Cole yelled from across the road. "Don't do it. Stay
n the car."

Harry stepped out and faced the western-dressed man.

The smell was much worse.

"That's Dick Chambers," Al said. "He's been dead for thirty
years. I was in high school, when a state trooper shot him."

Hank Milan stared at the sheriff for a moment. He shook
his head in disbelief.

"You want to mix it up, hotshot?" the cowboy challenged
Harry, then shoved him back against the car.

"You are not real!" Harry shouted.

"Oh, yeah?" the cowboy said, then knocked the crap out of
Harry, a big cold fist slamming into the agent's jaw.

Harry was knocked to one side, off balance. He felt an ooze
of blood from a cut lip. Burton was out of the car in an instant,
pistol in hand.

"Freeze, you asshole!" Burton shouted, leveling the autoloader at the cowboy.

The cowboy laughed at him. "Screw you, fancy pants. You
can't hurt me. Hell, I been dead thirty years." He jerked a
longbladed knife from a belt sheathe.

Burton shot him.

The slugs passed right through the cowboy, silently passing
through several cars and trucks, and slamming into the right
headlight and radiator of the car in which George and Scott
were sitting a hundred or so yards down the way.

"Goddamn!" Scott yelled, as he and George bailed out into
the soybean field.

The cowboy laughed, a foul odor springing from his open
mouth.

"Stun guns!" Cole yelled. "Use a stun gun on the thing."

Burton was momentarily frozen, standing staring stupidly at his pistol.

Fremont took a wild swing at the cowboy and fell right through the man, landing on his stomach in the gravel of the parking lot.

"Shit!" he hollered, crawling to his hands and knees.

"Stun guns!" Cole shouted. "It's the only thing that will work!"

The cowboy turned to face Fremont, the knife flashing wickedly in his hand.

Fremont jerked out his pistol and blasted away. The slugs passed through the cowboy and perforated the car they'd been sitting in.

Burton hit the gravel of the parking lot and bellied down as the slugs whined and howled above him. "Jesus Christ, Harry!"

Cole ran across the road and onto the parking lot. The band was playing, and the singer singing the old Buddy Knox hit, "Party Doll."

"Shit!" Fremont yelled again, jamming the pistol back into leather as he began scrambling away from the cowboy, tearing his trousers and skinning his knees and hands on the gravel.

What had once been Dick Chambers whirled around as Cole neared. Cole sidestepped and hit the creature under the chin with the souped-up stun gun.

The head exploded in a blinding shower of sparkling dots.

Burton and Fremont stared in shocked disbelief at the scene before them.

Minus a head, the cowboy began running wildly. And as had happened before, what was once unreal became real. The cowboy ran right over Fremont, who was just getting to his feet. Fremont was returned rather rudely to the gravel.

Burton, remembering the line about discretion and valor, crawled under the car and stayed there.

That which was once Dick Chambers ran all around the parking lot. He ran through some of the ghost cars and trucks and into others.

Cole chased after it, finally catching up. He jammed the stun gun against the man's back. The headless being exploded into thousands of sparkling dots that slowly fell to the ground, reassembling into a stiff corpse, dressed in rotting and ragged clothes.

Fremont managed to get to his feet and was leaning against the interagency car, under which Burton had crawled. "Charles? Charlie? Where are you?"

"Under here," Burton called, his voice muffled.

"Under where?"

"Under the damn car!"

"What are you doing under there? Never mind. I know. If I'd had any sense, I'd have been under there with you."

"Hang on, I'm coming out."

"I wouldn't," Fremont muttered.

Burton brushed himself off and looked around. The red neon sign over the door of the club was still flashing. But the music had stopped. The old cars and trucks were still in the parking lot. Burton touched one. It was real to the touch.

"Incredible," he said.

Fremont walked over. He was holding a handkerchief to his mouth. "I can tell you firsthand that ghosts can knock the shit out of you."

Scott and George walked up. "You two catch any of my bullets?" Burton asked.

"One headlight did, and the radiator."

"Wonderful," the IAD man said.

The entire group had walked across the road and were now gathered in the parking lot. Cole strolled over. Burton looked at the stun gun in his hand.

"I never would have believed that thing could do what it did."

"It displaces the electricity that makes up one's soul," Cole said.

"Really?" the Episcopal priest said drily. "We'll have to discuss that . . . theory some day. At length."

Cole grinned at him. "Can you come up with a better explanation right off the top of your head?"

Hank cleared his throat, opened his mouth, and started to speak. He abruptly closed it and said nothing.

The windows in the front of the roadhouse suddenly slammed open. The front door banged open. The walls of the old road-house seemed to swell for a few seconds. The interior of the club glowed a deep red. A large burp sprang from the nightclub.

"Was that what I thought it was?" Al asked.

"I think so," George said.

Something flew out of a window and landed at the feet of Katti.

"Oh, gross!" she said, looking down.

It was a human arm, rotting and putrid. The smell nearly made them all sick.

The old nightclub belched again, a long drawn-out, deep, ugly sound in the summer night. Another burp, and the building began disgorging human body parts, arms and legs and hands and feet and rotting chunks of human flesh, flying out from the open windows and front door.

The pieces of long-dead body parts began peppering the group standing in the parking lot, landing on them with sickening wet, slopping, smushing sounds.

The smell was terrible.

The rotting body parts forced the group further back, until they reached the blacktop and were out of range of the belching expulsions.

Laughter suddenly ripped the night, and the clear sounds of a coin being dropped into a container of some sorts reached the group.

A needle touched a record.

The night was shattered by the sounds of "Purple People Eater."

"I never knew the devil had a sense of humor," the priest said.

The body of Dick Chambers rose stiffly to its feet and slowly turned, facing the group.

"Oh, shit!" Al said.

The rotting corpse began lurching toward them.

"What do you have to say about the situation now, Hank?" Cole asked the priest.

"I say, fuck this!" the priest replied, and got ready to make a run for it.

The corpse came closer.

"Shotguns," Al said. "Get the shotguns and blow it to pieces."

The building ceased its disgorging of rotting body parts.

Dick Chambers stopped his lurching advance.

The music faded away.

The night was silent.

"What the hell is that moving over there?" Jim asked. "By the right side of the building."

"It's a man, I think," Al said.

Gerald Wilson stepped into the red glow of the flashing neon sign. His clothing was ripped and dirty, his face and hands grimy, his hair matted and tangled. Even from this distance, those who knew the man could tell his madness had pushed him past all point of reasoning.

He grunted incomprehensible words as he advanced toward Dick Chambers. Chambers had turned to face Gerald.

"Who is *that?*" Hank asked.

"It's a long story," Al said.

Before anyone could say more, Gerald lifted his rifle and shot the ragged rotting corpse in the chest. The round staggered Dick, but did not knock him down. That which was once human grinned in the neon glow.

"I wonder what he's smiling about?" Burton asked.

"If that's a grin, I'd hate to see a frown," Fremont replied.

Chambers began advancing toward Gerald.

Gerald emptied his rifle at the walking corpse, each impacting bullet blowing dust out where it exited the back. Chambers kept walking toward Gerald.

Gerald dropped his rifle and jerked out his pistol, putting a full clip into the lurching form. The bullets staggered the walking dead, but did not stop it.

"Gerald!" Al yelled. "Get over here with us, man. Come on, Gerald. Get over here."

If Gerald heard the words, he did not acknowledge them.

Dick Chambers reached the insanity that once was Gerald, and wrapped its stinking arms around the man.

Gerald struggled, but could not break free.

"Come on!" Cole said, and started running toward the struggling shapes under the red neon. Several of the group followed.

A sudden and very powerful blast of hot stinking wind knocked them off their feet and to the gravel parking lot. The men struggled to get up, but could not.

The wind became stronger and hotter, bringing with it the smell of burning sulphur.

Hank Milan walked to the edge of the parking lot and began praying.

From inside the club, there came a terrible, almost deafening roar of anger and rage, and the wind reached tremendous speeds and flattened the Episcopal priest, slamming him to the ground and knocking the wind from him.

"Hank!" Bev screamed the word, and ran to his side. The wind lifted her off her feet and tossed her aside like a rag doll. Bev landed heavily on her side and cried out in pain.

The corpse had lifted Gerald off his feet and was carrying him up the steps to the yawning door of the roadhouse. Horrible grunting noises were coming from Gerald's mouth.

Screaming and howling and shrieking ripped the night, the devilish sounds coming from inside the building. The neon sign over the door began blinking on and off. But the message had changed.

HELLHELLHELLHELL

The blood red words were flashing so fast they became an unreadable blur.

Wild wicked laughter cut the night.

Dick and Gerald disappeared into the roadhouse.

The windows banged shut. The front door slammed closed.

The howling and shrieking faded into nothing.

The wind died away.

The smell of sulphur dissipated.

The neon sign went dark.

Gerald began screaming. A wail of agony. A lone voice of anguish in the night. A voice filled with unspeakable terror and horror and unbearable pain. A red glow appeared in all the windows. Flames seemed to dance inside the club. Gerald's howling grew in intensity. None of those outside had ever heard anything like it.

Hank had caught his breath, crawled to his knees, and was once more praying.

The hideous screaming stopped with a low blubbering moan of pain.

Silence.

The old cars and trucks in the parking lot began fading into nothing.

The roadhouse became a mist in the night.

The parking lot became weed-grown.

Then, nothing but silence.

Fremont broke the silence. He looked at Scott and George and said, "You two have my apologies. I mean that. And I'll back your reports about these sightings all the way to the top."

"Did any of this really happen?" Burton blurted the words. "I mean . . . Oh, hell, I don't know what I mean!"

"Here is Gerald's rifle and shotgun," Cole called, the beam of light from his small flashlight pocking the night with a shot of illumination.

Hank Milan helped Bev to her feet. Her left arm was going to be badly bruised from landing on it.

"What did we just see, Hank?" she asked the priest.

He looked at her and his eyes were haunted. "Hell on earth," he replied.

Eight

arry Fremont's heated words over his car phone reached them
l. The discussion had been going on for several minutes.
remont concluded the conversation with, "With all due
spect, I don't particularly give a big rat's ass *what* you believe!
know what I saw, felt, experienced, and smelled. And further-
ore, you can go teach your grandmother to suck eggs!" He
unched the END button and stared at the cellular phone for
moment. "Asshole!" he summed it all up.

"Calm down, Harry," Burton told him. "Unless you want
retire immediately upon your return to Washington." .

"Calm down my ass! That incompetent fool hasn't got sense
ough to pour piss out of his shoes before he puts them on.
hat's the AG's pet. He's an idiot. Son of a bitch came from
cotton patch in Alabama, and he ought to go back there!"

Harry got out of the car and walked around and around it
r a few moments, mumbling to himself. When he once more
d control of his temper, he called his partner off to one side.

"We're going to write this up exactly as it happened, Charles.
ll right?"

"Suits me. Hell, I've always wanted to end my career in
argo."

Harry smiled. "I don't think it will come to that. But it i going to be interesting."

"After tonight, Harry, *anything* we encounter will be tame.

Everybody in the parking lot paused at what they were doing as the very faint sounds of guitar music sprang out of the nigh Someone was doing a very respectable job of picking: "Detou There's A Muddy Road Ahead."

The music drifted around them for a moment, and then fade away.

"Someone is trying to tell us something," Al was the firs to speak.

"I wish those people you spoke of could have made it, Bob, Cole said.

The Memphis cop shrugged his shoulders. "Like I saic they're up in Canada working with the RCMP."

All eyes swung to Hank Milam. The priest gave them a very jaundiced looks. "Look, people, I'm a preacher. Don expect any miracles from me."

"Can't you, ah, exorcise this place?" Charles asked.

Harry gave his partner a very strange look.

"Are you kidding?" Hank said. "Even if I believed i that—which I don't—you exorcise the demon out of th living, not the dead. How the hell would you exorcise ghost?" He paused for a second. Shook his head. "I don know what to tell you about this . . . situation. It's the damnes thing I've ever seen."

Chuckling flowed out of the darkness, deep and evil.

The priest pointed a finger at the night. "That, folks, is goin to piss me off very quickly." He stepped away from the grou extended his right hand, and gave the chuckling the middl finger. "Up yours!" Hank shouted to the night.

The chuckling stopped.

"Are you sure he's really an Episcopal priest?" Harry aske anybody who would answer his question.

"Oh, yes," Bev said. "Very well liked, too. But as I tol the others, Hank is something of a character."

Charles looked at the stocky priest. Hank was now giving the night two rigid digits. "I will certainly agree with that."

"What about Gerald?" Cole asked.

The sheriff shrugged. Sighed. "How 'bout if we say he's still missing? I mean, technically, he is."

"That's fine with us," Harry said. "I can assure you, the Bureau is certainly not going to make my report public." He smiled. "Although I would like to see the Alabama dickhead's face when he reads it." He quickly added, "Excuse my language, ladies."

"You're a dickhead!" the voice jumped out of the darkness.

Harry turned around slowly, doing a full three hundred and sixty.

"Yeah, you," the voice said. "Here's a present for you and the rest of the group. I hope you enjoy it . . . once you find it. Enjoy the search."

A long ugly belch erupted from the night. A very foul odor assailed their nostrils, then was gone.

"Something tells me Gerald is no longer missing," Cole said, shining the beam from his flashlight all around the weed-grown parking lot. The others clicked on their flashlights. Charles turned on the headlights of the car. There was nothing in the parking lot.

Hank Milam was only halfheartedly searching. The priest was deep in thought. "Voices from the other side," he muttered. "But from the other side of *what?* Why didn't they die? Did they make a pact with Satan while still on this earth? And why here? Why here right on this particular parcel of land?"

Cole broke into his thoughts. "None of us are that interested in *how* they got here, Hank. Just in how to get rid of them."

"We might not be able to solve the latter, until we figure out the former," the priest replied. "But that's just a theory. I'm shooting in the dark on this one."

"We, Hank?" Bev asked.

"Yeah, kid," Hank said. "We. I'm in."

"There is something to be said about strength in numbers," Harry spoke the words softly.

A loud and long and very wet fart cut the night.

A terrible odor caused them all to wrinkle their noses and fan the air in front of them.

"You are one thoroughly disgusting son of a bitch!" Hank called out.

"Sticks and stones may break my bones, but words will never hurt me!" the voice taunted.

"Ormeormeormeormeormeorme!" a dozen voices chanted in unison, male and female.

"I feel sort of sorry for you," Katti spoke softly. "All of you."

Everyone in the group looked at her.

"What'd you say, *bitch?*" the heavy voice asked.

"I said, I feel sort of sorry for you," Katti repeated.

"Fuck you!"

"You wish," Katti taunted the unseen. A heartbeat later she was knocked flat on her back, and cold hands were tearing at her clothing.

Cole stepped up and jammed his stun gun around until he hit a solid but invisible object. He hit the juice. The night exploded in a shower of sparkling dots and a wild scream of agony. A dozen small sparkling shapes bounced around on the parking lot, seemingly seeking each other out. They came together, and a rotting corpse began to materialize on the ground.

"The director of the funeral home is not going to be happy with me when I bring in another one of these," Al said.

Bev and Gary were helping Katti to her feet. Her blouse was hanging in tatters, and she worked frantically to hold her torn jeans together and on. They led her off to the Bronco, parked across the blacktop.

"And stay with her," Jim told his operatives.

Burton and Fremont opened the trunk of their car and got their shotguns, just in case this corpse decided to get up and take a stroll around the area.

"You know this one?" Cole asked.

Al shook his head. "I don't think so. But look at that suit. Or what's left of it. That's 1940's style. Look at those shoes."

"There's a car coming up the road," Bob said.

"I have an idea," Cole said. "When the car gets close, we'll all turn on our flashlights and wave our arms and shout at it. I want to see what happens."

Nothing happened. The car drove right on past them, the driver not even turning his head.

"You're becoming a real pain in the ass," the voice popped out of the darkness. "And dangerous with that damned contraption you carry around. But don't get too smart for your own good."

Cole held out the stun gun. "You don't know what this is called?"

The voice did not respond.

"Interesting," Cole whispered. "The bartender in that club I stopped at had never heard of Bud Lite. So they're locked into the era in which they died."

"How does that help us?" Fremont asked.

Everybody picked up on the "us." Harry and Charles were with them.

"I don't know. It's just another piece to the puzzle."

"Hey, Al," Gary called from across the road. "Your radio is squawking."

"Answer it," Al yelled.

A few second later, "There is some sort of emergency out at the Staples mansion. Victoria specifically wanted you to come out."

"Tell dispatch we're on the way."

"What about this corpse?" Charles asked.

"Oh, hell, stick it in the trunk of my car," Jim said. "We'll drop it off at the funeral home on the way back."

"We'll have to ride with you guys," Scott said to Fremont. "Our car's 10–7."

"You want us all to go out to the mansion?" George asked the sheriff.

"Why not? It might spook Victoria into doing something stupid, if she sees all of us in force. But I wouldn't count on it. That is one cold bitch."

"Get that disgusting lump of whatever it is out of my bed, goddammit!" Victoria shrieked at Al before he could even open his mouth to ask what was wrong.

"What lump?" Al asked.

"I think I know," Cole muttered.

Katti had been dropped off at the motel, Bev staying with her.

"I was in bed reading, when all of a sudden this . . . *thing* appeared! It's horrible. Disgusting. It stinks so bad, I vomited. Get it out of my bedroom!" she roared. She looked at Fremont and Burton. "Who the hell are you?"

"FBI," Fremont said, as they produced their credentials.

"Federal Bureau of Incompetence," Victoria sneered.

"Where is your bedroom?" Al asked.

Victoria pointed. "Down that hall and to your right. I'm not going back in there."

It was Gerald Wilson. Or what was left of him. The stiffening lump was burned so badly, it was difficult to tell exactly what it was. But they all knew it was Gerald.

"You!" Victoria commanded, standing in the hall and pointing a finger at Fremont. "Go outside and see if there is a hole in my roof, where that asteroid came crashing through."

"It isn't from space, Victoria," Al called. "It's Gerald Wilson."

Victoria turned deathly pale, clamped a hand to her mouth, and went whooping and barfing and hollering up the hall, moving very well, considering the stitches up her butt.

Al used the phone on the nightstand to call it in. "Get the coroner out here," he said, then hung up. He turned to the FBI. "Maybe we can't charge Victoria or her friends with anything—yet—but it's going to be real interesting listening o her try to explain how Gerald ended up in her bed, burned almost beyond recognition.''

"Have you taken into consideration how *we* are going to explain it?" George asked.

Al smiled. "That's the beauty of if. *We* don't have to."

The story spread all over the county early the next morning, and by noon, newspaper and TV reporters and their camera crews from Memphis, Little Rock, St Louis, Nashville, and a dozen other smaller towns and cities were in the area. Then the story about the ghostly appearance of the old roadhouse, the rockabilly music of the fifties and early sixties playing in the night, and all the strange disappearances over the years, was told to the press.

By dark, all the motels in town were filled to capacity, and the late arrivals were spread out in nearby towns.

Victoria had ordered the gates to her estate closed, and had hired guards from a security agency in Memphis to protect her privacy.

But that wasn't shielding her from investigation. The FBI was working quietly and skillfully (which they can do extremely well, if they so desire) on the suspected, or alleged, snuff and kiddie porn aspect of her life. Victoria was about to have her life investigated all the way back to the moment of conception.

But when it came to Victoria's friends, the Bureau was having to walk very light looking into the personal lives of US senators and representatives and federal judges who—on the surface at least—had done nothing wrong.

A few other noteworthy events had taken place: Carlos "Brother Long Dong" Washington had dropped out of sight. Rumor had it he was somewhere in Los Angeles. A nationwide search was on for Luddy's cousin (on his mama's side), Floyd Mason. But nobody held out any real hope there. Floyd had been very careful not to leave any paper trail. No money had been paid under his social security number for several years, and it was assumed Floyd had taken another SS number . . . which is very easy to do. Albert Pickens and Nick Pullen were model citizens, rarely leaving their homes to do anything other than go to work. Arlene Simmons suddenly became a doting wife, which surprised the hell out of her long-suffering husband. Ex-chief deputy Win Bryan went to work for Victoria, oversee- ing some of her many farming operations. Like the others, he, too, became a model citizen.

All in all, it was just downright boring in northeast Arkansas and southeast Missouri . . .

Until a group of reporters, print and broadcast, decided to have a beer bust out at the old roadhouse site . . .

Everybody concerned thought that would be a really neat thing to do . . .

Party while waiting for the ghosts to make an appearance . . .

And they wouldn't need any recorded music, since the ghosts would provide that . . .

Chuckle, chuckle, chuckle . . .

Anything to break the monotony of this hick town . . .

Yeah. Right.

"They're going to do *what?*" Sheriff Pickens asked.

"Have a barbecue and beer bust out where that old club used to stand," Deputy Frank Bruce repeated. "They're going to have it at night."

"You have got to be kidding!"

"No, sir. They're planning it for tomorrow night. That's a Saturday. And, ah, you, ah, know that's when most of the past sightings have occurred."

A redneck, good ol' boy, Bubba and Mary Lou party night. Yee-haw!

The sheriff called his legal counsel.

"Can't stop them," the lawyer said. "I checked it out as soon as I heard about it. They got permission from the guy who owns that land. Guy Lansing."

"Shit!" Al said.

"That's right. One and the same. The man who ran against ~~y~~u three times and lost big-time each time. Guy doesn't like ~~y~~u very much, Al. Anything he can do to make you look ~~ba~~d, he will." The lawyer paused. "About all these so-called ~~si~~ghtings." He cleared his throat. "Ah, Al, you, ah, don't really ~~be~~lieve in ghosts, do you?"

Al didn't hesitate in replying. He was, after all, a politician. ~~"O~~f course not, David. Don't be ridiculous." The sheriff strug~~gl~~ed to contain a very deep sigh.

"That's good, Al. Something like that could really hurt your ~~re~~election bid."

Al didn't tell his friend, but after this term was over, he was ~~th~~rough with it. Pulling the pin. Hanging up his badge. He'd ~~ha~~d it.

"Yeah, David. Right. Talk to you later."

Al leaned back in his chair and stared at the ceiling. "There's ~~go~~nna be hell to pay tomorrow night," he muttered. "And there ~~is~~n't a damn thing I can do to stop it. Not one damn thing."

Nine

"It doesn't surprise me a bit," Cole said, when Al broke the news of the beer bust and barbecue to him.

Al smiled. "I take it you are not a big fan of many members of the press?"

"Oh, a lot of them, probably most of them, are all right. For a pack of liberals, that is. For the most part, your locals are okay. It's the national's that give me a pain in the ass."

"Have you heard the news in the past hour or so?"

"No. Katti and I laid down for a nap and slept for over two hours. What's going on?"

"The FBI just arrested two punks. Both of them broke down and confessed to the rape and murder of the sisters. Most of the Bureau people are getting ready to pull out."

"Did they say *why* they did it?"

"Said the sisters refused to give them some pussy. So they decided to take it. Said they didn't mean to kill them. All that was an accident."

"Sure it was."

"Right."

The two career lawmen sat in silence for a moment, both of them wondering what in the hell was wrong with this nation.

Crime stats in all categories were up. The country had taken a moral nosedive. And it appeared to be getting worse, not better.

Cole broke the short silence. "What about the reporters and their beer bust?"

Al shrugged his shoulders. "There is nothing I can do. Except hope for the best."

His secretary buzzed him. "FBI to see you, Sheriff."

"Send them in."

It was Fremont and Burton. "We're out of here, Sheriff." Burton said. "Something's come up. George and Scott will be at the Memphis office for a few days, in case you need them."

The men shook hands. Fremont said, "Good luck to you all. I really want to know how this turns out." He gave Al his card. "You can reach me there."

Al nodded. "How about Victoria Staples?"

"Oh, we're still on that. Very quietly. But that investigation might take months. Don't worry. If she'd dirty—and we know she is—we'll get her. It's just going to take some time."

Neither man asked if the Bureau was leaving some people behind, undercover. They knew the agents wouldn't tell them if they did ask. It wasn't that the agents didn't trust the locals, they were just staying on the safe side.

After the Bureau men had gone, Cole said, "Have you made any statements to the press yet? About the roadhouse, I mean."

"I told them there have been reported sightings along that stretch of county road for years. Nothing confirmed. And that is going to blow up in my face, and I know it." Again, he shrugged his shoulders. "But this time around, I don't care. I'm hanging it up after this term. I'm tired of the hassle."

Al was trapped between a rock and a hard place, and Cole knew it. If he told the reporters they were in grave danger by going out to the roadhouse site, he would be publicly ridiculed, on the air, by the very people he was trying to help. And when some of them did get hurt, or killed, by events at the roadhouse—and Cole felt sure that was going to happen—Al would be blamed for not warning those involved.

All in all, Al was in a lousy situation.

The phone rang, and Al listened for a moment. He hung up and sighed, then cussed for a moment. "Somehow it leaked that we had a couple of bodies over at the funeral home," he said wearily. "The families of Hensley and Chambers went over there and demanded to see the bodies. There was a young attendant on duty. He let them in, and the families went ballistic. The press is all over the goddamn place. They'll be here in a few minutes, wanting an explanation and a statement."

"Hell, just tell them you found the bodies and were holding them, pending an ID."

"Unfortunately, the young attendant showed the families the ID tags. I'll just tell the press the family had not been notified, because the investigation was still on-going. If they don't like that, they can go to hell. The Hensleys and the Chambers are a bunch of goddamn trash anyway. They've been inbreeding for a hundred years. Half of the kids they have are idiots."

Cole chuckled at the expression on the sheriff's face. "We have an area like that, where I come from. We used to refer to it as the land that time forgot."

"That's it exactly—"

A babble of voices from the reception area cut him off. Al stood up. "Well, wish me luck."

Cole slipped out the back way and returned to the motel. Katti and Bev were out doing something. Jim and Gary had gone roaming around out in the country. Cole found the Episcopal priest in the coffee shop, sitting with Bob Jordan, and joined them, bringing the priest and the cop up to date.

"I don't blame the sheriff for wanting to keep it quiet," Hank said. "Nobody likes to be laughed at, and that is exactly what the press would do."

"Screw the press," Bob said, summing up what a lot of cops felt about the media. "Liberal bunch of sobbing sisters and hanky-stompers."

Hank chuckled. "Well, that much hasn't changed since my days behind a badge."

Both men looked at the priest. Cole said, "You were a cop?"

"For eight years. Eight long years. Dallas PD. I'd been on

the force for only a few months, when Kennedy got shot. I go
my degree by going to school at night, then left the force and
went to the seminary. I still wasn't sure I wanted to wear a
collar, so I bummed around for a year. Finding myself, you
might call it. Met a wonderful lady and she convinced me to
take the big step, marriage and the church. We had a very good
life together. I miss her terribly. Beverly has convinced me that
life goes on." He smiled. "And yes, we are seeing each other
socially. Not often, and nothing serious yet, but we see each
other."

"I think that's great," Cole said. "I never thought I'd ever
remarry, until I met Katti. Now we're talking about it. When
this . . . thing is over."

Hank toyed with his coffee cup. "Cole, does Katti realize
that her brother, what's his name? Tommy, yes. That Tommy
might never be free of his entrapment? That he might forever
be trapped between worlds, so to speak?"

"We've discussed that. But she refuses to accept it. Says
she's going to find some way to free him. Put his soul to rest."

"I'll ask for some help," the priest said. "From a higher
power."

"But no guarantees," Bob said.

"The Lord works in mysterious ways, my friends. And I am
of the firm belief that many things are the work of the Lord,
but man doesn't realize it and takes credit for it."

"I won't argue that," Cole said.

"What does Al have on the agenda?" Bob asked.

"Nothing until tomorrow night. Then he's convinced that
all hell is going to break loose."

"And it might not be confined to just the roadhouse site,"
Hank said the words very softly.

"What do you mean?" Bob asked.

Hank sighed, frowned, and shook his head. "I've done a lot
of rethinking and reshuffling of opinions and personal theories
over the past days. I think the Devil is alive—in a manner of
speaking—and doing quite well for himself. This nation of
ours, once the greatest in all the world, is literally falling apart

Spiritually, morally, socially, you name it, we're sliding right down the toilet. And I think Satan has a direct hand in it." Hank paused, his face a study.

"Say it all, Hank," Bob urged.

"I don't quite know how to say it. But whatever happens out at that old roadhouse tomorrow night—if anything—could spread. It could be, well, uncontrollable."

Bob and Cole exchanged glances, Cole saying, "I'm not sure I know what you mean, Hank."

The priest shook his head. "I'm not sure myself," he admitted. "I do know that I've got a bad feeling about what I believe *could* happen. And I stress *could* happen."

The Memphis cop studied the priest for a moment. "Do you know more than you're telling us, Hank?"

"No. Absolutely not. You recall that I scoffed at all this when I first arrived. It's just a . . . well . . . a feeling I have. What was it the voice said to you, Cole? Don't get too smart for your own good?"

"Yes. I don't think I'll ever forget it. But I don't know what he, it, meant by that."

"Oh, that was clearly a warning. After all the antics of the other night—the devil having fun, in his own evil way—I read that as the voice telling you that things could get a lot rougher, if the devil so desired." Hank waited until the waitress had refilled their coffee cups and was out of earshot. "And here's something else to think about: maybe the devil is tired of this game, in this location, and wants to exit with a big number. Leave with a bang. I think he's building up to something. Why else would he remain virtually unseen for all these years, and then expose himself to a few people bent on destroying his little playhouse? Have any of you thought about that?"

Before either man could reply, the foyer of the coffee shop filled with people and the waitress pointed them out.

"The press," Bob muttered. "I know that woman from Memphis. Susan Marcotte. She'd sell her soul for a story."

"She might get a chance to do just that," Hank said. "She's certainly come to the right area."

Cole looked the group over. "There's some top guns in that bunch. Laura Lordan, Kenny Gant, Cindy Callander. They work for the big networks."

"And here they come," Hank said.

"We really hate to interrupt you . . ." Cindy said.

"I just bet you do," Bob muttered.

Kenny Gant narrowed his eyes at that remark, but said nothing. Yet.

". . . But we've been informed that you are with a ghost-hunting group. Care to comment on that?"

"No," Cole said.

"Come on, Mr. Younger," Laura Lordan urged. "This is off the record. We're not recording or filming."

"Off the record's ass," Bob mumbled.

Susan Marcotte had walked up in time to hear Bob's remark. "I see your attitude toward the press hasn't changed any, Detective Jordan. What's a Memphis cop doing in Arkansas?"

"I'm looking for leprechauns. I'm told there is a big market for them in Ireland."

"Ha-ha," Susan said. "That's very funny. A cop with a sense of humor." She turned to Cole. "Is your name really Cole Younger? Like the famous outlaw?"

"That's right."

"Where is the woman who is looking for her missing brother?" Kenny asked.

"I don't know what you're talking about."

Anna Freeman, a TV anchor out of St. Louis, joined the growing circle around the table and stuck a microphone under Hank's nose. "What is your name, sir?"

"Hank."

Another reporter walked up. "I know you," he said to Hank. "You're a priest. My wife's parents go to your church in Memphis. What are you doing here, Father Milan? Do you think there is something to this ghost business? Is that why you're here?"

"Which one of those three questions do you want me to answer?" Hank asked.

A camera clicked on, and Cole said, "That's it. We're out of here."

The three men stood up and, without another word, pushed their way through the ever-growing knot of reporters and walked outside, the reporters right behind them, shouting questions.

Jim Deaton was just pulling into the parking lot, when he saw what was causing the crowd. "Oh, hell, Gary. Let's get gone from here."

"You going to come to our barbecue tomorrow night?" a man called to the trio's back.

"I wouldn't miss it for the world," Hank called over his shoulder, as he and Bob got into the priest's car and Cole into his Bronco.

The reporters were still shouting questions as they drove away.

Saturday's dawning was hot, and as the sun climbed toward noon, so did the temperature. The afternoon yawned on. No wind. Not even a small breeze to give some relief. Several times that afternoon, Cole drove past the old roadhouse site. Someone had rented or borrowed a big grill/smoker. Tables had been rented or borrowed, and ice chests full of beer were stacked around, cooling. Portable lights hooked up by the power company. The reporters were really going all-out for this party. Why not? Nothing else to do.

At five o'clock, one of the big network reporters spotted Cole and Katti having glasses of iced tea at a small cafe on the outskirts of town, and asked if she could sit down.

"Sure," Cole said. When she was seated and had ordered iced coffee, Cole asked, "Where is your cameraperson and tape recorder, Ms. Lordan?"

"My camera*man* is taking a nap, and my tape recorder is on the seat of my rent-a-car, Mr. Younger."

Cole smiled and studied the woman. In her early thirties, he guessed. Honey blond and very attractive. She wore blue jeans and a denim shirt, both of which she filled out rather nicely.

"Not into political correctness, Ms. Lordan?" Cole asked.

"Personally, I think it's probably one of the worst things to happen to this country. And that is damn sure off the record."

Cole and Katti both laughed, both of them taking an instant liking for this network reporter.

"You certainly can't be a liberal Democrat," Katti stated.

"As a matter of fact, I've been a very conservative Republican since I was old enough to vote. But I try to keep that from my bosses, and my reporting neutral. I like my job."

Cole said, "Go with us to that party tonight, Ms. Lordan. I—"

"It's Laura, please. Why?"

"Cole and Katti then. Why? How open-minded are you?"

"Try me."

"Laura, I'm a retired cop. Over twenty years behind a badge. I'm a realist, if you ever met one. Katti is a writer and journalist. Bob Jordan is a working cop out of the Memphis PD. Jim Deaton and his crew are P.I.'s out of Memphis. You've met Sheriff Al Pickens. Hank Milan is an Episcopal priest. Frank Bruce and Tom Starr are deputies. We're all reasonable people. None of us have any mental illnesses that I am aware of. We're not often given to soaring flights of fancy." Cole looked around. They were seated in a back booth, well away from any other customer. "I have always liked your reporting, Laura. You seem to be a fair person. So sit back, sip your iced coffee, and listen to one of the wildest tales you have ever heard."

"And every word of it is true," Katti added.

Victoria walked through the rooms, lovingly touching each article she came to. The chains, the whips, the instruments of torture. The sexual objects. She'd had countless hours of amusement in these rooms. She stopped in one of the film rooms and closed her eyes. In her mind she could hear the wild screaming and shrieking of those chained and tortured victims of her years-long perversion. Oh, my, the fun she'd had in these rooms. She especially liked to imprison big strong virile men and have her pleasure with them, reducing them to sobbing quivering masses of begging and pleading and broken useless slabs of meat.

She almost had an orgasm just thinking about it.

She walked on. My, but her climate-controlled and lusciously appointed basement rooms were filled with such delicious memories.

And she had it all on tape and film. Hundreds of thousands of feet of all those wonderful moments of pain and pleasure, blood and sweat, screaming and torture, sex and perversion, those exquisite last seconds before death took a subject, the hauntingly beautiful faces just as death touched them. Oh, my, that was wonderful.

And she also had, tucked safely away, totally unknown to the participants, thousands of feet of film of all those in her group ... in very interesting positions, and with even more interesting partners. Senators, congressmen, judges, men and women of high power and importance.

She giggled at the thought. A little ropy sliver of slobber leaked out of one corner of her mouth.

Of course, Victoria was quite mad. Dangerously so. Had been for most of her life. And the events of the past weeks had done nothing except push her further and deeper into her dark and dangerous madness.

She walked on down the long basement corridor. Pausing at first one, then another heavily locked door. This was a part of the basement that only she and a few others knew about. Whimpering moans reached her as she flipped on the lights. Cries for mercy and pity fell on deaf ears.

The long corridor had cells on each side, where Victoria kept her favorite victims, insuring each a very long and miserable life, until she decided to fatten them up and clean them up for their final film appearance.

"Darlings!" Victoria cried. "Mother's here!"

The moaning and pleading voices fell silent.

Victoria reached for a whip on the wall and took a key out of her jeans. "Now we have some fun," she said.

Ten

Cole talked for about fifteen minutes. Laura Lordan listened intently, then sat very still for a moment after Cole had finished his retelling of events, beginning with his trip up to Illinois to pick up a prisoner and bringing her up to date. After a moment, she smiled.

"You're putting me on, right?"

"We're telling you the God's truth," Katti said.

"Would you feel better about this if you heard it from an Episcopal priest?" Cole asked.

Laura thought about that for a moment, then shook her head. "I . . . guess I believe you at least *think* you saw all those things."

"We don't *think* we saw them, Laura," Cole said. "It happened just like I told you. Don't join the other reporters tonight. Tell them you don't feel well, and go with us and stay with us across the road. Maybe nothing will happen tonight. But don't count on it."

She thought about that for a moment, then slowly nodded her head. "All right. On one condition."

"Name it."

"We talk to the others and give them a chance to make up their own minds."

"No way," Cole said flatly. "Kenny Gant is a jerk and so is Paul Ackerman. I don't know about Cindy Callander."

"Cindy's all right. I've known her for years. But you're right about Kenny and Paul. I can just barely tolerate being around them. They're both liberal crybabies. I thought they both were going to have a snit when the Republicans swept the elections last year. It was really pathetic the way they acted. But I don't feel right about not letting Cindy in on this."

Katti and Cole exchanged glances. "All right," Cole relented. "Just tell her you're not going with the others; you're riding with us and we're going to give you a story. Make up something. Bring her along when you join us this evening."

Laura nodded her head in agreement. "All right. But I've got to tell you, I feel rather foolish about this."

"Would you rather feel foolish for a few hours, or get seriously dead?" Katti asked. "And would you like to go over to the funeral home and see what is left of Gerald Wilson? It isn't a very pretty sight."

Laura fiddled with her now empty glass. "No," she said softly. "I'll see you two back at the motel."

After Laura had left the fast-food place, Cole said, "You sure you want to go out to the club tonight?"

"Positive."

"Let's go find the others."

They were all at the motel dining room. The reporters had finally decided they weren't going to get anything out of the group and wandered off, most back to their rooms to get ready for tonight's party.

Cole told the group about Laura.

"I don't trust reporters," Bob said.

"Neither do I," Al said. "But it might be wise to have some of them on our side in this thing."

"My thinking exactly," Cole agreed.

"Are they taking their camera operators with them tonight?" Bob asked.

"I guess so. Laura and her crew can ride with Katti and me. Who wants to take the other one?"

"I will," Hank said. "But I've got a very bad feeling about not just tonight, but what might happen in the days and weeks to come."

"I told Katti about your theory of it spreading," Cole said.

"I told the rest of the group," Bob said.

Al looked at Hank. "God help us all, if you're right."

Hank was thoughtful for a moment. "Al, what kind of reserve force do you have?"

"Not much of one. 'Bout twenty pretty good ol' boys. It's pretty loose. I figure I could count on about half of them, if it got down to the crunch. Why?"

"Put them on standby, Al. Can you do that? Would you do that?"

The sheriff nodded his head. "Sure. I guess so. Like right now, for tonight, you mean?"

"Yes," the priest said.

"Well . . . it's pretty short notice. But, okay. Hank, you're beginnin' to spook me. What do you know that the rest of us need to know?"

"Just a very bad feeling. And I have learned to play my hunches. You're a cop. You know what I mean."

Al chewed his bottom lip for a few seconds. Sighed. "All right, Hank. I'll call them out and put them on standby at the jail."

"What are you expecting, Hank?" Bev asked, putting her hand on his.

"A breakdown of civility. A breakdown of law and order. Domestic violence. Looting. Drunkenness. Local at first, then spreading, if we don't contain it. I . . ." He hesitated. "I feel like a fool for saying these things. But I am firmly convinced that they not only could happen here, but that they will."

"I'll start setting things up," Al said. He pushed back his chair and left the table.

Cole met the priest's eyes. Deeply troubled eyes. "Someday we'll have to have a long talk, Hank. Then you can tell me how you reached this awful deduction."

"I don't know how, Cole. I guess it came to me in my sleep."

"Maybe the Lord told you," Bev suggested.

"Maybe He did," Hank whispered.

When Cole and Katti stepped out of their motel room that evening to join Laura and Cindy, who were waiting under the overhang, they both noticed a slight odor to the air.

"What is that?" Katti questioned.

"I don't know. Unless there's been a fire, I suppose. Smells like chemicals to me."

"Sulphur," Hank Milan said, stepping out of his room. "That's burning sulphur."

Cindy and Laura exchanged glances. "What would cause that?" Laura asked. "A plant close by, perhaps?"

"No," the priest said. "The devil at work would be more like it."

Cindy crossed herself and Hank smiled. "A good Catholic, hey?"

"I don't know how good," the reporter replied. She fixed her eyes on the priest. "Are you deliberately trying to frighten us?"

"I hope so, ladies. We'd all better be good and scared this night, and ready to run for it."

"Run where?" Katti asked.

Hank's smile faded. "That, my dear, is a damn good question."

The two reporters gave Hank a very strange look, but said nothing.

"Where are your camera people?" Cole asked.

"They wanted to go to the party," Laura replied. "They left about an hour ago."

The others drove up, and everybody was introduced all around. Cole glanced up at the sky. It was still light, but the sky held a peculiar flatness to it. Dull. And something else, too. Ominous, the thought came to him. Somehow, the sky looked . . . evil.

Cole cut his eyes to Hank. The priest was looking at him as

if reading his thoughts. He turned to look at Katti. She had a very worried expression on her face.

"Where are Tom and Frank?" Cole asked the sheriff.

"They won't be coming along. We've had some trouble in the county, and they have to work the field."

"Trouble?" Hank asked, moving closer.

"Oh, nothing serious. Just a sudden rash of domestic violence more than anything. Those inclined to it have picked today to start beating up on each other. Probably going to be a full moon tonight. People do strange things when the moon is full."

Everybody looked up at the sound of heavy metal music hammering the late afternoon. They could clearly hear the music before the vehicle came into sight. It was a carload of teenagers, the car radio turned up as high as the speakers would permit. They began circling the motel complex, tossing empty beer cans out the lowered windows.

On their next pass, Al yelled, "Pull that car over!"

The driver gave him the middle finger, accompanied by a sneer. The others in the car laughed.

Al's mouth dropped open in shock at the brazen contempt just shown him. "That's Sidney Brown's boy," he finally found his voice.

Sidney Brown's boy put the pedal to the metal and left a smoking trail of rubber behind him, as the car fishtailed out of the parking lot and onto the highway.

"It's started," Hank said, when the loud music and squalling tires faded away.

Before anyone could reply, Al's walkie-talkie squawked. "Yeah, what?" Al keyed the mike.

"The chief of police just killed his wife, and then stuck the shotgun in his mouth and blew the back of his head out," dispatch told him. "And the second shift didn't show up for work."

Al was too stunned to reply for a few seconds. "Jesus Christ!" he blurted. "Ah, okay. That's ten-four. Who's working the murder/suicide?"

"Frank."

"Call in everybody. Put half the reserves assisting the PD, and keep the others on standby."

"Ten-four, Sheriff."

"I'll be out in the country, keeping an eye on these nutty reporters."

"Ten-four, Sheriff."

Al slipped the handy-talkie back into the padded case on his belt.

"Had the chief of police been ill?" Bob asked.

"No. Not that I was aware of." He shook his head. "Frank will be a seasoned veteran after working that murder/suicide. A shotgun is real messy."

"I'll tag along, if you want to go over to assist Frank," Cole told him.

"No. He can handle it. It seems straightforward to me. Tom will help him, if he needs it. Let's head out, folks. It'll be dark by the time we get there. Jesus! What else is going to happen tonight?"

At the mansion, Victoria took a long hot shower. As she soaped and rubbed, she made a mental note to call Nick over to do something with the body of the young woman she'd left dead in a basement cell. She stepped out and toweled off, thinking: Kids nowadays just couldn't take a good whipping like they used to. Not much fight in them either.

Win Bryan was restless, pacing the floor of his den. He needed some action. He plopped his cowboy hat on his head and went off in search of some of his buddies. See if they couldn't scare up something to do.

Albert Pickens got in his pickup truck and headed into town. He was feeling . . . well, sort of weird.

Arlene's husband was out of town on a business trip, and Arlene was bored. Really bored. What she needed was some long-dicked ol' boy to roll around with for a time. That always took the edge off. She took a quick shower and headed into town.

Federal judges Warren Hayden and Jefferson Parks were meeting with state judges Silas Parnell and Roscoe Evans,

Senator Charles Bergman, and state senator Conrad Wright and state representative Maxwell Noble. They knew they were all under some sort of investigation and had to plan some strategy. They were meeting at a plush hunting camp that belonged to a large corporation, located just a few miles from the site of the old roadhouse. They'd cook up some steaks and have some bourbon and talk this thing out. Men from a private security company out of Little Rock had been hired and were stationed all around the camp, insuring they would not be disturbed.

An electronics expert had swept the camp and found no bugs. He had then disconnected the television, since technology is now so precise that satellites can be programmed to monitor conversations through a home TV (Big Brother really is everywhere). He disconnected the phones (just because your phone doesn't ring does not mean someone is not listening). The expert set up a digital phone system (which, to date, cannot be monitored, something that Big-Brother's-watching-you-and-snooping-in-your-life federal enforcement agencies are really pissed about).

"Hell, we're secure," federal judge Warren Hayden said. "Might as well have a party, while we're here."

"I thought of that," Senator Bergman said. "Some high-class whores from Memphis will be here in about an hour. Let's get the talking out of the way, and then we can party. Nice thing is, I figured out a way to have the taxpayers foot the bill for the fucking."

"Don't the taxpayers always get fucked by us?" Maxwell asked with a laugh.

"Sure," Bergman said. "They're just too goddamn stupid to realize it."

Groups of teenagers were gathering in various locations in town. They were all feeling a little bit . . . well, weird. Restless. Dangerous. Something was happening they didn't understand. The strange feelings in them had started about noon, and had been slowly building all day.

And it wasn't just the kids who were being affected. All over the county the behavior of many of the citizens was turning decidedly bizarre. Husbands were beating the shit out of wives, wives were beating the shit out of husbands. Siblings were squaring off against each other. Every since about noon, liquor sales had been setting new records all over the county. People who had never consumed alcohol before, were swilling it down. By seven o'clock, every bar and roadhouse in the county was jam-packed with people.

Out at the old roadhouse site, the steaks were just being put on the grills.

The sun was blood red and going down.

Eleven

The group left behind them a town filled with many people who had grown sullen and dangerous. The mood had not affected those who were truly sincere in their worship of God and did their best in day-to-day living—true believers aren't perfect, just forgiven—but there aren't many of those types of people around. Lots of people profess to be good Christians, Jews, Hindus, Moslems, Buddhists, and what have you . . . few really are. And the devil loves a hypocrite. Satan knows that eventually all hypocrites will be his anyway, so why not have some fun while their hearts are beating, pumping blood, and their flesh is unrotted?

Of the cops who didn't show up for the second shift, one had decided (although the decision was not entirely his own) to play Russian roulette with his 9 mm. He lost. Another had taken his deer rifle and climbed up the back stairs to the second floor of a downtown department store. He had a knapsack filled with ammunition and a wicked glint in his eyes. He was going to have some fun. Another cop stood in the blood-splattered kitchen of his home, over the body of his wife. Or what was left of her after he'd used a meat cleaver on her until he became arm-weary.

"Bitch!" he said to the unrecognizable mess scattered all over the floor—arm here, hand there, foot over in the corner. He tossed the cleaver on the butcher's block and went to get his guns. He didn't like his next-door neighbor either, so by god, this was a good time to settle that score, too. He didn't think to change his clothing, covered with his wife's blood.

Another cop who had not reported for work sat on his front porch and rocked and hummed softly. He had a .357 mag in his lap, and was really getting tired of his wife's bitching.

"You lazy bastard!" she screamed at him. "I come home from work and rush around ironing your goddamn cop shirt so's you'll look halfway decent, and then you don't even go to work! What the hell's wrong with you, you worthless dick-head?"

The cop stopped humming.

"Are you listening to me, you asshole!"

The cop stopped rocking.

"Are you gonna be docked for this? You stupid bastard, we can't afford it, not since you went out and bought that damn bass boat without talking to me about it. And I hate bass. You hear me, I hate bass!"

The cop lifted his pistol—cocking it as he lifted—and shot his wife in the center of the forehead. She slid down the door jamb and came to rest on her butt, her mouth open and her eyes staring at nothing, a large hole in her head.

"I like bass," the cop said. "Always have. Good eatin' fish."

Just down the street, a father was tearing at the clothes of his teenage daughter. To stop her screaming, he finally slugged her, knocking her to the floor. "You give that pussy to all the boys in town, Marie. Now by god, you can give me some!"

He stripped her naked and fell on her.

His wife might have had some objections to that, but she was sitting in the den, staring at the TV. At least her head was. It was sitting on the coffee table where her husband had placed it after neatly decapitating her with a machete he'd brought back from Vietnam. He'd spent several hours that hot afternoon putting a real good edge on it.

"Come on, baby," the father urged. "Move your ass. You're just like your mother, when it comes to screwin'. Lay there like a damn log."

The daughter silently wept while her father drove in and out of her, grunting and sweating.

Downtown, a gang of young people had decided it would be fun to smash some windows. Somebody else thought it would be fun to loot some stuff after the windows were smashed. And the first place they picked was a sporting goods store.

Filled to overflowing with rifles and pistols and sharp knives and camp axes and machetes.

They were really going to have some fun tonight. Fun being relative to one's state of mind, of course.

"Hey, Laura!" one of the reporters called to her from across the road. "You and Cindy come on over and join the party."

Laura and Cindy waved at the crowd and stayed on their side of the road.

"Bring on the ghosts!" a reporter yelled, waving a can of beer.

"Let's hear the ghost music!" another reporter shouted.

Nightfall had brought no relief from the heat and humidity, and had done nothing to dispel the odor of burning sulphur that hung heavy in the air.

Jim walked up to Cole. "Radio says it's raining all around us. Temperatures have cooled off twenty or so degrees."

"But not here," Cole replied.

"No. Not here."

Laura was standing beside Katti, pointing out the reporters across the road. "That's Doris McCoy out of Nashville. Chris Arkin and Robert Fassert with her, also out of Nashville. That's Arthur Strother out of Little Rock. Anna Freeman out of St. Louis. Susan Marcotte and Don Potter out of our affiliate in Memphis. Paul Ackerman from Atlanta. Eddie Whitfield from Little Rock. Ray Blackwell and Eddie Frazier are network. And the one acting like a fool is Kenny Gant."

''Kenny is a conceited turd,'' Cindy added.

''Get out of here, Sis!'' the voice came to the group. ''You must leave.''

''What the hell is that?'' Laura questioned, looking all around her.

''My brother,'' Katti said.

Those party animals across the road apparently had not heard the warning from the other side of life.

''Tommy?'' Katti called.

''Right here, Sis,'' the voice was stronger.

Cindy began murmuring a prayer.

''Why is it people never think to talk to God except in moments of great stress?'' Hank questioned.

Laura rubbed her arms. They were covered with goose bumps even though beads of sweat were clinging to her forehead.

''It's opening tonight, Sis,'' Tommy said, his voice almost normal. ''The door. It's going to open. I might be able to get through. But you and your friends have got to leave here. It's too dangerous.''

Both Cindy and Laura had enough presence of mind to click on small but very powerful cassette recorders in their purses.

''The radio in my car just quit working,'' Gary said. ''The entire electrical system is down.''

''Then it's too late for you,'' Tommy said. ''Don't go across the road. Whatever happens over there, stay where you are. *Don't* cross that blacktop!''

''Tommy!'' Katti called.

''You remember that ID bracelet you gave me when I graduated from college, Sis?''

''Yes.'' Tears were flowing from Katti's eyes.

''Remember it. That will be the sign I've made it out.''

''How, Tommy, how?''

''Remember it. I love you, Sis. Good luck.''

Katti called and called, but Tommy spoke no more.

Al first tried his walkie-talkie, then the radio in his car. Nothing worked.

The vehicles would not start.

"Shit!" Hank said.

"Are you really a priest?" Laura asked him, her voice shaky.

"Bet your butt, I am. Why?"

"You just seem a bit . . . unusual for a priest, that's all."

"Ummm," Hank replied.

"Was that really your brother?" Cindy asked Katti, her voice as shaky as Laura's.

"Yes. Come on, Tommy," she urged. "You can do it. Come on, come on."

The sounds of a steel guitar drifted softly out of the night, the sounds coming from across the blacktop. It was the old Santo and Johnny hit, "Sleepwalk."

"Oh, my god!" Laura muttered.

The reporters across the road had stopped their laughing and joking. They stood quietly, looking all around them, trying to locate the source of the music. The beer and barbecue was forgotten.

"Look!" Cindy cried, pointing.

The old roadhouse was slowly materializing in a mist. The red neon sign above the door began blinking on and off.

"What the hell is going on?" Paul Ackerman shouted, his voice reaching those across the blacktop.

"It's a damn trick!" Ray Blackwell said.

"You wish," Cole muttered. "Get out of there!" Cole shouted. "Get out of there! Cross the road. Come on, people. You're in danger!"

The soft notes of the steel guitar faded, and a rockabilly band and singer started hammering out "The Twist."

The reporters started laughing and attempting to dance to the old tune. Most of them had been small children when Hank Ballard wrote the tune and Chubby Checker recorded the monster hit back in the early sixties.

Old cars and pickups began taking shape in the parking lot, the grass and weeds disappearing and hard-packed gravel taking their place.

Some of the dancers stopped to look at the old vehicles.

"Stay out of those vehicles!" Al shouted. "Don't get into them."

Kenny Gant opened the door to a '57 Ford Crown Vic. "How are they doing this?" he asked. "What is this, some sort of mind control? This is really weird. Fun, but weird."

"Don't get in the car!" Hank yelled. "For God's sake, man Listen to me."

The music softened and the voice of Chuck Willis filled the night: "What Am I Living For."

Al Pickens straightened up and strained his ears. He thought he had detected the sounds of gunfire. Very faint, but it was definitely gunfire.

Kenny Gant sat down in the front seat of the car.

"Get out of there, you fool!" Cole shouted.

Kenny lifted his hand and gave Cole the finger.

"Well, screw you, too," Cole said.

The door slammed shut.

The club had fully materialized.

"Hey!" Kenny shouted, hitting the door, trying to open it "Somebody get me out of here."

Other reporters gathered on each side of the car, struggling to open the doors. They would not open. Kenny was shouting and cussing. "Break the glass!" he yelled. "Somebody get a brick or something and smash the goddamn glass."

Paul Ackerman grabbed up a heavy ice chest and smashed it against the window glass. No effect. He smashed it again and again. The glass would not break.

"It's getting hot in here!" Kenny shouted. "I mean, really hot. Get me out."

The inside of the car began to glow.

Kenny started screaming. "The goddamn car's on fire. Get me out, get me out!"

Flames began licking up from the floorboards.

Kenny's shrieking was louder than the music.

Hank Milan began softly praying for Kenny's soul.

"Do something!" Susan Marcotte screamed at the group across the blacktop.

"There is nothing we can do," Cole called to her. "You were all warned."

Kenny's hair was on fire. His howling was painful to the ears.

Wild laughter sprang from inside the old roadhouse.

Kenny's face began bubbling as the flames touched his flesh and cooked it.

The walls of the roadhouse seemed to swell, and a loud belch emanated from the open windows and doors.

The fire in the car went out. The doors popped open. Kenny was ejected from the front seat, landing hard on the gravel.

Smoke drifted from his clothing, but he was unscathed, not a burn mark on him. His flesh was untouched, his hair still perfectly combed. He sat up and looked all around him. His eyes were wild. Then he started screaming and babbling, at first incoherently, then about demons and monsters and the fires of hell and seeing Satan.

"Let's party, people!" a voice ripped the night, overriding Kenny's wild and confusing babblings. The band started playing "Let The Good Times Roll."

"Boogie, boogie, boogie!" the voice yelled.

Anna Freeman's shorts were torn from her, and her blouse ripped to shreds by invisible hands. She was spun around and around in the gravel by the force. She stood still for few seconds, in bra and panties, too shocked to move.

"Would you look at the garbanzos on that bitch!" the voice shouted. "What a set of jugs!"

Red-faced, Anna began gathering up her torn clothing and covering herself. Eddie Whitfield took off his shirt and handed it to her just as the music changed.

The voice of Narvel Felts, a living legend in the rock and roll and country field and still performing, came clearly through the night. "Honey Love."

"*Now* will you get the hell out of that parking lot?" Cole shouted to the reporters. "Move, damnit, move! Leave your cars and run for it. Come over here."

A few of them did just that, making a dash for the other side of the blacktop.

Only those few made it.

A hot wind began blowing around the parking lot. It kicked up whirlwinds and dust devils that created clouds of tiny rocks and dust.

Then the rains came.

Didn't take the reporters and camera crews long to figure out it wasn't really rain that was drenching them.

It was urine. Hot, stinking piss.

Across the road, standing with the group, Susan Marcotte was shaking with fear and anger. She directed that anger toward the sheriff.

"You son of a bitch!" she shouted at him.

"I warned you," Al said. "That was all I could do. Don't put the blame on me."

Across the road, the stinking rain had stopped, and now the wind had picked up, a strong, hot wind. Each time the men and women would try to cross the road, the wind would drive them back.

The front door to the roadhouse banged open. The neon sign flashed its welcome.

One of the camera crew from a satellite truck lost it and began screaming, running toward the open door.

"No!" Cole shouted at her. "No!"

The young woman jumped for the steps, and the doorway was suddenly filled with men. They dragged her inside, and the door slammed shut.

The music stopped.

Her screaming and shrieking filled the strange night.

"She worked for ABC," Laura said. "A technician. Sally something-or-another."

"Reynolds," Cindy said.

Sally shrieked for several minutes. Her screaming was punctuated with painful protests.

Her screaming suddenly stopped.

Those in the parking lot and across the road waited.

The door opened.

An ugly belch filled the night.

Sally was hurled out onto the gravel. She was naked. She

began crawling around on her hands and knees, weeping uncontrollably. Don Potter ran to her, taking off his shirt as he ran. He covered her with it and helped her to her bare feet just as the wind began to howl.

The stinking wind knocked those in the parking lot to the gravel, and began rolling them across the road. The big smoker-cooker was picked up and hurled across the road. It landed on the hood of the sheriff's car, smashing the hood and the windshield and sending hot coals and ribs and steaks flying all around the group.

The lids to ice chests flew open and cans and bottles of beer became minibombs in the night.

"Hit the ground!" Jim yelled, just as a set of drums came flying out the open door, cymbals clashing and banging together in the hot wind. The drum set crashed on the blacktop. The cymbals rolled around for a few seconds, then toppled over.

A flying bottle of beer knocked Chris Arkin to the ground, cutting a gash in the back of his head.

A can of Bud hit Arthur Strother in the back and knocked him to the blacktop, bringing a grunt of pain.

"I hope nobody over there smokes Camels," Hank said, belly down in the turn row. "Have you ever seen a pissed-off Camel? They can spit for fifty yards."

"I cannot believe you are really a priest!" Laura said.

"Forgive me for not wearing my collar. I'll try to do better."

The minibomb beer barrage stopped. The wind died down. The music began to fade.

"What's happening?" Someone asked.

"It's settling down, I think," Cole said. He raised his head and looked across the road.

The old cars and trucks in the parking lot were beginning to fade. The roadhouse was gradually turning misty. The sign over the door was still blinking its red welcome, but it, too, was beginning to fade.

Weeds were beginning to appear in the parking lot.

"Oh, dear God!" Doris McCoy cried out, pointing. "Look at that!"

It was Tommy Baylor, running down the center of the black top, his face and shirt bloody. "Wish me luck, Sis!" he called. He smiled and waved at Katti.

"Tommy!" Katti called.

Tommy leaped high into the air.

He vanished before their astonished eyes.

Lightning lashed the sky, a furious display of power. Thunder rumbled and rolled all around them. Bolts of lightning struck so close to the men and women, their flesh tingled from the impact and their hair was filled with electricity.

The lightning strikes began coming so fast they were impossible to count. A rolling, crashing, deafening cannonade of thunder filled the air, trembling the ground beneath their feet, shaking the vehicles parked in the turnrow.

Susan Marcotte put her hands over her ears. "Stop it!" she screamed. "Stop it!"

The lightning and thunder picked up in intensity. There was no doubt in the minds of anyone in the group that Satan was deliberately mocking her words.

Hank Milan rose to his knees and began softly praying.

The Prince of Darkness showed his contempt for them all. The dirty rain began anew, drenching them all with stinking piss. Excrement began falling from the sky, the turds plopping all around them, hitting the ground with plopping sounds.

The stench was horrible.

Several of the men and women began vomiting.

Cole grabbed Katti by the shirt and dragged her under his Bronco.

The rain of filth ended as abruptly as it began. The lightning ceased its dancing across the skies. The thunder was stilled.

The men and women began standing up, looking all around them.

"Did this really happen?" Laura asked, her voice tiny in the night.

Hank kicked a turd in her direction. "Look at that and make up your own mind."

Twelve

Mysteriously, the electrical systems in all the vehicles were suddenly operational.

"What the hell?" Jim muttered, cranking his car.

Cole's radios were working and the frequencies assigned to the S.O. were jumping. "It's a war zone in town," Cole yelled to Al. "Dispatch says everybody's gone crazy."

Kenny Gant and Sally Reynolds were put in the back of a station wagon. "Follow us," Al told the driver. "We'll head straight for the hospital."

"All right, Sheriff," the man said in a very subdued voice. "Whatever you say. Sheriff? How . . . I mean . . ." He waved a hand toward the weed-grown parking lot.

"I don't know," Al told him. "I just hope to hell we can make it back to town. I'll be in that Bronco. Let's go."

When the smoker/grill had landed on Al's car, it had shorted out the electrical system, rendering the unit inoperable. Al got his guns from the wrecked car and jumped in the Bronco. Katti and Laura were in the back seat. Laura appeared to be in mild shock. Cole had been monitoring the radio.

"Every available unit from the state police is coming in," Cole told him. "Tom was unable to reach us, so he called them in. A commander of state police is in town now, and he's thinking of asking the governor to call out the national guard."

"Jesus Christ!" Al reached for the mike and got dispatch. "What's going on there?"

"Good to hear your voice, Sheriff," dispatch said. "We were really worried about you. The whole county's gone nuts. People shooting and stabbing one another, raping, looting, smashing windows. You name it, it's happening here."

Al shook his head. "Hank was right," he said to Cole. "We've got to control this situation." He keyed the mike. "That's 10–4. My ETA is fifteen minutes. Call the hospital. Tell them I'm bringing in two people, man and a woman, both in shock."

"Hospital is full, Sheriff. They're taking only emergency cases."

"Shit!" Al yelled. He punched the talk button. "Put the highway cop on."

A second later: "Al? Andy Boyce here."

"Andy, get the governor on the horn. Have him call out the national guard. I want this county sealed tight. No one in, no one out. I want roadblocks on every road, every path, every pig trail. I'll explain when I get there. Just do it, Andy. Please?"

"All right, Al. No problem. We have a unit right here in town."

"No!" Al almost shouted the word. "Not the local people. We can't use them. They might be, ah, uh, *infected.* Get someone else."

"Infected?" the highway cop said. "Ah . . . okay, Al. Will do. I'll start using my people to set up roadblocks on the main arteries right now."

The caravan was stopped by the state police just at the city limits.

"Oh, hi, Sheriff," the young highway patrolman said, relaxing when he saw who it was. "We got a real mess in town. And getting worse. All these people with you?"

"Yes. And once we cross your roadblock, no one leaves. Okay?"

"Right, Sheriff. Captain Boyce told us. Uh, Sheriff. Do you now what's going on?"

"Son," Al replied. "You wouldn't believe me, if I told you." Ie waved Cole on, and the highway cop stepped back and let 1em through.

Cole let the sheriff off at the station, and he and Katti and 1e others went back to the motel to shower and change clothes. 'hey all stunk like a backed-up sewer.

The town was a mess. Store windows smashed out. Some arked cars and trucks had been set on fire. Only about half f the fire department had reported for duty, and the fire chief /as having to rely on as many volunteers as he could muster p to try to control the arson fires.

The front office of the motel was dark, the lights out. A sign n the door read: CLOSED. NO LONG DISTANCE PHONE ERVICE AVAILABLE IN THE ROOMS.

"We'll take turns showering and standing guard," Cole said. 'You ladies go first."

"You don't give me orders," a reporter said belligerently, etting all up in Cole's face.

Bad mistake.

Cole hit him with a big, flat-knuckled fist. A hard right cross the side of the man's jaw. The reporter went down like a ack of potatoes and didn't move.

"We're all under a strain," Don Potter said. "It's a tense ime."

"Yeah? Well, I just *un*tensed him," Cole said, looking down t the nearly unconscious man.

Katti winked at him and unlocked the motel room door.

The reporter Cole had decked moaned, and several of his riends helped him to his rather shaky feet.

"You got anything else you want to say to me?" Cole asked im, his nose about an inch from the reporter's nose.

"Ah, no," the reporter mumbled the words. A thin trickle f blood leaked out of one corner of his mouth.

"Fine. Keep it that way and we'll get along."

"Bully!" Susan Marcotte said.

Cole smiled, very thinly, and spoke about a dozen words in fast Cajun French. He turned his back to the woman and walked off.

"What'd he say to me?" Susan demanded.

"Among other things," Hank Milan said, "he told you to go fuck yourself. However it does lose something in the translation."

Cindy shook her head. "Damndest priest I ever encountered," she muttered.

All over the town and county, the players in this life-and-death struggle paused for a couple of hours to catch their breath. Had they not done so, they just might have been able to fulfill the silent orders that came from the dark part of the Other Side.

As it was, their pausing gave the authorities time to get into place.

A national guard military police unit had been called up, and was rushing in from a town about forty miles away. It was a small, undersized company, but was being beefed up by another guard unit coming up from the southwest.

After a quick shower and change of clothes, Laura Lordan and her cameraman asked if they could ride with Cole and Katti.

"Sure," Cole said. "Get in. I'm going down to the sheriff's office."

"Thanks," Laura said, climbing into the back. "I feel safe around you. You appear to be, ah, very capable."

"I think so," Katti said softly.

Laura got the woman-to-woman message in those words loud and clear.

It went right over Cole's head.

"This is Eddie King," Laura said. "My cameraman."

Cole nodded at the young man. "Everybody buckled up? Okay." He dropped the Bronco into drive and headed out of the parking lot.

Before he got out of the lot, his radio squawked. "Cole,"

the voice of Al Pickens jumped out of the speaker. "You 10–8?"

Cole grabbed the mic. "That's 10–4."

"I gotta use you, Cole. Sorry."

"That's all right. What's up?"

"Katti with you?"

"Ten-four."

"Have her open that city map I gave you and find Elm street. It's 802 Elm. Check out a signal 45."

"Ten-four. Rolling." To Katti: "Find it?"

"Yes. Turn right on Green and then left on Elm. What's a signal 45?"

"Shooting."

"I'm logging you as 28," Al's voice again popped out of the speaker. "That'll be your assigned number, until this mess is over."

"Ten-four," Cole acknowledged.

"Twenty-eight? This is Captain Boyce. I'll back you up on this one. ETA two minutes."

"That's 10–4."

"And watch out for bodies in the street," the captain came back. "One of my people ran over a body just a few minutes ago. Sort of spoiled his evenin'."

"Gross!" Laura said.

"Squashed his head flat with the left front tire," the captain added.

"Barf!" Katti said.

Cop talk can be dark indeed. But it's a very necessary defense against losing your mind. And your stomach contents.

Cole angled to the curb across the street from 802 Elm. The front rooms of the house were lighted, and Cole could see someone moving around inside. Captain Boyce pulled in right behind him. "Stay in the car," Cole told his passengers. He got out and shook hands with the captain of Arkansas State Police.

"Al briefed me as much as time would permit," the trooper said. "It's, ah, hard to believe."

Cole nodded in the dim light of street lamps.

"Don't shoot, officers," the woman's voice came from behind them and spun them around, pistols raised. "I'm the one who called it in," she added.

"Step forward into the light, ma'am," Boyce said. "And keep your hands in front of you."

The woman advanced slowly, stepping into the light. She was unarmed, and very frightened.

"You heard shooting, ma'am?" Cole asked.

"Heard and saw it. Mr. McClinton shot his wife and two sons. I saw them through that front window. He—"

She was interrupted by a shotgun blast from the McClinton house. Both men ducked into a crouch.

"Wonder what he shot at?" Boyce asked.

"Not at us, that's for sure."

"Come on."

Cole told the woman, "You stay here."

The men walked across the street and up the driveway. Both of them looked through a window.

"I have never gotten used to seeing people with half their head blown off," the highway cop said.

After killing his wife and two sons, the husband had propped them up against a wall. Neatly. All in a row. The shot they had heard came when the husband stuck the muzzle of the shotgun in his mouth and blew out the back of his head.

"It was your call, Cole. What do you want to do?"

"We'll call it in, and eventually somebody will come around to pick them up."

"The funeral homes are full. I've been to all of them. They've got bodies stacked all over. It'll be late tonight, maybe even sometime tomorrow, before these bodies are picked up." He shrugged. "Nothing we can do about that."

"With the temperature as high as it is, in a few hours, these people aren't going to be pleasant to be around."

"Yep. And if they aren't picked up until sometime late tomorrow, the maggots will be crawling and the blowflies busy."

The men walked across the street. The woman who had called the shooting in was still standing there.

"You go on back in your house, ma'am," Boyce told her. "Lock your windows and doors. "Do you own a weapon?"

"I have my husband's old double-barrel. Twelve-gauge."

"Can you use it?"

"I sure can."

"Is it loaded?" Cole asked.

"What the hell good is an unloaded gun?" she responded.

Both men chuckled. Boyce said, "Thank you for calling this in, ma'am."

"They're all dead over there, aren't they?"

"Yes, ma'am. All dead."

"It's the devil's work," the woman said. "It really is."

"Yes, ma'am."

She turned and walked slowly back to her house. Cole and Captain Boyce looked at the other houses close by. They were all dark.

"You keep that shotgun handy now, you hear?" Cole called to the woman.

She waved and kept walking.

Cole called it in to dispatch. The dispatcher said that the sheriff was out on patrol—some trouble out in the county—and added, "twenty-eight, see the man at 1107 Windsor Drive. Possible signal 44."

"Stabbing," Boyce said. "Well, let's go."

But before they could get to their cars, dispatch radioed, "Captain Boyce, 10–19, please."

"Let me go see what that's all about. I'll catch up with you, Cole."

Cole nodded and watched as the trooper drove off, back to the sheriff's office. He got back in his Bronco and told Katti to find Windsor Drive.

"I heard the call," she said. "Windsor Drive is all the way across town. Here." She showed him the map.

On the way over, they passed several burning houses. The

fire department was spread so thin, all the firemen (most of them volunteers) could do was keep it from spreading to other houses.

Cole stopped three times to check out bodies. One in the middle of the street, one lying dead on the sidewalk, and the other hanging from a tree limb.

Eddie King was filming it all.

The man at the address on Windsor Drive was hysterical, and Cole hated to deal with hysterical people. You didn't know what the hell they might do.

Cole finally got him calmed down enough to make sense.

"My wife, she don't like guns. So when I gave up hunting, I sold all my guns. I didn't want to, but I did to please her. All I had to protect us tonight was this here." He whipped out a long butcher knife that almost put Cole into cardiac arrest. Cole took the knife away from the man as gently as possible, and the man said, "Phil over there, the dead guy, he was my neighbor for years. We got along fine. I don't know what caused him to go off his nut like he did . . ."

It was a story that Cole was to hear several dozen times during the long night that stretched before him. Neighbor turning on neighbor, husband turning on wife, wife turning on husband, brother killing sister, sister killing brother. At three o'clock, Cole drove back to the sheriff's office for something to eat and some coffee.

"Chain him to a goddamn tree if you have to!" Al was on the radio, talking to a deputy. "But don't bring him back here. We're full. City's full; we're all overflowing with nut cases."

George Steckler and Scott Frey had arrived. They both smiled and shook hands with Cole. George saying, "I think the Bureau ordered us in here hoping we'd get eaten by a ghost . . . or whatever ghosts do with victims."

"He's learning fast now," Scott said, jerking a thumb toward his younger partner. "Center for Disease Control is flying people in at dawn. They seem to think some sort of virus bug is causing all this." His tired eyes twinkled, and he smiled. "When the SAC heard me tell them it was being caused by the devil, he immediately ordered us in here."

Cole introduced the Bureau men to Laura. "She's all right, guys. Good people. She won't do a shaft job on us."

"That'll be a refreshing change," Scott said with a tired smile.

"Oh, *shit!*" they heard Sheriff Pickens yell over the phone. "Well, let them kill each other then. Hell, no, I won't send anybody out there." He slammed down the phone and told a young woman, "I'm not here. I'm out of pocket, understand?"

"Yes sir."

Al walked over to Cole. "You remember me telling you about the Chambers and Hensley families?"

Cole nodded.

"They live right across the road from each other; way to hell and gone out in the country. They just declared war on each other. Sounds like Heartbreak Ridge out there. Hell with 'em. I hope they kill each other off." He wiped his face with a handkerchief. "Jesus, what a night!"

"National guard in place?" Cole asked.

"Yeah. Finally. We've got every road and pig path in the county blocked off. Governor is sending in more guard troops right now to beef things up." A deputy handed him a clipboard. Al scanned it quickly. "Over three hundred dead so far. And still counting. God only know how many more are dead in their homes and not listed on this. Eighty fires reported by 3:00 AM——"

"Are you fucking *serious?*" one of the women answering the bank of phones suddenly yelled.

The buzz of conversation stopped, and everybody turned to look at her.

"They're doing *what?*" she shouted over the phone. "Clyde, have you been drinking?" She listened for a moment, her face turning beet red. "Clyde, don't you tell me to stick this phone up my ass, you damned old drunk. You—" She listened for another moment. "I just don't believe that . . . What? . . . *What?*

. . . Well, fuck you, too! Clyde? Clyde?" She held the phone out at arm's length and stared at it for a moment.

"What's the matter, Jane?" Al called.

"That was Clyde Farmer." She shook her head. "But he didn't sound drunk to me."

"What'd he say?"

"He said the dead are crawling out of their graves and walking around . . ."

Everybody stared at her. George's mouth dropped open.

"He said he put up with that damned old bag he was married to for forty years. Said he was so happy when he buried her, he stayed drunk for a week, partying. Now she's back, trying to get in the house. Said she was butt-ugly alive, looks even worse now. Said she was on the back porch, beating on the door and grunting."

"This I have to see," Cole said. "Where does he live? I'll go check it out."

"We'll tag along with you," Scott said.

Al sat down and put his face in his hands. "Dear god! What else is going to happen?"

Thirteen

Katti insisted on coming along. But she did agree to ride with Bev and Hank Milan. Al rode with Cole, George and Scott following in their own car. None of them saw any walking dead during the ride out to Farmer's house, about two miles outside the city limits.

"Jane did say that this Farmer person drank a lot, right?" Cole asked.

"He doesn't drink that much," Al said glumly. "But he is a practical joker." He shook his head. "No. He wouldn't joke about something like this."

"Twenty-eight, where are you going?" the voice of Captain Boyce popped out of the speaker.

"Come on along, Andy," Cole told him. "We have reports of people climbing out of their graves and walking around."

Andy did not respond for a few seconds. "Ah . . . 10–9 on that."

Cole repeated it.

"I'm right behind you," Andy said.

Those out at the hunting camp were asleep. They had drunk too much and fallen asleep in the arms of their paid lovers. They were blissfully unaware of what was taking place all around them. All that was only a few hours away from changing. Dramatically so. The security people they had hired out of Memphis had said to hell with it, and were asleep in their cars.

Earlier in the evening, Nick Pullen had run into Albert Pickens, who had linked up with Arlene, who had found a couple of her less than moral female friends, and the five of them had headed out to Victoria's place. Victoria, on her way into town, had stopped Win Bryan, and he had followed her back to her mansion. The seven of them had then proceeded to have their own little party, and were all passed out in a drunken stupor. They did not know the town and county had erupted in violence and madness.

That was about to change. Abruptly. And with startling consequences.

Cole turned into the driveway of the Farmer house, his lights on high beam. It appeared that every light in the frame house was on and burning brightly.

Cole pointed to Hank, sitting behind the wheel of his car. "Stay here and keep the motor running. If things go bad, get the hell out of here."

Jim Deaton and Gary Markham were answering a call on the other side of the county.

They could all hear the hammering and grunting coming from the rear of the house.

They could also smell the rank odor of rotting flesh.

Clyde Farmer stepped out onto the front porch. The older man had a bottle of whiskey in one hand and a pistol in the other. "It's about goddamn time you got here, Al!" he hollered. "Now, I don't know what the hell's going on, but I do know it ain't normal. They's a half a dozen of them damn things on my back porch. They done busted out all the winders, and they're smellin' to high heaven. They stink so bad I done puked up my supper. Get 'em outta here!"

"Drunk," George said.

"Yeah," Cole agreed. "But what is causing that smell?"

"They can be kilt!" Clyde hollered. "But you gotta shoot 'em right 'tween the eyes. I done shot two. But as bad as I ated that bitch I was married to, I just can't bring myself to shoot her. If I could have, I'd a done it years 'fore she croaked.''

''Shotguns,'' Al said. ''Everybody get shotguns and stuff your pockets full of shells.''

''You don't believe—'' George began his sentence but did not finish it.

''I don't know what to believe.''

''Jumpin' Jesus Christ!'' Captain Boyce said, pointing toward the rear of the house. ''What is *that?*''

Al sighed. ''Henry Harper. I attended his funeral about ten years ago.''

The gaunt figure of a man stood in the light at the rear of the house. His face was mottled with rot, and his clothing was ragged.

''What the hell has he got in his hand?'' Scott asked.

Henry lifted the hand in question. He was holding a human arm.

''He tore that offen old lady Mosby,'' Clyde called from the porch. ''After I shot her off the porch. You 'member her, Al.''

''Dead for years,'' Al said softly.

''He's eatin' on it,'' Clyde yelled.

''Oh, shit!'' Boyce said.

Henry Harper started lumbering toward the front of the house. Other shapes appeared out of the darkness and followed his lead. Stumbling and staggering and lurching toward Cole and the others.

''Jimmy Jenkins is with 'em, too,'' Clyde hollered. ''But he wasn't dead yesterday, 'cause I saw him downtown. I think if they scratch you or bite you or something, you can get infected. Then you're one of them. I'd be careful, if I was you boys.''

''I just cannot accept this,'' George found his voice. ''I see it, I smell it, but I cannot accept it.''

''You'd better accept it,'' Scott told his partner. ''And do it real quick.''

Henry and his friends were making slow progress, but heading their way, stumbling along, grunting and making other disgusting subhuman sounds as they lurched along.

"There's Jimmy," Al said. "Clyde was telling the truth."

The young man was dressed nicely, in pleated pants a dress shirt. But his face was deathly pale, his eyes strang looking, and his lips blood red.

Al shucked a round of double-ought buckshot into his twelv gauge riot gun. "Shoot them," he said wearily. "Head sho Let's put them back into their graves, where they belong."

The night roared with gunfire. Heads exploded from t impacting buckshot. The walking dead flopped on the grour jerking in their second death spasms.

Just to see what would happen, Cole deliberately fired in the chest of one rotting man. The buckshot knocked him dow but did not kill him. Howling, his breath fouling the night, crawled to his knees and rose to his shoes. He staggered towa the living.

Cole took aim and blew the man's head off.

"You didn't get 'em all, Al!" Clyde called from the por "Two, three of 'em took off toward the woods out back."

Al walked to the rear of the house, staying wide of the rotti bodies on the side yard, sliding fresh rounds into his shotg as he walked. The back of the house was ruined. The walki dead had managed to break down the back door and smash the windows.

Laura and Eddie had pulled in to the drive just in time film the last few minutes of the hideous scene.

"Dumb move," Cole called to them. "It's very dangero out here."

"News is news," Laura said. "Besides, all the other cre are out and working. They're all over the county."

"Goddammit!" Al yelled, returning from the rear of t house. "Don't you people ever listen to warnings from la enforcement?" When he did not receive a reply, he turned Clyde. "You can't stay here, Clyde. Those . . . things might back. Get in the car. We've opened shelters in town."

Clyde was standing over the nearly headless body of h wife. "Maybe this time, goddammit, you'll stay in the ground he told her.

* * *

Federal Judge Warren Hayden got up to go to the bathroom. He was still drunk. He staggered down the hall, wondering why the rear window of the hall was wide open and letting skeeters in and good cold air from the central air out. He stumbled toward the window and put both hands on the sill, steadying himself for a moment. He wrinkled his nose at the foul odor that assailed his nostrils.

"Phew!" he said.

A second later he was staring into the dead eyes of a man he'd sentenced to life in prison, back when he was a district judge. The man had died there, and the body brought back home to be buried. Judge Warren Hayden had known all along that the man was innocent of the charge. Warren had been part of the frame-up in order to get a piece of the man's acreage . . which had been turned into a subdivision. Made him a lot of money.

Which wasn't going to do him a bit of good now.

Cold, clammy, rotting hands closed around the judge's throat. Gagging, Hayden fell back, dragging the walking dead with him. They tumbled to the hall floor.

Grinning, the undead opened his mouth and kissed the judge on the lips. A soul kiss. Lots of tongue action. Several maggots dropped from one mouth to the other.

Now the judge and the walking dead were kindred spirits. As one.

One of the whores from Memphis had been in the hall bathroom. She heard the noise and stepped out, stark naked. She froze at the sight. Opened her mouth to scream. Hayden's hand reached out and closed around a rather shapely ankle. She started screaming just as more of the walking dead began climbing into the hall. A naked man grinned at her, the odor of the grave almost causing her to puke. Then she saw he had a huge erection, and really started hitting the high notes. Cold rotting flesh pressed against warm living flesh. Putrefying lips touched hers. A rotting tongue slipped between her wet lips, just as the walking dead got his first piece of nooky in more than ten years.

Judge Roscoe Evans was the next to step out of his bedroom and into the hall. He took in the copulating scene through disbelieving eyes. Roscoe was sexually kinky to the core, and would try anything once, but this was ridiculous.

Wearing only his house slippers, Roscoe let out a bellow of fear and took off up the hall and into the den. He tore open the front door and ran out into the night, shrieking at the top of his lungs.

Conditions rapidly went from bad to worse inside the hunting camp.

Untangling himself from the naked flesh of the women who sprawled on the big bed and on him, Nick Pullen crawled out of bed and started for the bathroom, when he heard a noise from the living room. Naked, he padded up the hall toward the lights that someone forgot to turn off.

He stood in the archway and stared in utter disbelief. The room was filled with rotting, stinking, men and women in various stages of ragged dress. The smell was awful.

As if controlled by one mind—which they were—the walking dead began lurching and staggering toward him.

Nick found his voice and began screaming. He turned and ran into the first room he could and slammed the door, locking it securely. Breathing a sigh of relief, he turned away from the door. He almost passed out from shock.

Half a dozen ... *things* stood there, grinning at him, the rotting lips pulled back in hideous smiles. They began to shuffle and lurch and stagger toward him.

"Oh, my god, no!" Nick managed to say.

It was the last comprehensible sound that would pass his lips.

* * *

Sheriff Al Pickens sent squad cars all over town, with deputies on the speakers, warning people: Stay in your homes, lock the doors and windows, and don't open them for anyone. He instructed his deputies to tell the people that someone had contaminated the water supply, and whatever the contaminant was it had driven some people insane. They were easy to spot by the lurching, shuffling way they walked. Don't get near them, and whatever you do, don't let them in your house or let them get their hands on you. Shoot if you have to, and always aim for the head.

After his people had left, Al said, "I never thought I would ever give instructions like that out of this office."

"What else could you do?" Hank asked. "The people had to be warned."

"Yeah. But what do you really think they're going to do, when they see their Uncle Joe or Aunt Faith or father and mother or brother and sister who have been dead and buried for ten or so years? Shoot them?"

"Point taken," the priest said.

"Sheriff?" dispatch called. "Frank reports some really weird goings-on out at the Staples Mansion. Those . . . ah, things are lurching around all over the place."

"Good," Al said.

Cole and the others in the group nodded their heads in agreement with that.

"Sheriff," dispatch softened her voice. "Frank also said that Albert's pickup truck is parked out there."

Al's face did not change expression. He nodded his head. 'I made up my mind several days ago that somebody behind a badge would probably have to shoot my son, before this was all over. I just may be the one to do it . . . whatever form he appears in. What other cars or trucks are out there?"

"Arlene Simmons's car. Nick's truck. Win's truck."

Al looked at Cole and the FBI agents. "We might as well take a drive out there and see what's going on."

* * *

The guards at the hunting camp had been the first to become one with the walking dead. Of all the people in the lodge, only two made it out safely: Roscoe Evans and Silas Parnell, both of them on foot, and both of them naked as the day they were born.

They literally ran into each other limping and slapping mosquitoes, as they made their way down a gravel road that led to the blacktop.

Bob Jordan, riding with Chief Deputy Starr, spotted the two men. "What the hell is that over there?" he asked, pointing to a side road leading off from the blacktop.

Tom pulled over and put the beam from his spotlight on the two dark shapes.

He chuckled. "District judges Silas Parnell and Roscoe Evans." His smiled faded. "Big corporation owns a hunting camp several miles down this road. I bet that's where they've been, partying with whores until those things attacked . . ." He trailed that off.

Bob took it. "And they got out alive. So that means whoever they were with, didn't."

"Yeah." Tom got on the speaker. "Come on over here, gentlemen. I've got a couple of blankets in the trunk."

The two judges started limping over to the car.

"They're normal," Bob said.

"Sort of," Tom replied. "What they are is a couple of ass holes." He got out and opened the trunk, getting blankets while Bob stood off to one side, shotgun ready in case the two men were infected.

Bob relaxed when Silas said, "Something terrible has happened down at the hunting camp. This is going to sound awfully stupid, but——"

"Creatures attacked you," Tom interrupted. "Human beings that look like zombies."

"Why, yes. But——"

"It's happening all over the county, Judge." He held out the blankets. "Wrap up in these and get in the back seat. I've got to call this in."

"Those things might be all around us," Roscoe said, wrapping the blanket around him.

"Probably are," Bob said. "But they can be stopped."

"What in God's name are they?" Silas blurted.

"People who have crawled out of their graves," Tom told the man. "We call them walking dead. The undead." He shrugged his shoulders. "That's the best we could come up with on such short notice."

"Does this have anything to do with the old roadhouse?" Roscoe asked.

"It has everything to do with it," Bob said.

"It's all over, gentlemen," Tom told the woebegone-looking pair. It was getting light in the east; dawn was breaking. Both Tom and Bob had been in touch with the sheriff's office moments before the judges were spotted au natural. "The walking dead have attacked the people out at Victoria Staples's. We know that Albert Pickens killed Tommy Baylor. We know that snuff films were being made out at the mansion. The FBI called us less than thirty minutes ago. Carlos Washington aka Brother Long Dong was picked up in Los Angeles and spilled his guts. Do I have to read you two your rights?"

"We know our rights, young man," Roscoe said, doing his best to maintain some dignity. "We certainly don't need to be reminded of them by the likes of you."

"We also have Doc Drake in custody, Judge," Tom didn't let up. "He told us all about your bunny suit."

All the hot air went out of the judge.

"Fuck it," Silas said, crawling into the back seat of the squad car. "They can't prove a damn thing, Roscoe. All they've got is hearsay."

"Yeah," Bob said. "That's what the sheriff said. He said that he doubted any of this would ever come to court. But you two are through."

"Don't count on that," Silas said.

Bob smiled. "Let's take them back to the hunting camp and dump them out, Tom."

"That's a damn good idea."

"Wait!" Roscoe screamed.

"No!" Silas shouted.

Tom got a small cassette recorder out of his briefcase in the trunk and made sure it was loaded with tape. "You have a lot to tell us, don't you, gentlemen?"

"Yes," Roscoe blurted, his eyes wild with fear. "Where do you want to start?"

"First we start with this: You have the right to remain silent. If you give up that right . . ."

Fourteen

When Victoria, naked, eyes wild, face pale, lips blood red, came stumbling out of her mansion, grunting and mumbling, slobber leaking from her mouth in stinking ropes, Cole shot her.

The richest woman in the state died for the second time in two hours. Cole and the others hoped she would stay dead.

It was the beginning of the end of a long night of terror. But the day wasn't going to be much better, as the hunt for the walking dead intensified.

At the mansion, Nick Pullen was shot dead by Agent George Steckler. Arlene was killed by Agent Scott Frey. Sheriff Pickens put Win Bryan out of his misery.

Young Albert Pickens was found huddled in a closet in the basement of the mansion. Physically, he was all right. Mentally, he was a nightmare. EMT's called to the scene had to pump him full of tranquilizer before he could be transported to the hospital.

The basement was a chamber of horrors.

Victoria had been holding several prisoners in the cells. They were all right, just scared and confused. The undead had been unable to get to them, because of the heavy locked doors.

"This is incredible," Scott said. "I've never seen anything like this."

"Silas Parnell and Roscoe Evans were picked up out in the country by Tom and Bob," Al said, after using the phone to call in. "They're spilling the whole miserable story now. It jibes with what Brother Long Dong and Doc Drake said."

"Great God!" George thundered from a room just off the projection room in the basement. "There must be millions of feet of film in here. And still shots. There are some really prominent people involved in this . . . sickness."

The men gathered around and began looking at the 8 x 10 glossies.

"This is going to end some careers," Cole summed it up.

"Amen. Well, all this is now yours, boys," Al told Scott, dropping the ring of house keys into the Bureau man's hand. "And welcome to it. Come on, Cole. Let's go meet the CDC people. I really want to hear their explanation for all this. Then I'm going to grab a shower, some food, and sack out for a few hours."

"As soon as our people from Memphis, St. Louis, and Little Rock get here," Scott said. "I plan on doing the same. See you, guys."

Back at the motel, which had been secured and was being patrolled by national guard troops, Cole showered and laid down beside Katti.

She turned in his arms. "Is it over, now?"

"All but the mop-up. And that's underway right now."

"Are you going to be a part of that?"

"Not unless the sheriff asks for my help. I don't think he will. He's got hundreds of people at his disposal, and the number is growing by the hour."

"What now?"

"I want us to go home." He smiled. "And get married."

"Oh, I *know* we're going to do that. I mean, right now."

"You have something in mind?"

"If you're not too tired."

He wasn't.

Fifteen

Bad water.

"Are you serious?" Cole asked Scott.

"That's going to be the official government stance. Sure as hell wasn't my idea."

"Five hundred or so people dead, the downtown area looking like Beirut, corpses rising out of graves and lurching around attacking people, ghosts appearing out of a roadhouse that has been gone for ten years . . . and bad water caused it all?"

"Extremely stupid, isn't it?" George said. He shook his head in disgust.

"What about all that film the reporters shot?" Katti asked.

Scott shrugged. "Let them go on showing it. Freedom of the press and all that. It's already being attacked by some as a big hoax. And we've been instructed to have absolutely no comment on anything we might have witnessed here pertaining to the, ah, supernatural."

Cole smiled. "Bad water." He laughed out loud.

"The public will buy the story," Al said. "You just wait and see. By and large, they'll accept it. Hell, it'll be old news in a week."

Jim Deaton and his crew had returned to Memphis. Bev had ridden back with Hank.

Bob Jordan had gone back to Memphis, but not before predicting the government would try to cover all this up with some outrageous story.

"People just want their lives returned to normal," Al said. "I think they're ready to accept just about anything and get it over with."

"How's your son?" George asked, his voice softening.

Al shook his head. "Prognosis is not good. I think he'll be confined to a mental institution for a long, long time."

All the major players in the porn and snuff film business— with the exception of Long Dong, Doc Drake and a few others—were dead. Those left alive were facing long prison terms.

"How about the old roadhouse site?" Scott asked.

"I was out there earlier this morning," Cole said. "There is a huge burn mark, where the club used to sit. The burn goes down several feet. It took a lot of heat to burn the earth down that deep. I've never seen anything like it."

No one asked what might have caused the burn. They all knew who was responsible for that.

Judges Parnell and Evans were in jail, awaiting trial for their part in the snuff and porn films.

Several sheriffs and deputies and chiefs of police in north Akansas and southeast Missouri were in jail on various charges, all related to the snuff and porn film business.

Cole stood up and shook hands all the way around. "I guess this wraps it up, guys."

"Stay in touch, Cole," Al said.

Cole walked out into the sunshine of summer and drove back to the motel. Katti was waiting. They packed up and were on the road thirty minutes later.

They drove past the old roadhouse site one more time, slowly, but not stopping.

Katti said nothing as she stared at the huge burn mark on the earth.

Once they were past the old site, she said, "There are dozens of these clubs, Cole. All over the nation. What about them?"

"I don't know, Katti. When I brought it up, Scott and George were sort of evasive about that. I don't think the government wants to get involved in the ghost-chasing business."

The press had hung around for a few days after that bloody night of terror, then vanished after hearing what the government's official stance on the matter would be.

Few people had noticed it, and the press had not reported on the strange scorched areas, but all over the South and in parts of the West, where dozens of old roadhouses used to stand, there were deep burn marks in the earth.

Katti was silent on the ride back to Memphis, and Cole did not attempt to make any conversation. He knew she was thinking about her brother Tommy.

They stopped at a supermarket in Memphis and bought groceries, before heading on to Katti's house.

There was an message on her answering machine to call the garage where Tommy's car was in storage.

"Miss Katti," the man said. "I'm sorry, but I don't know what happened. I called the po-lice and they come out and done all sorts of investigatin', but they can't explain it either."

"What are you talking about, Sam?" she asked.

"Your brother's car, Miss Katti. It just disappeared. And no one can explain it, neither. None of the doors shows any sign of being opened. That would have set off the alarms. That Mustang sure wouldn't have fit through no window. And nothing else is missin'. It's like it just vanished into thin air! The insurance people come around, and they can't explain it, neither. But they'll pay off. 'Cause it damn sure is gone. I'm terrible sorry about this, Miss Katti."

"That's all right, Sam. It wasn't your fault. I'll come down and sign whatever papers have to be signed. Thank you, Sam. No, put it out of your mind. It wasn't your fault."

When she hung up and turned to Cole, he was pointing to something on the dinner table.

Katti picked up the shiny object. It was an ID bracelet. There were happy tears in her eyes as she held the bracelet. TOMMY was engraved on the front. She turned it over. LOVE, KATTI was engraved on the back.

She smiled at Cole. "Some stories do have happy endings," she said.

Please turn the page for a preview of
William W. Johnstone's stunning blockbuster
HUNTED
coming in December 1995 from Pinnacle Books.

"He is somewhere in this area," the men were told, their eyes
on the map, on the spot touched with a pointer.

"He really exists, then?"

"Yes. For years I've thought it was nothing more than rumor
and myth. I couldn't get people into Romania to dig around
until the Ceausescu regime was overthrown and the country
opened up. But he is real. He is alive and well and has been
so for nearly seven centuries. He's about five–ten, well built,
muscular, with dark brown hair and very pale gray eyes. He
speaks a dozen or more languages and he is a very dangerous
man. The ultimate, consummate, eternal warrior—always bear
that in mind. The man has fought in every major war since the
thirteenth century. He's been a teacher, a priest, a writer, a
singer, an actor. He was a gunfighter in the wild west here in
America. He's worked as a mechanic, a bookkeeper, a salesman.
He can do practically anything. I've recently discovered that
while working in Colorado during the gold rush, he found a
very nice vein, staked it out, dug it up, and with the help of a
San Francisco law firm, invested the money. That investment
has grown over the years. He does not have to work. He's

changed his name, again, and got a new social security number. Then he dropped out of sight. Questions?''

''He has to be taken alive?''

The man who was paying the bounty hunters' salaries gave the questioner a pitying look. ''I just told you, he can't die. He cannot be killed. At least not by any method that I am aware of. If he has a Achilles heel, it has never been found. I want him for study. The man holds the key to eternal life. I want to be the one who unlocks that secret.''

Robert Roche looked at each of the twelve men standing around him. ''You gentlemen come highly recommended. You are supposed to be the finest mercenaries in all the world. You're being paid well, certainly more than you have ever received for any job. Now prove your worth.''

A dark-complexed man with hard obsidian eyes spoke up. ''What have you not told us about this man?''

''What do you mean?'' Roche questioned.

''There is more that you do not tell us. Why?''

Roche hesitated for a second, then said, ''Because it is unsubstantiated rumor, that's why.''

''What is the rumor?'' the hard-eyed man pressed.

Roche sighed. ''The man you are searching for is rumored to have the ability to change into animal form.''

''Shape-shifter,'' the questioner whispered. What animal?''

Again, Roche hesitated. With a sigh, he said, ''A wolf.''

The Indian's eyes narrowed. ''He is a brother to the most intelligent, dangerous and cunning predator to walk the face of the earth. You will never have this man. You are wasting your money.''

''Then you refuse to take the job?'' Roche snapped out the question.

George Eagle Dancer smiled. ''I did not say that. I will take your money, and I will do the best I can. And I alone will survive the hunt . . . along with the shape-shifter. The rest will fail.''

''If there are no more questions? You know your assignment. Find this man and bring him to me,'' Robert Roche said.

"Everything you asked for in the way of equipment has been
purchased and is at your disposal. I don't expect to see you
again until this is over. Good day."

Darry Ranson sighed and cased his binoculars. He lay for a
time with his forehead on the cool ground. He was so tired of
running. Centuries of running. An endless roll of years, unable
to establish any sort of permanent home or relationship. And
it just got worse as technology advanced. It hadn't been so bad
before the telegraph and telephone and the industrial revolution;
life was slower and easier and it had been much simpler to
lose one's self. It was getting more difficult each year.

He raised his head and gazed down into the valley. Two
more men had joined the others, and Darry felt sure there would
be still more. The men had gathered in a small circle and were
squatting down. One was pointing toward the west. That was
all right, for Darry's cabin lay to the south of the valley. But
they'd get around to it, sooner or later.

He wondered just how good these men were. That question
was answered a heartbeat later when a voice said, "Mike? You
copy this?"

Ranson tensed, not moving a muscle. He didn't even blink.
How in the hell could a man get this close to him without his
knowing it?

"Yeah, Mike. You can see for several miles up here. There
are no cabins in this valley. No signs of human life at all.
None."

How close was the man? Not more than three or four yards
at the most, Darry guessed, for the voice was clear.

"Yeah, OK," the man radioed. "I see Doolin and Blake.
They're comin' out of the timber to the north of you. OK.
Right. I'll start workin' my way down to the valley floor.
Jennings has already started down. Sure. Let's give Mister
Roche his money's worth. Webb out."

Darry listened as the man turned to leave. He moved well,
his boots making only the tiniest of whispers. If the rest of the

man-hunters were as good as this one, Darry was in for a tim
of it.

Six teams of two each. At least twelve men were huntin
him. Damn! And the reporter and her camera-person. He'
have to run. He'd have to pack up what he could, put his dog
in the bed of the truck and leave. He had no choice in th
matter. None at all that he could see.

Or did he?

Darry lay on the ridge and thought it out. His cover was a
good as it had ever been. His driver's license was valid. I
would take some organization like the FBI to discover that hi
past was non-existent—at least on paper—and it would tak
them several days to do it.

These men hunting him were not government hunters. H
was sure of that. Someone named Roche was paying them. Bu
why? He could not remember anyone named Roche in his pas

Roche Industries? The words popped into his consciousness
Robert Roche, he had read somewhere, was the richest man i
the world. Worth billions and billions of dollars. He owned al
sorts of factories and construction companies and real estat
and . . . hell, Darry couldn't remember all of the article. Bu
Robert Roche's holdings were vast. Worldwide.

Could that be the Mister Roche the man-hunter was referrin
to?

Probably.

But why?

Darry made up his mind. He was not going to run. Not jus
yet. He was weary of running. He'd stick around as long a
possible. Maybe he could bluff his way through. He'd done i
before.

But the man-hunters didn't worry him nearly as much as th
TV reporter. He could not allow his face to be shown nation
wide. Somebody in his past would recognize him. Then ther
would be hell to pay.

Darry stood up and checked the valley below. The hunter
had moved on; tiny dots in the distance, slowly working thei
way west.

He looked up at the sun. High noon. What was it that Afri-
caner had told him during the Boer War? Yes. It was always high
noon in Africa. The same could be said for Darry's situation.

Then Darry remembered something about the hunters. They
all had a short, tube-like object carried on a strap. What the
hell was that? What was inside that tube? Some sort of weapon?
He'd better find out. He decided to pace the man-hunters. They
had to camp somewhere. And when they did, he'd be there.

Darry, as his Other, covered the distance very quickly, loping
along on silent paws. He encountered no other wolves, for the
other packs had heeded his earlier warning about the danger
of man and were laying low, staying close to the den and
hunting only small game.

Darry smelled blood and angled off, coming to the spot
where the man had been killed. His body had been removed,
but the blood smell was still strong. Not more than several
hundred yards away, he could smell men and hear the murmur
of their voices. He edged closer and listened.

"I am not moving from this spot," he heard one say. "I'll
be goddamned if I'll be a part in the killing of innocent people.
I won't do it."

"Same here," another agent said. "I'm staying put, eating
these lousy field rations, and keeping my ass out of trouble.
This whole thing stinks to high heaven."

"Look, we're under orders to . . ."

"Fuck orders!" another agent blurted. "I was up north of
here on Ruby Ridge a few years back when we attacked the
people in that cabin. It was a goddamn federally-sanctioned
assassination and that's all it was. You can call it whatever you
like, but it was an assassination of family members whose
views went against what some asshole liberal bureaucrat in
Washington think they should be. Shoot a kid in the back and
then blow his mother's face off while she's holding a baby in
her arms. Goddamn! That was a set-up, bait and hook, just like
this is."

Darry moved on, silently leaving the camp behind him. H visited other camps that night, listening to the federal agents men and women, talk and grumble and bitch about this assign ment. He quickly reached the conclusion that about ninet percent of them believed this operation to be a cover-up fo the Bureau's mistakes. But that still left about a hundred hard core agents who had to kill those civilians involved or fac dismissal and/or prosecution.

Darry headed for his cabin.

NOW THERE'S NO NEED TO WAIT UNTIL DARK!
DAY OR NIGHT, ZEBRA'S VAMPIRE NOVELS
HAVE QUITE A BITE!

THE VAMPIRE JOURNALS (4133, $4.50)
by Traci Briery

Maria Theresa Allogiamento is a vampire ahead of her time. As she travels from 18th-century Italy to present-day Los Angeles, Theresa sets the record straight. From how she chose immortality to her transformation into a seductive temptress, Theresa shares all of her dark secrets and quenches her insatiable thirst for all the world has to offer!

NIGHT BLOOD (4063, $4.50)
by Eric Flanders

Each day when the sun goes down, Val Romero feeds upon the living. This NIGHT BLOOD is the ultimate aphrodisiac. Driving from state to state in his '69 Cadillac, he leaves a trail of bloodless corpses behind. Some call him a serial killer, but those in the know call him Vampire. Now, three tormented souls driven by revenge and dark desires are tracking Val down—and only Val's death will satisfy their own raging thirst for blood!

THE UNDEAD (4068, $5.50)
by Roxanne Longstreet

Most people avoid the cold and sterile halls of the morgue. But for Adam Radburn working as a morgue attendant is a perfect job. He is a vampire. Though Adam has killed for blood, there is another who kills for pleasure and he wants to destroy Adam. And in the world of the undead, the winner is not the one who lives the longest, it's the one who lives forever!

PRECIOUS BLOOD (4293, $4.50)
by Pat Graversen

Adragon Hart, leader of the Society of Vampires, loves his daughter dearly. So does Quinn, a vampire renegade who has lured Beth to the savage streets of New York and into his obscene world of unquenchable desire. Every minute Quinn's hunger is growing. Every hour Adragon's rage is mounting. And both will do anything to satisfy their horrific appetites!

THE SUMMONING (4221, $4.50)
by Bentley Little

The first body was found completely purged of all blood. The authorities thought it was the work of a serial killer. But Sue Wing's grandmother knew the truth. She'd seen the deadly creature decades ago in China. Now it had come to the dusty Arizona town of Rio Verde . . . and it would not leave until it had drunk its fill.

Available wherever paperbacks are sold, or order direct from the publisher. Send cover price plus 50¢ per copy for mailing and handling to Penguin USA, P.O. Box 999, c/o Dept. 17109, Bergenfield, NJ 07621. Residents of New York and Tennessee must include sales tax. DO NOT SEND CASH.

THE BLOOD BOND SERIES

by William W. Johnstone

The continuing adventures of blood brothers, Mat Bodine and Sam Two Wolves — two of the fastest gun in the west.

BLOOD BOND   (2724, $3.95

BLOOD BOND #2:
BROTHERHOOD OF THE GUN   (3044, $3.95

BLOOD BOND #3:
GUNSIGHT CROSSING   (3473, $3.95

BLOOD BOND #4:
GUNSMOKE AND GOLD   (3664, $3.50

BLOOD BOND #5:
DEVIL CREEK CROSSFIRE   (3799, $3.50

BLOOD BOND #6:
SHOOTOUT AT GOLD CREEK   (4222, $3.50

BLOOD BOND #7:
SAN ANGELO SHOOTOUT   (4466, $3.99